THE DEMON KNIGHT SERIES

BOUND TO YOU

ALYSON CARAWAY

PRESS

Published by Vulpine Press in the United Kingdom in 2020

ISBN: 978-1-83919-036-0

Cover by Adam Seal and Claire Wood

www.vulpine-press.com

To my mom

Five years ago, I wouldn't allow you to read past the first page because I couldn't handle the embarrassment. Now, I hope you're up there, reading it in its entirety and cheering me on from the skies. I'm looking forward to hearing about how Heaven really is some time.

ACKNOWLEDGEMENTS

This book and I have gone through a lot since I started writing it five years ago. I was a newlywed then, living in a small, one-bedroom co-op, oblivious to what it would be like to lose a parent to cancer or to become a mother myself. Now, my beautiful little girl sleeps in our three-bedroom home as I write this and reflect on how much life has changed and who has helped me along.

First, I'd like to thank my wonderful husband, Adam, who has supported me since I wrote the first sentence. He's seen the extreme highs and lows that come with writing a book, and has been there to see me through every emotion. He is why I can write romance.

When I decided to try and make something of this book, I found my tribe in the Long Island Romance Writers chapter of RWA. Without them, these pages would never have made it to print. I am so lucky to have such an incredible group of mentors, friends, and cheerleaders to guide me into becoming a professional author. I can't wait to share this book with you just as you've shared yours with me.

To my family, especially my sister, Lauren, who bought champagne to help celebrate the sale of this series even though she makes me feel awkward about writing smoochy scenes. Dad, if you're reading this, thank you for your wonderful support, but please don't read any further. I'll know if you did because you'll be red as a tomato next time I see you and you'll regret it, and I'll regret it, and it will be even more awkward than it is with Lauren. Love you!

To my writer friends outside of LIRW, especially those who helped me fall in love with writing back in the days of AOL chats. I will forever love and cherish the text adventures we went on after school. I've lost touch with so many of you, but thank you to Matt, Ken, Jeff, Tony, Jerry, Steph, Alex, and David for writing with me. You were my tribe before I realized what that meant.

To my real-life friends who read my drafts, checked up on me, or followed the journey along the way, thank you. Erin, Laurissa, Molly, Stephanie and Kelsey—you ladies are amazing.

To whoever created Twitter pitch events and #IWSGPit, you are the real MVP. Without you, Libby Iriks would never have seen my pitch, liked it, and much to my amazement and delight, acquired it. Libby, thank you for taking me and my characters under your golden angel wing at Vulpine Press. You have made this publishing journey so wonderful and fun, and I have already learned so much from you. Thank you for making my dream a reality!

And thank you, reader, for furthering that dream along. I hope this is the first book of many, many more to come!

PROLOGUE

Ouranos lay there, with his broad, muscular chest and hard stomach fully on display, looking every bit the god he was. His eyes were smoldering, begging for Coriel to strip down and jump into bed with him, but her anger trumped all feelings of lust.

Ouranos sighed. "They didn't mean it, Coriel."

He propped his head on his hand, and with his elbow pressing into the mattress, the gray silk sheets slipped down his side, settling just above his narrow hips.

Coriel continued to pace at the foot of the bed. "The rest of the team thinks the upcoming elections will be rigged and that I'll make archangel, but only because you and I are sleeping together. It's like they've forgotten I survived a fight against the demon knight Oriax, or that my decision to reposition Diniel's squad a few weeks ago didn't save their lives."

She unfurled her golden wings and scoffed. "I earned this golden down before you and I ever met. Have they forgotten that, too?"

"Of course not. They're just jealous. You're a smart, talented, sexy little creature with the ability to charm a god." He winked and smoothed out the sheets before him. "Now, come charm me, little canary."

Coriel scoffed but couldn't keep her smile at bay. Sky-blue eyes that matched her own twinkled back at her, and she took a moment to appreciate just what her charm had brought her—a beautiful deity with a chiseled build, golden hair, and tanned skin. Though most gods lacked wings, Ouranos had two breathtaking sets with orange and red down that reminded her of the Manusyan sky at sunset. He was truly a sight to behold, and he was all hers.

She jumped onto the bed and knelt before him, taking a moment to appreciate his fresh, clean scent before she leaned forward and planted a searing kiss on his lips. He sucked on her lower lip and ran his tongue across it, then wrapped his arms around her small frame and pulled her closer.

Heat ignited low in her belly, but she had one important thing to ask him before she gave him what he was seeking. Coriel planted her hands on his chest and pulled her head back, allowing her lips to fall from his.

"You think I can be archangel, don't you?"

Ouranos kept his eyes closed and lips parted. When his brow furrowed, Coriel's heart sank. He was clearly struggling to come up with an answer that would please her.

After a long moment, he finally opened one eye and said, "I will talk to Michael."

Coriel frowned and pushed off his chest, increasing the distance between them. "About what?"

"About making you arch, silly."

"Heavens everlasting, Ouranos," Coriel said, kicking away the sheets he'd tried to trap her in before rising on her bare feet. "Are you serious? Were you listening to anything I said?"

His sigh made her see red.

"You're young, Coriel," Ouranos explained. "Angels are usually a couple centuries old before nominating themselves for the position. You were created, what, two decades ago?"

"That means nothing! Pahaliah is young and she's been nominated as well."

"Let me talk to your high archangel. You have the talent and drive to be a great arch. Just let me seal the deal with Michael."

"No. I'm earning this without your help. If I hear so much as a whisper that you did anything to influence the election, we're done. Say nothing, do nothing. I will rise to power on my own."

She crossed Ouranos's chambers to the door, collected her boots, and shoved her feet inside them.

"Where are you going?"

"Hunting. If I don't take off a demon's head soon, I'll end up taking off yours."

Ouranos matched her irritated tone. "Is that any way to speak to your god?"

2

"You are the god I sleep with, not the one who commands me. The only god I need answer to is Wodan, and he encourages beheadings. While you avoid speaking with High Archangel Michael, I will avoid recommending your head to the god of war."

She swung the door open and stopped on the threshold to look at him over her shoulder. "Deal?"

"I'm only trying to help you, Coriel. Give it some thought while you're destroying demons on Manusya. I know how badly you want this. When you return, I will make sure you are appointed arch."

Rage roared inside her like a forge. "Go to Hell!"

CHAPTER 1

THIRTY YEARS LATER

"Try it again," Coriel said, peeking out from behind a large punching bag that hung from the ceiling.

Diniel nodded, fists at the ready. He focused on a spot around his eye level, shifted his weight from one foot to the other a few times, then let loose on the bag.

Coriel smiled as she swayed to the rhythm of his punches. "Shoulder. Chin. Cheek. Stomach. Good, yes!"

She was trying to trip Diniel up, but he never missed the correct spot on the bag. With a smile, she bobbed, matching the rhythm of the fight and sinking down into a battle stance before shouting, "Let's go!"

And so began their dance. Diniel turned, slamming his forearm against the bag as Coriel did the same on the other side. They relied on the connection they shared as angels to keep in step with one another, on their hearts instead of their words to anticipate the other's movements. They were flawlessly in sync, using their momentum to send the bag into a wild spin as they rotated around it. They continued their assault until the chain holding up the bag whined, then broke, sending the entire contraption slamming into the ground.

Coriel leaped back with a delighted shout, laughing as the bag fell toward her and spewed sand at her feet. She gave it a few more punches, then a final kick for good measure.

"I think it's dead, Erelim Coriel," Diniel said with a chuckle.

She swiped a hand across her sweaty brow and smiled. "You know you don't have to call me that when it's just us. Coriel is fine."

Diniel shrugged. "The title suits you, though Archangel Coriel will suit you even more."

Coriel lifted her chin and placed her hands on her hips. "When I am archangel, I shall promote you from taqaphim to erelim so you can take my place." She motioned toward Diniel's silver wings. "Those should have been made gold a long time ago, Din."

"It doesn't matter to me what color they are. All I care about is being on that battlefield and demons dying by my hand. If I can save one human soul from corruption each time I take a demon's, I've done by job. Taqaphim or erelim, it doesn't matter. Make them white and call me a malakhim, even."

"Oh, stop. You don't mean that. You're a much better fighter than all of God Wodan's malakhim combined. Don't sell yourself short."

Diniel laughed. "I knew that'd get a rise from you. I'm only trying to tell you that titles aren't everything. You can accomplish whatever you want to, no matter the prefix before your name."

"Sure, sure. But still, when you and I finally slay a demon knight, we'd better be rewarded with better titles. I expect to be called Your Highness. What about you?"

Coriel smiled whenever she coaxed a genuine, jovial laugh from her friend.

"Sometimes I think the others are right when they say you don't listen."

"I listen when others say something I can agree with," she said with a wink. "Now, shall we go again? Swords this time?"

Diniel was reaching for his sword hilt when a gong rang and reverberated inside Coriel's chest. Diniel would have felt it too—all of Wodan's angels would have simultaneously received the call from his archangels.

The vibrations inside Coriel's chest translated to words in her mind.

Demons have been summoned to Manusya. Prepare for immediate deployment.

Coriel waggled her eyebrows at Diniel. "Come on. Time to dance for real."

She trotted past him and out of the colossal training center, then kicked off the ground, spreading her golden wings and beating them as hard as she could to be the first angel to the square. She grumbled when she found a handful of angels, including Erelim Tarael, already there.

Diniel landed by Coriel's side a few moments later. Like birds sensing their prey, several dozen angels amassed in the square, but this was only half of Wodan's army. The rest would join them soon.

The gong inside Coriel's chest sounded again.

Close the portal, exterminate the demons, keep the humans intact. The victory will be yours, angels. Now, go. Glory be to the gods and your strength.

Coriel dove into the plush clouds that made up the Heavens' solid ground and willed that they would let her through.

As she fell and the warmth of the Heavens' eternal sun grew distant, she held her breath and braced for the impact of the invisible shield that separated the holy realm from the terrestrial. The thunderous clap and violent jolt to her bones as she broke through the barrier always startled her, but it was just the rush of adrenaline she needed before a fight.

Frigid air assaulted her face as she passed into Manusya, the human realm, and she focused on how its gusts sailed over the down of her wings and stoked her growing demon bloodlust. Anticipation for the fight made her skin break out in goosebumps. She drew in a deep, focused breath to stifle her excitement and surveyed the battlefield below. As the archangels had described, demons were spewing from the ground like a geyser.

Coriel smirked wickedly as she watched their horned, dark shapes surround their cowering human victims. This was just how she liked her prey—demonic, reeking of evil, and appearing en masse. Thoughts of rending their flesh and saturating the soil with their sticky black blood only made her want to fall faster.

The summoners of these demons were a group of gray-hooded humans; they'd drawn a pentagram in an open field to create a portal to Hell. According to the information the archs were relaying, the humans' attempts to summon a demon or two had accidentally sprouted hundreds. That, at least, Coriel could confirm from the skies. There were over two hundred of the feeble-looking creatures crawling out of the shimmering hole, and they now surrounded their beckoners with curiosity.

Oh, humans … It was sad that they would never know how far angels and gods would go to stop them from destroying themselves.

6

Coriel turned her attention to the crudely drawn pentagram on the ground—a circle that looked more like an egg with a wobbly five-pointed star inside. The human who'd drawn it wasn't much for accuracy; certainly not the best candidate to be drawing these sorts of evil shapes in the first place. In the spaces between each tip of the star were smaller circles with different symbols drawn inside them.

As she continued to fall, she read the symbols one at a time and let out a disgusted sneer when she saw the mistake they'd made. Accuracy was paramount when drawing a summoning portal—it was amazing what one line or squiggle out of place would do. *These careless people deserve this,* she thought bitterly. Instead of writing the symbol for 'great one,' they'd managed to write 'great numbers.'

Well, they were certainly getting that.

To make matters worse, humans rarely thought to include the symbols for sending the creatures back to the underworld when they summoned them. But that's what she and several squads of battle angels were there to take care of—killing the hellish beasts and sending their spirits back to the Lake of Souls for cleansing.

Many of the demons began noticing the collage of gold, silver and white-winged angels descending on them like bees to a honeycomb. Coriel was proud to represent the gold in the sky, the mark of an erelim, the most elite of the Heavens' warriors. She was created by the gods for the sole purpose of protecting and purifying humans against the creatures of Hell, and as she watched the ground grow darker with screeching demons hemorrhaging through that portal, she had to take another breath to control her overwhelming desire for their blood.

At least three hundred demons will have come through by the time I destroy that portal.

That made three demons to every one angel; nothing they couldn't handle. She almost wished there were more and briefly considered stalling to increase the challenge. These were all lesser demons, mere foot soldiers, without a higher-ranking demon in sight—for now.

"Tarael, north!" Coriel commanded to her fellow erelim and pointed to the tip of the pentagram. He and his team were excellent at making impenetrable walls and could block any demons from escaping into the forest closest to that mark.

"That's not the order the archs communicated to me," Tarael shouted back.

"I know. Just do it."

The archangels knew little about being on the battlefield; she needed to make decisions in real-time to maximize survival.

When I am archangel, I will fight alongside my warriors and make better calls than our leaders do from the Heavens.

Their immediate supervisor, Archangel Pahaliah, would be upset at her for disobeying orders, but not for long; Coriel's impulsive decisions brought in far too many victories for that.

"Arael, Jariel, Cantrael! Fall in behind me!"

The erelim hesitated and stole unsure glances at one another, but eventually drifted into the formation she set. Coriel nodded in satisfaction, then threw her hands to her sides and crushed her wings to her back to descend faster than the rest.

Coriel aimed for the center of the pentagram, her feet meeting the ground with shocking force. Ripples of earth spread in all directions, obliterating the symbols and closing the portal while demons in the immediate area flew backwards. Half a lesser demon screamed in agony, its torso in Manusya while the rest of its body dangled somewhere in the depths of Hell.

Coriel smirked as her team fell in around her with one demon already dead at her feet.

This is for you, Ouranos. The god would have loved to see the Heavenly warriors landing with her at the center. *Where was he now?* She said a silent prayer for his return to the Heavens—the same way she'd begun every battle for the past three decades.

Coriel spotted Diniel landing gracefully beside her. He saluted, awaiting her next order. Her command from above had been to protect the humans, but she wanted to slaughter demons. She smiled at Diniel and tilted her chin in the direction of the demon summoners, who were cowering on shaky legs and hiding their faces in their hoods as they held each other.

"Keep them safe and get them to the forest, Din."

"Yes, Erelim Coriel," he said, giving her another salute.

That was her Diniel, the one angel who always trusted her decisions and never hesitated to change course at her command. The rest of the squad had much to learn from him. They listened, but they could learn to listen faster.

As Diniel lowered his arm and unsheathed his blade, he looked her in the eyes and nodded. "May the light of the gods bask us in its glory."

"Glory be to Wodan," she responded, and he was off, grabbing a few of her lowest-ranking white-winged malakhim along the way to assist.

With the humans taken care of, it was finally time to further indulge her bloodlust—she shook with the need to massacre demons. Reaching over her shoulder, she grabbed at the empty air and a sharp blade materialized from its invisible sheath. The angels surrounding her were already battling and she was all too happy to join them.

"Glory be to Wodan!" she shouted, loud enough for her entire squad to hear.

Before she was met with a response, Coriel began hacking down the creatures that threatened to corrupt the world she was sworn to protect.

Demons came in many shapes and sizes, but Coriel was much smaller than most of those she fought against—even among other angels she was tiny—yet she considered this an advantage. Every opponent underestimated her, and the exaggerated size of her sword only further threw them off. Made of destiel, a Heavens-forged metal that never dulled, its hilt was longer than her forearm and the blade was almost two-thirds her height. The golden wings carved into the hand guards matched her own, down to the way the feathers lay.

The sword looked as if it equaled her body weight—and it did—yet it was nothing but a blur in the sunlight as she sliced through one demon after another with ease. Each time it slid through a hissing, desperate beast, black blood poured from its body and the reeking scent of sulfur saturated the air.

Within a few minutes, so much slick, oily demon blood had spilled on the ground that Coriel could hardly stay standing. Taking flight, she eyed her next demon victim in the distance.

While she charged at the beast, a sudden pang burned in her chest, making her wince. She knew from the pain that two second tier taqaphim had fallen. She'd felt smaller vibrations when a few third tier malakhim were killed, but all of the first tier erelim were still in the fight. Coriel sighed, saddened that they'd lost some of their team yet was just as disappointed that there were no stronger demons to present her with more of a challenge.

The archangels would want as few casualties as possible, and Coriel would not allow for her change of strategy to be blamed for their losses.

"To me!" she shouted at her subordinates, seeing them wade too far from her in the endless sea of hell creatures.

She almost felt bad for the evil beasts as their desperation in this war grew. They were ravenous to kill angels, even if it meant dying by the hundreds to claim a small handful of the Heavens' malakhim.

With loud, commanding shouts, slicing blades and flying arrows, the angels were giving a swift end to the battle. The victory they were about to claim and the high she got from killing these beasts were the sweetest of drugs. And yet, she could not deny she admired the dark, muscular bodies of the humanoid demons that fought against her. Beings created outside of the Heavens should not be so delectable to look at. The corded muscles beneath their dark skin twisted and tensed with each swing at her, and the dark reds, oranges and yellows of their eyes were like pieces of Hell brought with them to the surface. And those long, poison-barbed tails?

What I could do with a tail like that ...

No one else knew just how often her mind drifted to demon appreciation when she fought, but it was becoming a problem.

Focus, Coriel, focus, she thought as she dragged her blade across the chest of another well-built demon.

She would not let her lust, a sin created by these creatures, be her undoing. All angels, and even the gods themselves, were tainted by the influence of demons; they just knew how to keep each other in check and had a myriad of rules and hierarchies to ensure the darkness didn't spread. Someday, they would return to a world of purity—that's what they were fighting for, after all. But when these sinfully attractive beasts had tainted the first god and his angels, the fall from grace had brought evil to the Heavens.

Mild admiration for her opponents was once again replaced by white-hot scorn as her focus returned to the battle, causing her to roar out another battle cry and continue her massacre.

Fewer screams were heard around the field as the angel-favored battle began drawing to a close. The ground was littered with countless demon bodies, a few angels peppered among them. Of the demons that were still alive, a few had fled. Some were mindlessly feasting on angel blood, no longer able to focus on the battle and too distracted to defend themselves.

Of those who continued to fight, one was stupid enough to take Coriel on. It ran at her, but she gripped it by a horn and used its own momentum to spin it, then jerk it against her with its back to her chest.

It screeched and struggled wildly until she held her sword against its throat, then it stilled. It had to be unnerving, feeling the blade and smelling the tainted blood of at least two dozen of its comrades right before dying.

Coriel had a feeling she'd made the most number of kills that day. She would add this one to the count once her question was answered.

"Who is your leader?" she snarled into her hostage's ear.

But instead of the feeble, quivering voice Coriel had expected, she heard a roar so loud it shook the ground and brought all on the battlefield to a halt. Every remaining fighter, angel and demon alike, turned north. The roar continued to echo in Coriel's ears as a hulking demon with bat-like wings sailed into view over the trees.

The tingle in her chest felt different from the archangels' usual signal, but the demon's name formed in its vibrations and her heart lurched against her rib cage.

"Demon Knight Zagan," she hissed.

She guessed her tone wouldn't have been far from the slithering sneer her hostage would have used had she not just sliced its throat open and added its blood to the pool at her feet. She no longer had need for the creature's answer; its leader had presented himself.

She'd been hoping for a challenge but had not expected an elusive demon knight to appear. They were the demon king's protectors, and rarely appeared on Manusya, yet were skilled at covering their tracks when they did. Coriel had only ever fought a knight once before and, based on the wave of fear detonating among the rest of the frozen angels, guessed she was one of the few who had even seen one.

Of all the demon knights, Zagan's power was the most notorious. His cruelty and ability to corrupt souls were legendary, but they had always been just that. Legends.

Powerful as the angels were, and as well as they fought, none of them seemed interested in taking the horner on. The wave of fear among the Heavenly swarm gave way to an overwhelming desire to flee.

"Stay calm!" Coriel cried to the others, though she was anything but.

Fascinated, she watched the demon—with his large frame and deadly Hell-red eyes—as he swooped down and landed in the center of the field.

The rest of the angels were moving again, and the knight was coming right for her, yet all Coriel could do was stand there and stare. She gasped as he closed the distance between them.

By the gods! And I thought these other creatures were works of art.

He had two sets of horns, pointed ears, and a chiseled body clothed in nothing but black pants that hugged sinful hips. The thundering sound of her heartbeat drowned out another loud roar from the knight. The ground beneath her shook and angels all around her scattered, but Coriel remained paralyzed. Something inside her had shifted at the sight of this demon—she was captivated.

All around her, Zagan's lesser demons arched their backs and yelled at the sky, their leader's arrival reinvigorating them to retaliate against the angels. The fight turned with the demons' second wind.

With nothing but his clawed hands and barbed tail, Zagan met the ground several hundred feet before her and began ripping through lower-ranking angels like he was shredding paper. Skin tore and bones cracked with every swipe of his huge arms. Each death sent a pang through Coriel's chest that begged her to snap out of her trance, yet she found herself unable to look away. His hardened torso expanded and contracted in tempo with her own gasps for air.

Zagan and his army continued to tear through her peers, pulling off their wings as if they were as fragile as a butterfly's before slicing their necks. A few demons lingered at each body, sipping at the silver angel blood that swirled and mingled with the oily blood already saturating the ground. She shook her head, astounded that she was still alive after standing there for so long, openly gaping at the demon knight.

He is the one trophy that would guarantee me a position as archangel.

Maybe that's why her body had seized. He was her ticket to a promotion and the reason songs would be composed in her name.

By the time she collected herself and slid into a fighting stance, Coriel had lost count of the number of angels they'd lost. When Zagan speared a malakhim with his tail, the pain in her chest was so intense she went numb.

Enough of this! What are you doing?

Coriel charged at the knight. Three angels took out two of the lessers beside Zagan, but he did not retaliate. Instead, his bright red eyes locked on hers and his menacing gaze pierced right through to her soul.

Gods, he took her breath away.

To keep from stumbling, she averted her eyes and recited her goal.

Kill the knight. Make Hell suffer. Become an arch.

Zagan's wings flared and he flew straight for her as she ran at him, her hands clutching her sword so tightly she thought she might dent the grip. They were seconds from tearing each other apart when a jarring thrum between Coriel's ribs made her stumble. The knight slowed, regarding her sudden pause with confusion.

Retreat!

She couldn't believe the message the archs were sending them.

"No!" she shouted at the sky.

Zagan resumed his advance, drawing closer with each flap of his gigantic black wings.

The archangels' instruction was the most nonsensical yet—running from the chance to end a demon knight when they had so easily slaughtered most of his army—but she felt the energy of the angels sigh in collective relief. Most took a few more swipes at their opponents before spreading their wings and kicking off the ground.

"Retreat, Coriel!" Erelim Tarael insisted from a distance.

His fear, and the fear of all the angels around her, dulled the rest of her senses.

"It's a trap. The battle was too easy and you know it!"

Battle angels of every rank were taking to the sky like doves freed from cages, but their numbers were smaller than she expected. They had lost so many.

Tarael kicked off the ground and joined their ascent before Coriel had a chance to respond. He'd made some sense, but her bloodlust was too strong.

She met Zagan's gaze once more. He seemed hell-bent on destroying her and ignored any other angels in his wake.

Yes, that's it. You're mine, horner.

She wondered how difficult it would be to cut through his hard, corded muscle when her blade met his chest. But before she could resume her charge, several remaining angels in her squad surrounded her, hooked their arms through hers, and took flight. When her feet left the ground, she gasped.

"No!" she cried again as she watched Zagan's red eyes grow distant. He'd been only a few steps from death.

"I can take him! I order you to let me go!" She continued to struggle in the grasp of her fellow fighters.

"Paha's orders," one insisted flatly.

"Since when have you ever known me to listen to Paha?"

His answer came through gritted teeth. "Since now."

Blinded by rage at her team's blatant insubordination, she writhed like a child in their grasp. All she wanted was to see Zagan dead, and by her own hand if she had the choice. Did they not realize they'd sacrificed her greatest chance of becoming an archangel?

And now, like a carrot on a stick before her hungry eyes, Coriel saw Zagan take off from the ground and follow them. He was nearly close enough to kick before they reached an altitude he wasn't able to meet. She stared into the flaming red embers of the demon's eyes as she was dragged up, up, further away from the snarling enemy. They were in the clouds before she could pull free of her squad. She cursed as she heard his roar, beckoning her to descend and fight.

"I can take him!" she shouted, tears of frustration stinging her eyes, desperate now that victory had slipped away.

Collective feelings of fear were replaced by a burn of annoyance from the angels around her. One cheeky taqaphim glared at her as they continued to drag her upward.

"We would love to let you fight to your death, Coriel, but High Archangel Michael would destroy us all. We had to bring you with us."

She fell silent at the mention of Michael, and as the skies of Manusya gave way to the blinding brightness of the Heavens, fat droplets of water struck her forehead and she was thankful for it. A feeling of warmth enveloped her and her comrades, and she closed her eyes, allowing the holy rain sent from the gods to close her wounds and cleanse her body of the rage and hatred that consumed her, as well as the sticky black demon blood that coated her skin. That same rain continued to fall to the human realm, where it would purify the battlefield, wash away the carnage, and dissolve the corpses left behind. She could picture the area being restored to its original beauty of fresh green grass and vibrant wildflowers—with Zagan flying away unharmed.

Though the rain had washed away most of Coriel's anger, she held onto the image of Zagan just steps from his death. Ending his life hadn't been her destiny today, but it would be her mission going forward—she would be the one to kill the demon knight.

As she prepared to suffer the wrath of the archangels for her actions, she kept images of donning archangel robes once she presented Zagan's head to the gods in the forefront of her mind. She would be the one to lead the Heavens to victory in this war.

CHAPTER 2

Before Coriel had even finished folding her golden wings to her back, her superior, Archangel Pahaliah, was pushing through the crowd and barreling toward her. Coriel sighed and shook her head as she watched the archangel approach with murderous intent in her jade eyes and thin, pursed lips. This would be Coriel's most painful fight of the day.

"Well, I hope you're satisfied with yourself, Coriel," Pahaliah said, her voice icy and thick with anger. "Diniel and the six malakhim he took with him, those you tasked with protecting the humans, were dead long before the battle turned."

Coriel's eyes widened and she went cold. How had she not realized Diniel was one of the angels she felt die? She knew her desire to kill had consumed her, and she wondered now whether she would have given it much thought if his death had felt like a boulder had hit her.

Oh, Diniel . . .

The satisfaction Paha obviously took at her shocked expression made her hide it immediately. Diniel's demise meant the humans hadn't escaped their death either; Pahaliah's cold glare confirmed it. Coriel sighed and stared at her feet. It didn't matter if they killed one demon or one million, or if all the angels died along the way—if a mission resulted in any human casualties, it was an automatic failure.

"I specifically assigned *you* the task of rescuing the humans!" Pahaliah cried, but Coriel was taken aback by the disappointment rather than anger in the archangel's voice.

"I don't know why you still can't see that saving humans is our number one priority. Michael made sure you were given the most important part of this mission because he believed you could handle it!"

Pahaliah tore her fingers through her light-brown hair and scrubbed them over her reddened face before letting out a loud grunt. "I knew he was wrong, but he convinced me you could do this. Why did we think you could handle protecting the humans, Coriel, why?"

Her shouts made the angels nearby turn and stare, and it took everything Coriel had to look back at Paha instead of yelling at them to run along.

Paha glanced at the crowd but continued their spectacle.

"Why did you stay to fight the demons? Because you wanted to play hero again in the center of the battlefield? Heavens everlasting, Coriel! We should have known better. I should have fought harder against Michael's wishes. As much as he and the other high archs have faith in you, you know it makes very little sense to me."

Coriel winced at the archangel's words. Yes, she knew her priority should have been protecting the humans from the demons. But if there were fewer demons in existence, wouldn't that make the job easier? Plus, those humans had summoned the hell creatures in the first place. As far as she was concerned, their souls had been too far gone to save anyway.

"But, Paha, the humans drew the penta—"

"No! No excuses! Each and every human life is sacred. We need to purify them all, no matter how strong you think the taint inside them might be. You must always have the utmost faith in them."

Pahaliah squeezed the bridge of her nose and closed her eyes. "Your chances are running out, Coriel. Michael can only defend you for so much longer. You are not an archangel. You cannot keep changing the specific orders we give to you and your team. And ordering around other erelim! Trust me, they will suffer the consequences for listening to you once again. If you want to continue to even *dream* of taking Michael's place someday, this behavior stops now."

Coriel could only nod. Pahaliah was obviously envious of her natural fighting talent and the knack she had for battle strategy. Paha was a stuffy, boring, rule-abiding archangel where Coriel was a charismatic, logical erelim with more drive than Paha could ever hope to have. Coriel should have been made an arch already, but Pahaliah had made it difficult for her to prove to the gods that she was worthy of the title. And since Ouranos had disappeared three decades ago, Coriel's goal was even further away. Many angels and archs believed that Coriel's relationship with Ouranos was the only reason she'd been promoted to erelim in the first place, and he was no longer around to prove otherwise.

At least Michael, the current high archangel of the erelim, saw through Paha's complaints and bad reports. Coriel was thankful for his continuous faith in her, but this time, she had to admit that Pahaliah was right. She'd never had humans die under her order before and would need to make sure it never happened again if she wanted to stay in Michael's good graces and see her name in the upcoming promotions.

Coriel sighed, hiding her guilt. "Who knew that a demon knight would—"

"Enough! I have every excuse to demote you to taqaphim, Coriel. I could strip the gold from your wings and replace it with silver, and then you would report to Tarael or Imriaf. Yet, I will show you mercy once again. I hope you take my gift and finally learn to protect the humans with your life."

Coriel opened her mouth to speak, but Paha's hand flew up to shush her. "That does not mean always focusing on the demons! In fact ..." Pahaliah reached over Coriel's shoulder and wrenched the invisible sword and sheath free from her back, and it materialized it in her grasp.

"On your next assignment, you will not be permitted to use weapons of any kind. You will obey this command, or so help me, we'll skip the demotion to taqaphim and make you a simple malakhim. Do I make myself clear?"

Coriel hated the smug look Pahaliah always gave her when she thought she'd won. Staring at her hands, Coriel refused to give her superior the satisfaction of knowing how upset she was at the loss of her sword. Though Paha waited for her to respond, Coriel let the silence between them linger. She answered just as the archangel was about to repeat her question.

"Yes, Pahaliah. I understand."

"Good. You are dismissed." Paha, with a curt nod and sword in hand, spun on her heels and left Coriel standing alone in the square.

***

Zagan rolled his eyes as he approached Jinn's Denn, Hell's most popular nightclub. He was here to see his comrades, but each time he dragged himself to his fellow knight's club, he questioned why he didn't just stay on Manusya. The line of lesser demons, all clamoring to be the next to enter, grew longer each time he visited. Would Jinn continue to let anyone into this place, or would he one day set some standards?

A shrill cry rang through the air. Reluctantly, Zagan turned to find a preta demon, with its lips curled in a sickening sneer, meeting the challenge of another who dared to push past him in line. The preta sank its teeth into the challenger's neck and whipped its head back. It smiled—as much as its species *could* smile—while it chewed on the meat it'd just torn from its victim. Blood sprayed from the challenger, his eyes going blank before he fell to the ground in a heap. Every other demon around them cheered. This was the fifteenth time in a row Zagan had come here and found an impatient demon trying to force his way into the club out of turn, and each time the demon had died trying.

Zagan walked past the line and approached the entrance, where three hulking blue demons bowed low and drew back the thick black curtain, giving him access into the club. Upon entering, his senses were assaulted with the heavy bass of dance music and the scents of sweaty demons, hell smoke and sex. The dancing orgy parted around him as he made his way to the corner reserved for the demon knights. The blinding, pulsing lights made his friends Oriax, Jinn, and Lamia look spasmodic as they waved and nodded to him.

Zagan didn't wave back. "They're imbeciles, all of them," he hissed as he sat down.

"Aww, what happened?" Oriax said with a mocking pout. He leaned casually back against the plush wall, light gray eyes peeking out from beneath his hood. "Your boys got spanked by a few angels again?"

Zagan snarled in response and moved his chair closer as Lamia poured a glass of cloudy silver liquid and slid it toward him. Zagan looked at the shimmering hellsglory, a cocktail of angel blood and milky-white liqueur, and hesitated. Whenever the strobe lights went dark, the contents of each glass glowed like a firefly in the night. He'd never noticed that before.

Swallowing, he slid his glass back to Lamia and shook his head. "I had plenty of the real stuff on the field, thank you."

Oriax gave Zagan a once-over as he pushed his burnt-orange bangs from his eyes. "Seven Hells, Zag, what's got your panties in a twist? You won, didn't you? And took out a third of the angels yourself, I heard."

"More than a third," he said, tapping his claw on the table, "and you know a true warrior only goes commando."

"Hm, maybe that's your problem. Your boys might need more protection." Oriax grinned. "Pun intended. But also? That's too much information."

"Far too much information," Lamia agreed with a nod.

Zagan couldn't help but crack a smile, which the two other knights returned in kind.

"Now, tell us what's really bothering you."

Though they weren't related by blood, Oriax, Jinn, and Lamia were the closest Zagan had to a real family. Few demon species remembered their parents. When they came of age—around two or three years old depending on the species—they were sent out to fend for themselves, to form their own bonds and make their own lives. There wasn't a group of demons more dedicated to one another than Zagan and his fellow knights were to each other, which was why it was so difficult to hide from them what was truly bothering him.

Zagan let out a heavy sigh. "I shouldn't have to swoop in and kill angels myself to ensure victory," he said, hoping they wouldn't call him out on his lame response. That was certainly not what bothered him most and they all knew it.

He was grateful Jinn decided to play along.

"Yes, well, that's what happens when you neglect your army," he replied dully as he reached up, grabbed a sconce on the wall behind him and pulled hard on it. He stretched his muscles to their limits, roaring in satisfaction as he closed his eyes and arched his spine. Several female demons, and quite a few males, turned and salivated as they watched the powerful fighter put his muscular form, adorned with silver jewelry and demonic markings, on display.

Zagan clicked his tongue in annoyance. "I was never trained by anyone, and I'm the best damned slayer there is. I don't need an army, and I especially don't have time to babysit lessers that can't fend for themselves."

Oriax shook his head and exchanged a knowing glance with Lamia. "Trust me, oh mighty Zagan the God Slayer, no one knows that better than us. But the king needs an army, and you were charged with running it. You don't wanna do it? Then now's the time to take *his* job."

Zagan leaned back and crossed his arms over his chest. "I do not want to be bound to this realm. The king is doing a fine job of doing nothing at all in Hell. Why take that away from him? Corrupting human souls on Manusya is far more fun than sitting here forever, commanding the demons those souls become."

Lamia shook her head. "Just take the throne and officially appoint me as general to the army already. I'm sick of picking up your slack and getting nothing for it."

"And what is it *I* get, exactly? The messenger constantly summoning me on behalf of the king. You can have it, but I'm not taking the throne."

"If you're so against leading the army, why did you even show up on the field today?" Jinn said.

"I'm glad you asked. It's the perfect example of the messenger being up my ass. He intercepted me on Manusya and interrupted my real work, insisting I join the battle because it was getting out of hand. Too many demons had been summoned and not enough were going to return alive."

Zagan had been in the middle of tainting human souls when the messenger found him. Though he'd been bothered by the disruption, he now found himself glad he'd followed the king's order. Had he not been at that battle, he never would have feasted his eyes on that beautiful little erelim.

"Well, be glad you still had soldiers to join," Lamia said. "If it weren't for me, the angels would have slaughtered all your lessers a long time ago."

"Killing angels is easy. It's in our blood. I ask again, why does any demon need to be trained in that?"

Lamia sighed. "The scent of too much angel blood overwhelms lessers. They essentially get drunk from the fight and need a leader who can snap them out of it."

It was nothing Zagan didn't already know, but that didn't mean he understood. "Whatever," he growled. "I didn't see *you* there."

Before Lamia could scold him further, Zagan was relieved to see Malarath—a scantily clad purple-skinned succubus and his favorite waitress—

striding over with her hips swaying provocatively from side to side. She reached the table and set a drink down before him. She always knew what he wanted without him needing to ask; a trait of her species he appreciated.

Zagan winked at her, and she giggled and winked back before sauntering away.

Oriax grinned. "She wants you, you know."

Zagan swirled his glass around a few times. "She wants anything that looks at her," he said, then took a swig of his apple brandy.

"Well, yes, but that still includes you."

Zagan let out a short laugh and shook his head. Malarath was beautiful, knew just what he wanted, and practically dripped of sex, but Zagan wanted a chase. Finding a female who didn't throw themselves at the knights the second they looked their way was nearly impossible, and while Oriax and Jinn enjoyed the perks, Zagan and Lamia had both decided they wanted more than that.

As he swirled his drink, Zagan couldn't help but think about the tiny, brown-haired erelim he'd spied on the battlefield. Even though she'd been created by the gods, the female was a work of art in both body and power. Though he'd just chastised his army for the same, he'd turned feral at the scent of spilled angel blood as he'd torn through her fellow winged warriors. But as soon as he'd laid eyes on her, he'd sobered instantly. She was a power-house despite her size, and even as she'd decapitated his soldiers, he'd found her breathtakingly striking—the most beautiful creature he'd ever seen. He would have served his pathetic army to her on a silver platter, one demon at a time, if it meant he could watch her fight for a while longer. The memory of her struggling in the arms of the other angels, trying to get to him and kill him, rage and determination in her eyes—and something darker, naughtier— had only further piqued his interest.

His thoughts surprised him. Never had he been so drawn to another creature. But she was an abomination of the Heavens; no matter how attractive he found her, he would never have her.

Maybe that was her appeal.

Zagan caught Oriax staring at him with a goofy grin on his face.

"I think you should go for it," Oriax said.

Zagan nearly choked on his drink as he took another sip. "What?"

"With Mal, doofus! You're thinking about her right now, I can tell. I know you told her you weren't interested before, but we're the king's knights, for fuck's sake. We take who we want, when we want 'em, y'know?"

Zagan frowned, confused, but then the conclusion Oriax must have jumped to became clear. O had assumed, no doubt from look Zagan had worn, that he'd been daydreaming about Mal, when instead, he'd been imagining how good that erelim would look on his cock.

"Uh, right." He wasn't about to admit he was thinking about an angel—with no intent to kill! No, what he had on his mind was far more physical. Far more fun.

"I mean, no!" Zagan corrected hastily. The last thing he needed was Oriax getting the wrong idea and trying to play matchmaker with him and the succubus. Mal was a sweet female and all, but not for him.

"No. Just ... leave it, O. I'm a big boy. The next in line for king, if you recall. I can handle myself, thanks."

Oriax shrugged, leaned back, and draped an arm over the booth. "If you say so, brother." A wicked smile curved his lips and bared his fangs, which gleamed in the lights over the dance floor. "More for me in the meantime."

"Have at it," Zagan said with genuine enthusiasm. Hopefully that would get his brothers off his back for a while.

"You'd better hurry up and pick someone, though," Oriax said, "or there won't be any females left for you after I'm done."

"Or males," Jinn added with a wink, and Lamia rolled her eyes.

"I'll take my chances." Zagan drained the last of his drink, then set the empty glass down and pushed to his feet. "I'm out."

"What? So soon? Have at least one more with us," Jinn said, throwing his arm up to get Malarath's attention from a nearby booth.

"Yeah!" said Oriax. "I won't give you any more grief about the ladies tonight, I swear. It's just, you've been a little moody lately, and every guy needs a little—"

"Afraid I can't. I haven't given my report to the king yet. I only stopped by for a quick drink and to see who was around. After I'm done at the castle, I'll be heading to the Moon Festival in Dellview." Zagan winked. "You know I can't turn down a jovial gathering at which to torment souls."

"Happy tormenting," Jinn said, his shoulders sagging. "But come back soon. We rarely see you these days."

Zagan nodded, but they all knew he'd stay in Hell for as short a time as possible. He was reminded why as he pushed his way out of the club. Bodies were bent over on the dancefloor, others pounding into them before turning and entering other bodies still. It wasn't a chase. It wasn't a challenge. Lust spurred on lust in these demons like oxygen feeding a flame. He wanted—no, he *needed*—more than that.

And he couldn't get that damned angel off his mind.

CHAPTER 3

The Heavens were built on fluffy white clouds, yet the ground held heavy marble structures built into stone cliffs that climbed high into the sky. Each building was an architectural wonder of columns, curved roofs, and intricately carved facades inlaid with precious stones, all surrounded by lush carefully tended gardens. Night never darkened the Heavens; everything was always bathed in light from the eternal sun. The constant, calming sound of running water could be heard everywhere as waterfalls cascaded down its many cliffs, running off the clouds and into the atmosphere of Manusya to help cleanse the world of its taint.

Like every other angel not currently on assignment, Coriel made her way to the city square to attend the daily vigil of angels.

"Erelim Coriel," a few said in greeting, bowing their heads as she passed by.

A fountain with cerulean water surrounded a stark white, impossibly high statue of the Supreme God. She paused for a moment in front of the massive sculpture and clasped her hands together in prayer, beseeching Him to safely guide Diniel's essence to the Lake of Souls so it could quickly pass through to a new incarnation.

Coriel found that, ironically, vigils held by humans on Manusya were more spiritual and beautiful than those held in the Heavens. Then again, humans held far fewer of these ceremonies than the angels did, which must make them more of an event for their kind. Angels perished daily at the hands of demons, corrupted humans, and manifestations—the half-demon, half-human breeds that were created when humans gave themselves to Hell's evil beasts. That was another argument Coriel would have to share with Paha; humans—half, full, or otherwise—killed angels more often than the gods and archangels cared to admit. Why was she expected to protect the malicious beings that often cared so little for her own kind?

She shook away the thought as a malakhim handed her a candle, as was customary, and she cradled it in her hands. It was a soft, chartreuse green, made of beeswax and bayberry, and was wrapped in a ribbon of the finest gold. Coriel fingered the shiny embellishment as she stood in quiet contemplation over Diniel and had to blink away a sting at the backs of her eyes. She flattened her palms together with the candle sandwiched between them, praying once again for her fallen friend. A warmth enveloped her and washed away her sadness; the gods could calm the fears and upsets of the angel population anywhere inside the city.

Now numb to her feelings, Coriel looked down at her candle as the wick ignited with a soft yellow flame. The additional light was barely noticeable under the undying sunshine of the Heavens, but its warmth symbolized the love and camaraderie the angels had for their fallen brethren. They all began to hum in unison; Coriel included. It was a song that sounded like the buzzing of a thousand bees, which, for a place that forced emotional comfort, could drown every human in tears of sorrow if ever they were to hear the tune.

The hymn lasted only a few minutes and died on a fading note.

"Safe travels, my friend," Coriel whispered before all in attendance blew out their candles at the same time. She usually wasn't so affected by the deaths of angels—it was part of the job, after all—but Diniel had died because of her inability to follow orders. Had she followed the mission, *she* would have gone after the humans. But she hadn't, and she would carry their deaths and Diniel's on her shoulders forever. She only hoped that when his soul passed into a new being, the Lake would be just and give him the brilliant life he deserved.

"Are you all right, Coriel?"

As gentle and filled with concern as the voice was, it made her jump and whirl around.

Her eyes widened. "High Archangel Michael!"

He was an archangel so tall she had to tilt her neck all the way back to see his face. He had golden wings similar to Coriel's, though with his rank, his looked as if they were inlaid with sparkling diamonds. Olive-green eyes gazed down at her as he waited for her to respond. After a moment of silence, he tilted his head to the side, causing Coriel to stammer.

"Am I all right? I, err … yes, I'm fine. Just … thinking about Diniel, and how I will avenge him."

"Oh?" cooed another diamond-winged angel.

Azazel took a few steps forward to stand beside Michael; two towering high archangels now before her like trees. Unlike her own high leader, Azazel's skin, eyes, and hair were all void of color. Everything aside from his wings was stark white, but even those had the white diamond speckles on otherwise golden feathers. Being a cherubim, he was able to shapeshift into a human, lion, eagle or ox at will, and Coriel always wondered whether those forms were also plain and colorless.

"Yes," Coriel replied, unable to hide her disappointment at his presence. She stood a little taller and crossed her arms as she met the head cherubim's gaze. "I am going to avenge Diniel's death."

Azazel's lip quirked. "And how, little erelim, do you hope to achieve such a thing?"

She lifted her chin. "I'm going to find the demon knight Zagan, and I'm going to kill him."

His lip spiked even higher, infuriating Coriel before the emotion was quickly suppressed. Did he think she was funny?

"But the demon knight Zagan is quite a powerful opponent. They say he's to be the next king in Hell. You plan on taking him down on your own?"

Is this a trick? Coriel bit the inside of her lip as she momentarily contemplated her retort, but as she opened her mouth to speak, Michael interjected.

"Coriel is a skilled fighter, albeit a little too eager to be the hero sometimes." His joyful eyes stole a brief glance at her, causing her to smile weakly as heat rushed to her cheeks.

"I have every confidence that if she had to, she could face and take down the horner on her own. Couldn't you, Coriel?"

Her smile broadened, pride surging and reinvigorating her, and she nodded. "Yes, High Archangel."

Azazel let out a dry laugh. "Hmph. You're right, Michael. I suppose she's conquered worse. Maybe he'll simply disappear like your last conquest, Coriel."

Coriel narrowed her eyes. She wanted to respond, but any mention or hint of Ouranos made her mind go blank. Thirty years ago, she had left Ouranos's temple in a huff, falling to Manusya to take her frustrations out on a few demons. When she'd returned, the archangels were surprised to find he wasn't with her.

"Ouranos was worried," they'd told her, "and he descended to find you, yet you have returned alone?"

And so began the rumors that Coriel had been so aggressive in her quest to become an archangel, her constant begging for Ouranos to support her had made him flee the Heavens for good.

She'd been fighting the rumors since then, but so many angels believed it, it might as well be true. She was powerless to prove them wrong.

Why can't the gods also suppress embarrassment?

Perhaps sensing Coriel's discomfort, Michael smiled in response and extended his hand to his fellow council member. "May the gods' creations guard your safety, High Archangel."

Coriel was all too relieved to hear the customary goodbye.

Azazel locked eyes with Michael and shook his outstretched hand. "Give it, and it shall be given unto you."

Coriel sighed softly as she watched the high archangel turn and disappear into the crowd of white, silver and gold. With only a nod of gratitude to Michael, she was quick to turn on her heels and peel off the other way, anxious to be alone.

***

Alexander was a manifestation who acted as Zagan's conduit for corruption. As soon as Zagan stepped through his hell portal and entered the forest surrounding the town of Dellview, he knew his protege was already at work among the humans, sniffing out souls that held a penchant for darkness.

Zagan spread his leathery wings and took to the sky. He landed in the trees a short distance away from the last house on the town's main road and drew in a deep, cleansing breath. Alexander's soul was deliciously dark, especially after the dozens of mass corruptions they'd performed together over the past couple of years. Zagan could do quite a bit of damage with it. Nurturing souls was an art; it took time to properly infect one, and to gain the momentum and influence necessary to affect the surrounding souls like a cancer. He was sure that with the evil already swirling inside Alex, he might have time to influence the entire town before the angels ever caught on to his game.

Zagan excelled not at raising an army of idiotic lesser demons but at corrupting the souls of humans, turning them to Hell's side when they entered the Lake of Souls. He'd recruited hundreds of humans that were reborn as demons over his two centuries of life. Without him, Hell would be sparsely populated.

A sign over the gate to the town read *Welcome to the Moon Festival!* It celebrated the gods and goddesses of the moon, but those deities were not here to protect the people from the darkness that surrounded them. Alexander was doing an excellent job stirring up panic among the villagers and festival attendees. Zagan spotted him making his way through the crowd. He would stop someone with a light hand on their shoulder, whisper in their ear, and each time the human's eyes would widen. Then they would spin on their heels and scurry about.

Soon, every human in the town had been alerted that Zagan would be making a guest appearance. A panicked soul was a moldable one, easy to influence when you gave it something to hold onto and feel safe with.

Zagan crossed his arms and watched the scramble.

"He'll be here soon! Quick, bring it all!" one man said to another.

"No, let's kill the demon. He's only one. We are many!" interrupted a third.

"Just ... just do it. Don't anger him, or the mannie." The man pointed at Alexander, the manifestation, over his shoulder with his thumb. "If we do this, maybe they'll have mercy on us."

A demon ... have mercy? Zagan nearly laughed out loud.

When he took off from the ground, the flap of Zagan's wings earned him a chorus of gasps and whimpers from the chaotic villagers. He saw Alexander look up at him and smile as he tore past the moon, intimidating the villagers from the shadows. Alex laughed and turned his attention back to the activity on the ground, grabbing a large wheel of cheese before running back toward the center of the commotion.

A table had been laden with a variety of wines, meats and cheeses, and there were tree stumps for seating. With the placement of one candle, the scene was set. People scattered in every direction, hiding in the same shadows Zagan was about to emerge from. Couldn't they guess that a demon would see even better in the dark than he did in the light? In the middle of the square, Alexander was now the only occupant at the table that could have easily accommodated twenty people or more. Sitting in the first seat in the far corner, he poured red apple wine for Zagan.

"Come, friends. Bask in the power of Demon Knight Zagan, the God Slaver!" Alex called.

The more corrupt souls, drawn to Zagan because of their darkness, emerged first, shepherding their significant others and children toward the table.

Zagan sat at the head of the unfinished wooden table with Alex at his right. He watched the villagers join them, eyes warily following along each of the four long horns that grew from his head. He made sure they saw his pointed black claws as he slid his wine glass closer. Leaning his head casually on his free hand, he lifted his glass and watched the wine slosh from side to side as he swirled it.

"And what is the meal?" Zagan asked.

Several of the villagers now seated at the table jumped at the sound of his rumbling voice.

"Steak, cheese, and summer vegetables as requested, my liege," Alexander said with a deep bow.

He motioned to the shadows and two wildly shaking women brought forth plates for each person at the table, setting Zagan's down first, then Alexander's, then the rest.

Zagan's gaze darted up to regard his partner in corruption. Some of the humans in this village would be a challenge to convert, but with this meal, they could win them all.

"Alexander Hillyard, a wonderful job with preparations once again."

Young Alexander—he couldn't have been older than twenty-three—smiled and bowed his head at the praise before reaching for the cheese wheel he'd brought to the table. Zagan had already begun tearing into his steak with his claws and looked at the yellow block of dairy that landed on his plate with disdain. He hated cheese; he only demanded it because the young man loved it so.

He watched his half-human conduit eat his own piece of wretched cheese with mild curiosity. Alexander had worn a hooded black trench coat over his black shirt and pants. His face was angular, his form lanky and lean, his soul dripping with darkness. Everything about him was unassuming, from his soft green eyes to his short black hair. He looked like an innocent human, spare the large fangs nestled between his other teeth, and yet here he was, stoking the evil within these villagers for a black-winged hell creature.

Zagan drained his glass of wine and slid it back to Alexander, who happily poured him another.

"Thank you," Zagan rumbled as Alexander slid the glass back.

Zagan found the steak dinner, combined with the scent of dark, terrified souls wafting through the air, delectable. He smacked his lips and slowly turned his burning gaze to the young boy and his parents seated to his left.

"A fine son you have here," he said, motioning toward the boy who clutched a small toy boat.

Zagan took another bite of his meal as he felt the mother's swelling sense of pride despite her horror.

"Th-thank you," she stammered.

He sensed a spark in the father's soul and mentally reached for it, pulling the darkness within him forward.

"He is not my son," responded the male, the potent stench of his rage filling Zagan's nostrils.

Alexander shivered when Zagan turned his eyes on him. But he wasn't looking *at* Alex; he was looking *inside* him, to where his soul sat, coaxing it to begin spreading its evils to those around him.

The woman flushed, seemingly perplexed, surprised and mortified all at once by her husband's sudden confession. Little did she know that Zagan brought out the worst in people; the poor man couldn't help himself.

"My apologies," Zagan said coolly. "*Your* son, my lady."

"P-please. Call me Adare," she said and then placed her hands on her son's shoulders. "And this is Rylen."

Zagan studied Adare first, then her companion. He leaned back and said casually, "Was it an affair?"

31

The man was all too happy to chime in, his face bright red as he leaned forward in his seat. "With a tailor's apprentice!"

The power behind his anger and jealousy was easy to encourage.

"Declan, please!" Adare gasped. Her eyes were wide as she gripped her husband's forearm and attempted to turn him toward her.

Declan shook the petite woman off with a small shove. "A tailor's apprentice, and who do you think is the one who made his sewing cabinet? His chair?"

Tendrils of Zagan and Alexander's corruption snaked around the growing spark in Declan as he continued. "And don't forget the gods-damned headboard that knocked against the wall as he fucked my wife!"

"Declan!" the woman cried again, crawling over him and trying to cover his mouth with her hand. She turned to Zagan, furiously shaking her head. "I'm so sorry. I don't know what's gotten into him."

Zagan shrugged and waved his hand dismissively. He knew exactly what had gotten into her husband; it was the same force making Adare desperate to shut her husband up to protect her pride.

Declan forced Adare off with another wild shove, nearly toppling over their plates and the stumps they sat on in the process.

"What's gotten into *me*? It was what you let get into *you* that's the problem!"

With a sweep of his arm, he cleared his dinner plate off the table and sent it crashing to the ground, rage consuming him as he stalked off—but not before tendrils of the evil that corrupted him had forced their way into Adare and her son.

The small boy cleared his throat, seemingly unaffected or unaware of the scene that had just played out before him. It was no wonder; he had just finished his second helping of the meal.

"May I have more, please?" Rylen asked, holding up his plate and tilting it so Zagan could see it was empty.

His mother looked mortified. "But, Rylen, you had so much already!"

She looked over at Zagan. "He never eats this much, I swear. He's the pickiest eater."

But it wasn't that Rylen was picky; the child had the scent of gluttony all around him. He liked what he liked and wanted to consume it in abundance.

"But it's so good!" the boy exclaimed.

When Alexander served him another piece of steak, Rylen shoved it into his mouth as if he hadn't eaten for days.

Adare launched at the boy, trying to make him slow down.

"My lady, please. Let the boy have as much as he would like." Zagan motioned for her to sit, and with a small nod, she obeyed and lowered onto the stump beneath her.

He nodded in approval. "Now, you eat as well."

Adare dug in without hesitation this time, smiling at her boy as he continued gorging himself.

"He's tall for his age," she said proudly.

Zagan nodded, smirking at the overwhelming scent of sin in the air. "I see that. Now, why don't you call the rest of your friends over to show them just how perfect your son is being?"

***

Hours later, Zagan and Alexander were once again the only ones at the makeshift table, clinking wine glasses together. Villagers, drunk on wine and corruption, wandered aimlessly around them.

"How was dinner, my liege?" asked Alexander.

"Quite successful."

Alexander smiled. "And the cheese?"

Zagan paused, then shrugged. "Fine, so long as you enjoyed it."

Alex laughed, then silence fell between them. In the silence, and with his head buzzing from the wine, Zagan's mind drifted back to the erelim female. What was the angel doing now, in the Heavens? Did she have a lover? As if he needed another excuse to take down the rest of her kind.

Alexander opened his mouth to speak again, but Zagan threw up one clawed finger, urging him to stay quiet. The boy's breath hitched and he squinted into the night, his dread-filled eyes scanning furiously for any movement. Zagan's pointed ears twitched, catching frenzied whispers that carried on the wind, and in the reflection of his wine glass, he spied two weapon-wielding villagers coming up behind him.

They chose pitchforks to attack the devil? How clever.

The humans were making a detrimental mistake. He would have scented the men in a couple more steps even if he hadn't seen them approach.

Damn it all. He closed his eyes and took a deep breath.

When the larger of the two men raised his tool to strike, he immediately gasped out in pain.

Zagan let out a small chuckle and shook his head.

In the light of the moon, the trembling villager, hovering a few inches off the ground, looked down to see Zagan's barbed tail piercing his heart. The other man stood frozen in place, wide-eyed and gaping at the sight.

Such prolonged corruption and rebellion from the humans would have tipped the angels off to Zagan's whereabouts by now. He had, with his own powers and the strength of Alexander's tainted soul, turned the souls of these people toward the dark as much as time had allowed. Now he only needed to put them back into the Lake so that they could be reborn, either as corrupt Manusyans or as demons to serve him in Hell. Some souls were still too pure to know their fate, but he'd done what he could.

Zagan sighed as his gaze settled back on the half-demon. "Oh, Alex. I guess this village has to go now, too."

But before Alexander could answer, four rusty metal points tore through his chest, and it took Zagan a moment to realize the second man had stabbed the boy through the back with his pitchfork.

No!

Zagan roared and the ground shook. He pushed to his feet and ran the man through with his claws, causing screams to erupt from the humans around him. He toured the village, extinguishing lives and piling the bodies on the long table. Minutes later, he stood atop the mound of lifeless villagers, covered in blood but with barely a scratch on him. Wings flared, he held Alexander in his arms and met the boy's wild, dimming gaze.

"I'm sorry, my liege," he gurgled, his chest spasming and his black clothes damp with blood.

"Look at me, Alexander Hillyard."

Alexander was a dedicated and talented servant. Together they had turned hundreds of pure souls to darkness all over Manusya. The half-breed was like a son to Zagan.

34

I could bind him to me.

Every demon knight held special powers unique to them. In addition to spreading the corruption of souls through a conduit like Alex, Zagan's other ability could only be used once—he could heal any creature, rendering them immortal if they weren't already, but doing so would force them into his servitude. He could make Alex healthy, but he would be forced to obey Zagan's every command.

Zagan felt the poison in his fangs and tail thicken as he prepared to bond Alexander to him. The young man's strength would return and his life would be spared. He could serve as Zagan's conduit forever.

But as he studied Alexander, questioning whether or not he should save him, he felt the poison thin again.

No. He has worked hard. The boy deserves his freedom.

"Thank you for all you've done, my son."

Zagan couldn't leave the boy to suffer and bleed out. Alexander's eyes went wide as Zagan took a deep breath, lifted his sharp tail, and punctured Alexander's chest, pushing the pitchfork out through his back. They both let out a small squeak, staring at each other as Zagan pumped him full of his regular, non-binding poison.

Tears welled up in Alexander's eyes, then his entire body fell limp.

Zagan held on to the boy's lifeless form for a while before extracting his tail. Then he straightened, exhaled the contents of his burning lungs in a shaking breath, and erupted in another loud, booming roar at the Heavens.

As if that were a challenge, a thunderclap from above answered his cry. Zagan could only laugh as a golden, burning stream of light burst from the stars. Oh, this was going to be good. Now, more than ever, he craved killing angels and drinking their blood to distract himself from his loss.

The angelic asteroid barreled toward the ground, briefly blinding him where he stood atop his throne of human carnage. It hit the earth quick and hard. The light faded to reveal a small, golden-winged angel, kneeling a short distance from his bloodied table and whispering a few words to herself. Her auburn hair fell over her shoulders as she stood and scanned the scene with a neutral expression.

When she met his gaze, Zagan froze. She was the erelim from the battlefield. *His* erelim! He narrowed his eyes as he regarded her.

What the fuck is wrong with you? You are next in line to become king, yet here you are, breathless before an angel.

Zagan was more than happy to take out his rage on this creation of the gods. "My my, erelim, haven't the Heavens run out of your pathetic lot yet?"

He waited for others to fall in around her, but no other angels came—she was alone.

CHAPTER 4

She should have been overwhelmed by the scene before her, yet all Coriel could focus on was how she'd fallen to Manusya without any troops surrounding her.

Where are you all?

This was nothing more than a prayer. She was no archangel, not yet, so her thoughts wouldn't reach her brethren. They had to be right behind her, though ... surely.

The demon knight Zagan looked even more menacing than when they'd last met. She scanned his body, studied the dead young man in his arms and the mound of human corpses beneath him. She swallowed the bile rising in her throat.

This close, Coriel could take in the demon knight's true size. He was nearly twice as wide and two feet taller than she, with two enormous horns protruding from his shining jet-black hair. Two more horns, about half the size, grew just above his long, pointed ears, and his lips were pulled into a tight smirk as he regarded her. Once again, he wore black pants and nothing else, leaving his chiseled torso and broad shoulders, decorated with swirling black marks, fully exposed. He was pure, devilish muscle. Every dip and groove in his body was purposeful, each sinful in its own right. His dark wings, larger than Coriel's, were rugged, leathery, and each armed with three spikes at their apex. They looked just as deadly as his tail.

Zagan radiated evil, even in the darkness—the epitome of Hell and everything she hated. She would not let herself get distracted by her inexplicable infatuation with him this time.

Needing to stall while she waited for her squad to fall in around her, she drew in a deep breath through her mouth, hoping to avoid smelling the stench of death around her.

"The archangels informed me that the man"—she dropped her gaze to the male in Zagan's arms—"was something of a pet to you. Yet you killed him with your own poison."

Shaking her head, she reached for her invisible blade, realizing too late that it wasn't there. Failing to hide her shock, she quickly schooled her features and cursed herself for her own stupidity. She hadn't been without her blade since her creation—she should have remembered Pahaliah had confiscated it.

Weaponless and without my squad ...

Fighting her growing panic, she kept her stance and expression as even as she could. She couldn't have been the only one to have heard the archangels' call, right?

She felt the blood drain from her face when Zagan's expression twisted into amusement. He knew something was wrong. From atop his corporeal mountain, he slapped at the bodies beneath him with his tail, like a cat waiting patiently to attack its prey.

"Alexander was a faithful servant."

He looked woefully down at the young man in his arms and gently set him down on the rest of the townsfolk. His eyes snapped back to Coriel's, and he grinned, exposing his fangs.

"And I will make *you* pay for what the humans did to him."

Zagan jumped from his perch and landed a few feet before her. Laughing maniacally, he swiped at her with his massive claws.

Coriel jumped back, flared her wings and flew toward the mountain of bodies. She wrenched free an ax she'd spied among the carnage and blinked away the stinging tears that refused to relent, her heart breaking for the poor villagers and the cruel demise they'd suffered. All at once, she understood why Pahaliah was so focused on the preservation of the defenseless beings.

And then it hit her.

She would be getting no assistance from her fellow angels; Paha was teaching her a lesson. The archangel must have waited until the demon had slaughtered every villager in Dellview before sending the dispatch instructions to

Coriel—and only Coriel. Clearly, Paha had banked on Coriel's eagerness to face the demon knight again, and her assumptions had been right; Coriel had dropped everything and descended without first assembling in the square or remembering she had no weaponry.

As Coriel descended, the archangel's telepathic voice had filled her in on Zagan's relationship with Alexander and what he'd done in the village. His actions proved to Coriel that these beasts weren't just fun to hack apart, they were completely incapable of compassion. Even though Zagan seemed to care for Alexander in his own demonic way, that was all it was—caring in its simplest form. But demons couldn't love. They could never be virtuous. Humans, though, no matter how much evil crept into their hearts, could always be taught kindness and humility—virtues Coriel also needed to work on.

Words had never been effective with Coriel, that much she could admit, so she understood why Pahaliah put her in this predicament. She needed to experience this revelation firsthand and carry it forward when she was reborn. She would no longer be the rebellious angel who only cared about the number of demons she'd killed in a personal quest for glory. If she was chosen to reincarnate as an angel, she would be a fierce warrior, hyper-focused on protecting the Supreme God's creations—humans.

Maybe then I'll become archangel ...

Coriel knew what she had to do. She didn't want to die, but with no sword or backup, death was imminent. Still, she'd damned if she didn't leave the filthy demon with at least one less horn or three before her soul left her body. Gripping the ax as tightly as she could, she dug her golden boots into a corpse and launched from the table. With a high-pitched yell, she spun and swooped, wings tucked tightly against her back as she jabbed the tool toward Zagan's face.

"Feisty little one, aren't you?" the demon shouted with glee, wrapping his tail around the ax's handle and ripping it from her grasp.

The tug sent her flying and Zagan took another swipe at her, tearing her skin open and causing her to yelp. She hit the dirt and went rolling, her arms wrapped around her abdomen, until she stopped with a *thunk* against one of the dead humans.

Holding her wound with one arm and gripping the table with the other for support, she scrambled to her feet.

"Why did you kill the boy?" she cried, slipping on one of the bodies but catching herself before she fell forward. The potent poison from Zagan's claws burned worse than any she'd felt before.

She gritted her teeth in agony. "Tell me why!"

Zagan regarded her through narrowed red eyes but then looked away. To her astonishment, he rose from his attack position, and his gaze fell on the boy's rumpled body. Coriel could have sworn she heard him voice a feeble sound. Zagan, evil personified and the creature that left beings across the three realms screaming with nightmares, whimpered.

Surely the poison is making me hear things ...

"The village failed," the demon knight said finally. "They killed him. I only ended his suffering."

He balled his claws into fists, and turned his gaze, colder than ever, on Coriel. "Erelim, bury him."

With the poison in her system, Coriel's vision had begun to fade, but she managed to stare up at the massive demon incredulously. Demons didn't believe in burying the deceased, let alone in asking angels for favors. Coriel felt, though, like she owed it to the boy to give him safe passage to the Lake of Souls. When a human was buried by a Heavenly creation, they were guaranteed a pure rebirth as an angel. It killed the angel doing the burial ... but now, Coriel had nothing left to lose.

* * *

Zagan could tell the erelim was trying to play off the effects of his poison. Her breathing had grown labored, she swayed on her feet, and as she looked at Alexander's lifeless eyes, her own could barely focus. Any other being would have already fallen victim to Zagan's attack. They'd be convulsing and vomiting and pleading for death by now.

When the angel fell to her knees, he thought she was finally succumbing, but she squinted and blinked as she took Alexander's head and placed it on her lap. She sandwiched one of the boy's hands between her own in prayer and began murmuring words in a language Zagan couldn't understand.

He stood before them, wings wrapped tightly around his body like a cloak, remaining quiet as the angel spoke her incantation. Relief washed over him when Alexander's body began to glow.

When the light faded, Zagan tilted his head to the side and took in the boy's peaceful features. He would return to his cave with that image of Alex and would do what he could to forget the contorted, lifeless way the boy had lain strewn among the dead.

I'm so sorry, Alexander.

He turned, ready to walk away, but he looked back over his shoulder at the angel. She still fought stubbornly against the poison in her veins.

"You have my gratitude, erelim. For this, I shall spare your life."

Her sunken eyes, with their lids half closed, widened as she met his gaze. They both knew he could tear her to shreds and indulge on her angel blood—the scent of it was stronger than the coppery human blood—though it was not what he craved from her now.

Her eyelids drooped again and she let out a small, humorless laugh. "You only claim to spare me because I'm as good as dead anyway."

He was surprised at her ability to still articulate her words.

Beautiful, and strong. A true warrior.

She swayed on her knees as she tilted her chin toward Alexander. "But before you leave me to die, we need to complete the burial."

"We?" Zagan growled. He'd asked her to bless the boy, yes, but he didn't want to be a part of the act.

Trying to focus on him, she labored for every breath. Her hair clung to her, drenched on her sweaty skin.

As Zagan watched her struggle, he supposed she was right—there was no way she could dig the grave on her own. He would have to finish what she'd started. After all, leaving a blessed human corpse unburied would make it rise into a creature neither angel nor demon wanted to deal with.

Dirt flew everywhere as Zagan tore his claws into the earth a short distance from where Alexander and the angel lay. The erelim was fading in and out of consciousness as he picked up Alexander and, kneeling beside the hole, spoke a few words into the boy's ear—the angel didn't need to hear his parting words to his faithful servant—then placed him in the grave.

When he turned around, Zagan was shocked to find the erelim on her feet.

"So, the demon knight Zagan has a soft spot for his pets," she mused. "Too bad no one else will ever know."

Chest heaving, she tilted her head back all the way, arched her spine, and groaned.

"I'm sorry, Diniel," she murmured, then coughed and closed her eyes, her entire body convulsing. She spat a wad of silver blood from her mouth before her eyes rolled back and she fell forward.

Zagan caught her in his arms, his heart thundering when he realized what he'd done. Now that he had a firm grip on her, her body limp in his arms, he realized just how tiny she was. Despite the armor she wore, he could detect her delicate curves, full breasts, pink lips and shining golden wings. Everything, even down to her long eyelashes, was the mark of a perfect specimen. And he drank her in.

Maybe the gods do create miracles sometimes.

She didn't have horns and bright yellow eyes like his last female. Her wings were the softest down, and she had no tail to speak of; everything about her was like nothing from the underworld, and he hated that she was the most beautiful thing he'd ever beheld.

I won't allow her to die.

If the other knights were here now, they would pummel him for that thought. He'd slaughtered countless angels without giving them a second glance, then he'd feasted on their blood and moved on to kill the next. What was different about this one?

Everything.

Seven Hells, he was getting soft. First, he felt affection for a half-human, then he'd asked the erelim to bury the boy, and now she'd captured his interest? But it was more than her gorgeous face and body that drew him to her. She was a ball of fire. Her pure hatred for the lesser demons had been obvious on the battlefield. She'd tried to hide her panic with smugness when no other angels came to her tonight, and the determination in her eyes as she'd fought the effects of his poison had been palpable. He wanted to see more of those expressions on her soft face.

I want her.

And, he decided, he would have her. He would not let this one go to the Lake of Souls just yet. Besides, a demon knight got whatever he wanted, and fuck if he didn't want her.

Zagan lifted the angel closer to his chest.

You're mine, erelim.

For the second time that night, his bonding poison thickened in his fangs.

***

Coriel wasn't sure how much time had passed from the moment she'd accepted her death to when a low, commanding voice jolted her awake.

"Erelim."

The insistence in the tone forced her to consciousness, though her body was weak.

"I told you I would spare your life. Now, drink."

Opening her eyes enough to peek through her lashes, Coriel found Zagan's wicked face hovering above her own. He cradled her with one arm and held the other over her stomach, bracing her at the hip. She caught the aroma of salty oil and sage—the smell of a much more potent poison than what had already burned her.

Groaning, she turned her head away. "No. I'm ... not an idiot, you ... filthy horner."

Still, the sweet scent of the liquid filled her nostrils. Her body craved it, and she couldn't muster the strength to hide how much it tempted her.

She turned away, focusing instead on the tombstone that had appeared over Alexander's grave. It was blank, but she studied it anyway, attempting to distract herself from the smell. She would choose death a thousand times over suffering whatever curse his sage-smelling poison carried.

Zagan chuckled. "So delicate, and oh so stubborn." Then, tilting his head to the side, he studied her. "Why were you alone tonight, warrior?"

Warrior, huh? At least someone *recognized that.*

She let out a humorless laugh. "Someone up there didn't want me becoming an archangel. Did it occur to you that perhaps you're doing the Heavens a favor by eliminating me?"

He arched an eyebrow. "If they wanted you dead, they're capable of eliminating you themselves."

She rolled her head along his arm and looked out into the distance. The sun was just peeking over the horizon.

"Sometimes, demon," she said, "the Heavens can be just as cruel as Hell."

His eyes narrowed at that. "If they want you dead, that only further encourages me to keep you alive. Plus, if you wanted to die, you would have given in to my attack long ago and we wouldn't be having this conversation. I am the antidote to my own poison, angel. Let me save you, and you can wreak havoc on those who have forsaken you. Is revenge not sweeter than surrender?"

He was right; she didn't want to die. Even as her vision had gone dark, she'd imagined killing Pahaliah for doing this to her. Now, this demon was giving her a way to live and seek vengeance. He would probably even help her with it.

I really am sick if I'm considering joining him.

The scent of sage grew stronger in the air and the demon knight's mouth flooded with taint. It slurred his speech when he said, "Come on, angel. Take back the Heavens."

Coriel inched closer to him as if an invisible force compelled her.

Take back the Heavens. Show Pahaliah I'm a force to be reckoned with.

She would make Paha sorry she'd ever been created.

Zagan planted a kiss on her parted lips, laughing into her mouth as his tongue brushed lazily over hers, coating it in his thick, spicy poison. She met his tongue with her own, greedily stripping it of his antidote and swallowing. She grew stronger in his hold, her vision clearing when she opened her eyes and looked upon him.

Laughing softly against her lips, he lowered her to the ground once she'd ingested enough poison.

"Good girl. Now, return to the Heavens. Heal, then find me."

He kissed her again, gently, and then stood. Spreading his leathery black wings wide, he smiled down at her, reiterating his command as he took off into the air. "Find me, my pet."

Pet? It sounded more like a promise than an endearment.

The word echoed in her mind as she lay shaking on the ground beside Alexander's grave.

CHAPTER 5

No ...

Gods, no!

Demons of all shapes and sizes had appeared in Dellview by the time Coriel got to her feet. She absently watched them devour the carnage their leader had left behind. The sickening sounds of smacking lips mixed with the crunching of bones and squishing of exploding organs between teeth made her stomach roil. Not that her stomach needed help with that; the spice-and-sage taste of Zagan's antidote still lingered on her tongue.

Adrenaline coursed through her as she tried to reconcile what had happened. She was convinced Zagan's antidote had done more than purge the toxin from her veins, but exactly what, she wasn't sure. All she knew was that she needed to remove it from her body immediately.

Coriel leaned over amid the demons' feeding frenzy, placed her hands on her thighs, and willed the contents of her stomach upward. It bubbled in her throat for a moment, then dropped to her core. Desperate to vomit, she stuck three fingers—coated in dirt, human blood, and gods knew what else—into her mouth. Tears stung her eyes and the taste of earth and copper joined the vile flavors already on her tongue, but no matter how hard she tried, she couldn't retch.

I should have known better.

Zagan had brought out her need for revenge and she hadn't been able to resist the temptation. Now, somehow, she was going to pay.

Coriel felt hot and cold, panicked and scared, as she straightened. She grunted and struggled out of each piece of her angelic armor, the clashing of metal spiking against metal ringing out among the sounds of feeding demons.

46

She couldn't get the damned useless gold, allegedly crafted for her protection, off fast enough.

When she had finally stripped down to her soiled white robes, she bent down and picked up an old pitchfork. Rolling her tongue across the roof of her mouth a few times trying rid it of the horrid mixture of tastes, she held the farming tool to her stomach and hesitated. Impaling herself and spilling her guts for the demons to consume would be a welcomed dream compared to the nightmare of living out her days cursed by a demon knight.

With a nod, Coriel sucked in a breath, preparing for the pain the tool would deliver when she drove it into her body, and violently thrust the points of the pitchfork toward her. With a gasp, every muscle in her body seized as the rusted metal kissed her dirtied robes. Coriel stayed there, hunched over, unable to force her body to obey her mind.

Whimpering, she psyched herself up and made another attempt.

But she froze. Another try. And she froze again.

Coriel screamed in frustration, knowing two laws, one of the Heavens and one of Hell, were against her—Heavenly beings were unable to commit the sin of suicide, and unless otherwise instructed, neither could any creature in the servitude of a demon.

A servant ... of Demon Knight Zagan? No!

Coriel thrust again, and her body seized. She screamed, rested, then tried again. And again. And again. Coriel lost count of how many times her body betrayed her, and so, giving up, she dropped the pitchfork to the ground alongside her armor.

As the demons continued to rent the flesh of the deceased humans, Coriel's vision began to fade. She felt herself losing consciousness but knew the demons would pay her no mind, even though they hungered for angel blood more than the taste of the humans. Lessers would never eat the flesh of a creature claimed by their knight.

Oh, Gods.

Zagan's words echoed in her mind as if he were beside her, whispering them into her ear.

"Heal, then find me."

Unable to fight her body's urges, Coriel's vision came back into focus and she kicked off the ground and soared into the sky.

No! No, stop!

But her body ignored her. Every part of her brain tried to fight the instinct, but the curse was dominant. Coriel was too tired, too shocked now, to fight anymore.

Is this what his poison does? Compels me to follow his orders?

Even the wind whipping through her hair brought Coriel no comfort as she ascended toward the Heavens. The holy rain didn't fall, but why would it? No one but Paha knew Coriel had gone to Manusya, so the gods would not know to cleanse her.

Paha.

Rage overwhelmed her, so strong it drowned her panic and sorrow. Pahaliah had meant to kill her, had wanted her to see the error in her ways, but had she considered the consequences to her actions?

Now I'm ... I'm ...

"Find me, my pet."

Coriel screamed as she broke through the gray storm clouds that had blown in over Dellview. Her entire body shook, her shoulders heaving violently up and down with angry sobs.

Sunlight met Coriel above the storm clouds and spread warmth across her face. Just as her sorrow had been overcome with rage, all her emotions were now overridden as the light of the Heavens blinded her. She wanted to keep her anger, though, and tried desperately to fight the feelings of calm, but the eternal sun vaporized her tears. The only evidence of her crying were puffy, swollen eyes and internal mortification.

Coriel ran to her chambers, shielding her face and her wound, already half-healed from the light and Zagan's kiss, but still evident from the stains on her robes. Other angels stared at her as she ran past, most likely confused by her appearance and offended by her blatant disregard. Or maybe they knew she'd been infected and cursed by their enemy. Maybe she looked different.

Maybe I grew a tail.

Her feet finally meeting the white carpet of her private chamber, Coriel slammed the door shut, crushing her golden wings against her back as she twisted the lock.

Heal.

48

How long did she have before she became a mindless puppet to the demon? A ... slave to Demon Knight Zagan?

You're strong, Coriel. You can beat this.

She checked her appearance in the mirror. Her sky-blue eyes stared back, albeit a dimmer hue than usual. Her long, loosely curled auburn hair remained the same. Dirt and blood—some hers, some human—caked and congealed on her face, and she rubbed at it furiously with her palms. It brought her some relief that her smooth, creamy skin still lay beneath the grime. Most importantly, she still had her golden wings to crush against the door and pad her panic. Thank the gods, she still had her wings. She was still herself. No horns, no barbed tail.

Maybe Zagan had only been screwing with her. After all, she'd buried Alexander at his request and he'd seemed genuinely appreciative, so maybe he'd only wanted her to leave before his minions came to feed. She knew what it was like to try to save face after doing something the rest of her brethren wouldn't agree with.

Yes, that must be it! She was fine. He'd simply instructed his lessers to leave her alone and pretended to all that he'd bound her to him. He was saving face.

She'd almost convinced herself when she heard Zagan's voice echoing in her mind again.

Heal, then find me.

"Ow!" Her hand flew up to her breastbone and she rubbed, suddenly feeling as if her chest was filled with embers that would ignite into flame at any moment. Pain turned into panic as the burning sensation grew between her lungs. Why were these feelings not extinguished by the Heavens? Because of the demon's curse?

"Heal."

She needed to heal. She needed to return to him.

***

49

In a fresh change of clothes and with her injuries fully healed, Coriel flew toward the archangels' council chambers. The urge to return to Zagan grew stronger with each moment she remained in the Heavens.

If I must return to the demon, I'm going to kill Pahaliah first.

Maybe that was what he really wanted, for her to kill an archangel or two before he tossed her aside.

If that's how I'm to be used, then fine.

She wanted to kill Paha, regardless of whether or not it was Zagan's curse fueling that desire, and if this was to be her final battle, so be it.

In her haste, Coriel nearly clipped her wing on one of the tall marble columns marking the archangels' council building. Bringing her shoulders forward, she angled her feet to the ground and landed with a soft click of her shoes.

As she continued on her warpath to Archangel Pahaliah's chambers, a male voice stopped her dead.

"Erelim Coriel, a word?"

Michael.

She cleared her throat. "Of course, High Archangel."

Pumped so full of adrenaline and rage that even the Heavens couldn't completely dampen the emotions, she wanted to tell him it could wait. Still, she forced a smile. This was Michael, after all—the high archangel who could ascend her to arch after Paha's demise.

Michael was eyeing her suspiciously. "Are you all right, Coriel?"

He seemed genuinely concerned. Everything with Michael was genuine. His eyes darted from her face to her wings, then bore into her eyes once more. She raised her chin and took a deep breath.

Take Pahaliah down.

Coriel would strip her of everything—from the title she didn't deserve to the soul her body would never again possess.

"Actually, High Archangel ... no, I am not all right. Pahaliah has done something most egregious and I believe it needs to be addressed immediately."

"Is that so? Please, step into my office and tell me of this egregious act."

Coriel was all too happy to follow him through the door, and her excitement over the meeting quelled the intense burning in her chest—for now. As

Michael made his way to the plush chair behind his desk, Coriel began explaining Paha's crimes.

"I was deployed last night. Did you know this?"

He tilted his head to the side. "Why, no. And it was Archangel Pahaliah who deployed you?"

Michael's ignorance only further confirmed Paha's wrongdoing. Coriel shook her head in disbelief.

"Yes. I was sent to Dellview. I was told the demon knight Zagan would be there."

Michael steepled his fingers and rested his chin on them. "Who else did she send without my knowledge?"

"No one!" Injecting more pain into those words than she'd intended, she straightened and gripped the back of the chair facing his desk. "Pahaliah was mad that I hadn't protected the humans in the field. She wanted to teach me a lesson, and so she waited for Zagan to slaughter an entire village of humans before sending me. I was resting after the last battle and when I woke up, all I knew was that Zagan had been spotted on Manusya. I didn't think. I just followed orders, High Archangel. And when I got to the human realm, just steps away from him, I realized I didn't have my sword. Pahaliah set me up to die."

Silence fell between them as Michael took in her words. "Well, I see you're here now. What happened with the demon knight?"

This was where she would need to dodge a few key details. "He had a manifestation with him, a young man, whom I assume he'd been grooming. But he'd killed him! The boy was dead before I arrived, but the demon seemed remorseful. I know it sounds crazy, but he asked me to bury him."

Michael leaned forward in his chair, incredulous. "He asked you to bury a half-breed? Surely he realized that would send the boy's soul to the light?"

Coriel could only nod. "He knew. I followed through with the request, and he let me go. Without my sword, doing as he asked was my only hope of getting out of there alive."

"But ... Coriel, if you buried the mannie, you still would have died."

Shit. She'd been so focused on trying to make it sound as if she'd escaped the demon and led a half-human's soul to salvation that she was blind to the fatal flaw in her story. But she couldn't tell him a kiss from the demon is what kept her alive ... and for a price.

"I thought so too, High Archangel. I was waiting to die, but the gods have been good and I have yet to perish." She forced a smile. "Blessed be the gods who protect their creations."

The doubt in Michael's expression deepened. "Yes. But you describe the impossible."

He stood, forcing Coriel take a step back. "There is something you fail to tell me."

She let out a small, nervous laugh behind her forced smile. "I survived, and I am here now. Is that not reason enough to rejoice?"

"No. It is not."

His coldness made her recoil.

"Coriel, you will tell me what really happened with the demon."

She glanced at her feet. Michael was good to her; if she confided in him, maybe he could help her.

"I was dying, High Archangel. Not from the burial, but from the fight I'd had with the horner. In exchange for burying the boy, he gave me the antidote to his poison." Speaking of it made her chest burn again. She rubbed between her collarbones as she studied Michael.

He watched her hand move from side to side and his eyes widened. "You carry his taint," he said, his words not quite a whisper.

Looking around as if to make sure no one else heard them, he walked toward her.

Coriel felt her burning heart plummet into her stomach. "I ..."

Michael moved past her to the door. She expected him to open it and leave, but he locked it instead.

"You know what this means," he said sadly as he turned to face her.

She froze. "No," she managed to whisper. "Michael, don't do this!"

But he gave a curt nod and grabbed her arm. "There is nothing I can do. You will be stripped of your name, title, and barred from the Heavens forever. We begin the falling ceremony now."

CHAPTER 6

She plummeted from the Heavens still breathing but feeling barely alive. Her body folded in half, and her arms and legs flailed about in the harsh wind as she fell toward Manusya.

She did not turn to see when she would hit ground. In fact, she hoped she would crash into the earth and die before she felt anything at all. Her soul would leave her, and she would be reborn in a new body, a new vessel with a fresh start.

But, as had been the case with everything these past few days, her wish was not granted. She hit the ground with a force that knocked the wind out of her, but death did not come. Instead, a fierce burning in her lungs showed her she was still very much alive as she struggled involuntarily for air.

Her wings had taken the brunt of the fall, sending plumage soaring upward before it fluttered back down. Though her vision was blurry from the tears in her eyes, she caught sight of her new gray feathers and couldn't suppress a whimper. The down of her wings was no longer a beautiful gold— that privilege had died along with Coriel, the erelim who dreamed of greatness. Gone was the fierce warrior angel who would bring down the demon knights and become archangel. Now, she was a nameless gray-winged forsaken. Never again would she look upon the majesty of the Heavens.

Arching her spine and craning her head back, she found herself gazing up at the tombstone of Alexander Hillyard.

So, I'm back in Dellview.

"Heal, then find me."

The burning sensation in her chest compelled her to call to Zagan. She sat up with a strained gasp and rubbed fiercely at her sternum in an attempt to ease the discomfort.

Call to him, her body told her. But her mind was strong; she would not give in.

She balled up the fabric of her simple brown tunic and shouted, though she bit back any real words that threatened to leave her lips. She sank her teeth into her tongue so hard that hot blood exploded inside her mouth, making her grimace. The bitter metallic taste of her new human-like blood was something she'd need to get used to. She wiped the side of her mouth with the back of her hand and looked down at the red stain it left behind. If she drew blood from anyone, she wanted it to be Za—Za—

"*Zagan!*" she cried, disgusted with herself as she spat out a red wad of saliva. His name had bubbled up like a sneeze she could no longer hold back. As soon as she'd spoken his name, the burning in her chest stopped, her breathing returned to normal, and the vice grip around her heart released. She closed her eyes and groaned as she hunched over in defeat.

A low chuckle emitted behind her. She braced herself, then slowly turned around to find Zagan crouched atop Alexander's tombstone, his arms draped over his knees and an amused expression on his face.

His eyebrows shot up as he regarded her. "Yes?"

She dropped her head and slid into a kneeling position.

Jumping off the stone, Zagan stood before her and dragged a claw along the underside of her chin. "Look at me, pet."

She tensed, though her head lifted at his command and her tears grew too fat to keep from spilling down her eyes. She wanted to fight—but what was the point now?

Zagan gripped her cheeks in one hand, moving her head from side to side as he leaned in close and looked her over.

"And the erelim returns to me as a reject of the Heavens. What did they call you up there, anyway? I assume it was not pet."

She choked on a whimper and her tears continued to fall. Coriel would have never cried in front of anyone, let alone the demon knight Zagan, but she was no longer that strong erelim.

"C-Cor ..." she stammered, though her throat tightened on the rest. As a forsaken, she would forever be unable to utter her full gods-given name again.

"Cor ...?" The demon lazily dragged his tail along the ground as he pondered. "It was probably one of those stupid names you angels always have.

Corion, Corael, Coriah, or some nonsense. Since you are no longer erelim, I will give you a name."

His eyes sparkled when she trembled.

"Cor … *Coryn*. A simple human name for a simple forsaken female." His clawed finger lost itself from her chin. "Yes, others will call you Coryn. But to me, you will simply be pet."

Coryn tilted her head up to the sky, feeling the hot burn of tears streaming down her cheeks. She gasped when Zagan's long tail came up to wrap around her neck, its tip bracing the back of her head and forcing it forward. She struggled to focus as he tilted his head to the side, studying her, and then he frowned.

"You really are nothing of your former self, are you? A shame. I've never bound anyone in this manner before, but from what I understand, you're compelled to follow my direction."

If he only knew. She dropped her gaze.

"Look at me, girl!" he roared, throwing her to the ground with his tail.

Growing more and more fatigued, she was only afforded a moment's hesitation before she let out a small grunt and slowly looked up at him again. He smiled in satisfaction, and she felt herself die a little more inside.

"Follow me."

Zagan spread his wings and took off into the sky, heading for the mountains east of Dellview without bothering to look back to see if she followed. He knew she had no choice, though she refused to follow without a fight. She dug her nails into the earth, determined to resist for as long as she could, but the longer she held back, the worse the burning in her chest became. She felt as if she'd anchored herself underwater and was about to drown. After only a few moments, her trembling hands released the earth, and she opened her wings and took off after him.

***

Zagan led Coryn deep into the mountains. The slopes were far too treacherous for humans to scale, and even other Manusyan animals were scarce on the steep mountainsides. Though defeated and miserable, Coryn took solace in the beauty of the range and its glittering, snowy white peaks that gave way to lush greenery. It was truly a sight to behold, and she couldn't help but thank the gods for such a gorgeous view to help ease her suffering, even if only a little. She vowed to grasp any potential moment of calm or appreciation; it would help her fight the curse and work out a way to detach herself from the monster she flew behind.

Following Zagan to a cave in the side of one of the steepest mountains, she landed inside, and Zagan wrapped his wings around his body and faced her. She knew she looked pitiful, but she didn't care. He didn't deserve her at her proudest.

Zagan sighed, and Coryn knew he was not impressed at having received such a broken creature.

"Come along, then."

He stepped into the darkness of the cave and Coryn followed, taking a few uneasy steps forward and squinting as she tried to spot him in the shadows.

"What's wrong with you?" he said only a few inches from her face, his breath startling her.

She recoiled. "Of all the things the Heavens allowed me to keep, it was my shitty eyesight in the dark."

Zagan laughed. "Cruel of them, but it's not only *your* eyesight that's shitty. All angels have trouble seeing in darkness. It makes killing them at night even easier than during the day."

With a wave of his hand, the torches hanging on the walls around them roared to life and illuminated the interior of the cavern.

Coryn's jaw dropped when the light revealed the opulence of the space. Furniture separated the cavern into different sections—a sitting area with plush couches and an ornate table, a kitchen with wooden cabinetry and a long dining table, and a bedroom with two four-poster beds, end tables, and chests.

Coryn blushed. Had he moved in another bedroom set just for her?

He made his way over to one of the chests and opened it, motioning for her to look inside.

"I have procured new clothing for you."

She pulled out a long, thick blue tunic and found it to be her size.

56

When she gave him a questioning look, he shrugged. "I have held you in my arms and slid my tongue into your mouth. Did you think I would not know the shape of your body?"

Her blush deepened, and for once in her life, she found herself speechless. She quickly folded the tunic and stuffed it into the chest, which she slammed shut.

Zagan chuckled. "Come this way, pet."

She glared at the back of his head as she followed him involuntarily. It was awfully chilly in the cave, and she wrapped her arms around her middle for warmth. She longed for that tunic now.

"C-Coryn," she insisted. "If you're to call me anything, at least call me that."

Stopping short, Zagan dropped his chin and then pivoted slowly around to face her.

"I will call you what I want to call you until you come at me as you did before. I am a warrior of my kind and we value strength. You no longer have yours. Show me you can get it back, and I shall call you by that name, though I suggest you do it soon. As a knight and the next demon king, I will not have a weakling bound to me. Build up your strength, and I will make you my angel of darkness."

Coryn glared at him, leaning away in a defensive stance even though she was sure he wouldn't physically attack her. "I thought you liked your victims battered and beaten, and their souls tortured."

"You are correct. I do like my victims that way. You, however, are not my victim. You are my pet."

Before she could respond, he turned away, motioning toward the rear of the cavern.

"Welcome to our home. We will move every now and then whenever we find new villages to corrupt, but for now, we will stay here. You may come and go as you please."

She didn't have to stay with him?

"I do not care if you spend the entire day away from me, but every night you will return, stronger and with more confidence in your forsaken form each time I see you."

He opened a drawer in the kitchen and extracted the only thing in it—a bejeweled dagger—and held it out to her. She took it tentatively, thinking it might be a trap.

"You will hunt. Kill your own kind, humans, large animals, even demons. I do not care what, just stop being so damned pitiful."

A muscle in her temple twitched and rage sparked deep in her belly.

His fangs popped out from behind his upper lip as he smiled. "You don't like being called pitiful, I see. Good. You are to kill one living thing of your choosing every day. And before you think you can be clever about it, I am not eligible to be killed."

Too bad, because she was already envisioning slamming the blade between his ribs.

"Your word will be enough to prove to me you did it. You have to follow my orders, after all. But every day, one death. I do not want a forsaken puppy. I want an angel of darkness, a warrior. I know you can be one. I would not have wasted my bond on you otherwise."

So, she didn't have to stay with him, *and* she could kill demons?

"Fine by me."

With her new weapon in hand, she abandoned the idea of exploring the rest of the cave and instead spread her gray wings wide, all too happy to leave the cave and take off into the open air.

CHAPTER 7

Coryn entered the cave with precious seconds to spare before the start of the new day. She'd followed orders, returning to the cave at night, but had waited until the final moments before the curse would force her to. If she had to deal with being bound to Zagan, then this was how she'd do it. She would follow his commands enough to skirt by while she looked for a way to break free.

Sure, she was testing the patience of her keeper, but some risks were worth taking, if only to preserve whatever sense of self she still possessed. Zagan needed to know that if she had a choice, she would not be here, and especially not with him. If he wanted to drag her into Hell, she would reciprocate.

She was annoyed to find no sign of him upon her return. So much for trying to rebel—he wasn't even there to witness her pitiful attempt. But just as she turned to watch the sunrise from the mouth of the cave, Zagan's giant wings covered the view.

He landed, smiled, and leaned casually against the wall.

"Why, hello there, little pet. Tell me of yesterday's kill. Human, demon, angel, or beast?"

Coryn dropped her gaze to her feet, the compulsion to tell him already taking root behind her ribs.

"You said you wouldn't ask about my kills," she said softly.

He chuckled. "My forsaken, I told you I would not require proof of your kill, meaning you wouldn't need to bring me the head of your victim or something similar. I never said you wouldn't have to tell me about them. Each one of those deaths will be etched into your soul. I want to truly corrupt you, not simply have my bond running through your veins."

She wanted to harness the anger that arose at his words, but the longer she refused to tell him about her kill, the more excruciating the burn in her chest. All at once the pain became too much to bear.

"Beast!"

She hated herself for giving in to the curse, even as her breathing returned to normal and her lungs cooled in sweet relief. The demon's lip quirked up on one side and his eyes glittered with amusement. More than anything she wanted to slice that smile off his too-handsome face.

"So you killed a beast?" he asked smugly.

She took a deep, restorative breath. "I killed a wolf in the forest at the base of the mountains."

"A simple kill, but I am pleased. What fun this bond will be." Laughing, he pushed off the wall with his shoulder and came a few steps closer. "You know, it's funny. You drank from me and it kept you alive, but you became bonded to me, your savior. You must obey my every command. Hell, I could tell you to strip and suck my cock and you'd have to do it eventually. Me? When I drink angel blood, it burns for a moment—gets me a little high, actually—and I heal, but I am bonded to no one. Your gods are cruel, are they not?"

Coryn tried not to show her annoyance, but as soon as her eye twitched, Zagan caught the motion, and a wide smile grew across his lips.

He leaned closer and, clearly taking enjoyment from taunting her, dropped his voice. "Make you strip. I very much like the sound of that. Should I do it?"

He pulled her to him, and she felt his erection against her thigh. A gasp escaped her lips, and he grew even harder against her. She wished she could say her body didn't respond, but arousal flooded her, shocking her. She'd truly lost control.

"Each time you try to subvert me, or come at me with that attitude of yours, should I tear you down a little more?"

She shuddered and her skin prickled as he leaned closer and dropped his voice to a whisper.

"I can think of so many ways to torture you, my beautiful forsaken. Shall I share you with my brothers? Or should I keep you for myself?"

"Do whatever you want, Zagan," she said, keeping her voice even so as not to betray that she was unbelievably drawn to him. "I can't do anything to stop you. Corrupt me, have the rest of your deplorable brethren do what they will to me—it will only bring me more joy when your kind is destroyed. One thing to keep in mind, though, as you make me your angel of darkness, try not to fall in love with me, because if you order me to pleasure you, that's exactly what will happen. I have been the lover to gods."

She wasn't sure why she told him that but enjoyed the twitch it sent down his cock. Was he imagining her now, pleasuring a god instead of him? Did that make him jealous?

"The skies on Manusya would crackle when I pleasured Ouranos."

He bristled. "The god who disappeared from the Heavens?"

It took effort to keep her shoulders from sagging—he wasn't jealous, and all the realms knew of the god's disappearance.

"In spite of the pleasure I gave him," she said quickly.

That Zagan wasn't enraged by her experience with the god angered her instead. She wanted him irritated that she'd been with another ... but why?

"If you share me with your brothers, I can't help when they fall in love with me too. It would be a shame if you all destroyed each other while fighting over a forsaken erelim."

Letting her smile stretch wider, she purposefully brushed the side of her leg against his erection. "A damn shame indeed."

Zagan growled, then there was a moment of silence between them before he matched her wicked grin with his own. "Continue to come to me with this much sin, with this much hatred ... and I may just fall in love with you either way."

His arms tightened around her and she fought back another gasp. *Yes,* she urged. This was what she wanted—his claim on her. She wanted him just as reliant on her as she was forced to be on him.

As if feeding off that need, he continued. "Your threats mean nothing. You belong to me, and I am a selfish beast. You will be mine, and mine alone. I will use you in whatever way I see fit."

He released her from his hold, and the sudden absence of him when he did was just as disorienting as when he'd grabbed her.

"Now rest. You may leave again when you are ready, but you must kill something more challenging than an animal this time. Human, demon, or angel. And from now on, you will learn the name of each victim before you kill them ... I want each one etched into your soul."

Zagan turned away and headed toward the mouth of the cave after he'd dispensed his new command. Coryn was shocked. She'd expected him to order her to her knees so he could make good on his threats. After the thick, hard erection she'd felt, the last thing she thought he'd do was leave. Breathless, she watched him open his wings and take off into the dawn.

Coryn stood frozen in place, her hand over her mouth. She should be relieved. She should be outraged by the way he'd treated her, yet she felt the need to press her thighs together to relieve the ache he'd caused at her apex.

You're so sick, lusting after him like this. She rubbed her thigh as if his cock had branded her there. *Think of Ouranos.*

To her surprise, thinking of the god doused her arousal entirely. She'd succeeded in easing her need, but it alarmed her all the same. Shouldn't Ouranos be the only one to cause her body to stir like that?

The extinguishing of her lust brought clearer thoughts.

She'd pushed him too far tonight, and now she had a harder kill to make before the sun rose again tomorrow. She only hoped she could find a demon to kill—preferably a lesser, for lesser demons had no names—or she'd be forced to take the life of an innocent.

***

Few things brought Coryn joy now that she'd been cast from the Heavens, but flying was one thing that still gave her pleasure. Feeling the wind in her hair and between her feathers was therapeutic and soaring through the air was the only way she felt like her old self.

I just can't look at the color of my wings.

While flying, she scoured the land for her daily prey, planning to spend as little time as possible in that cave.

Halfway through the afternoon, Coryn hit the jackpot—a lesser demon on the hunt in the woods just north of Dellview. This particular catch was a drude; a nasty, lanky thing with two short horns, a round face, huge eyes, and an emaciated body with sickeningly long claws and feet.

If she didn't feel enough like herself while flying, killing a demon would make it seem like nothing was wrong at all. Coryn swooped silently through the trees, feeling the familiar and delightful rush of adrenaline, and descended upon the creature. She ripped into his back with her dagger and sliced along his spine.

The demon squealed in pain, arched its back and, writhing wildly, fell to its knees, nearly impaling Coryn with one of its short horns. When it grew still, Coryn knelt behind it, and though she knew it was already dead, began stabbing into the creature's gray-green flesh. Rotten oily black blood spilled from every new puncture, and though it was satisfying, her angelic sword would have done a better job with the mutilation. Her strength wasn't what it used to be, either. She'd felt weak when she'd killed the wolf the day before, but she'd chalked it up to being tired and unmotivated. Now that she was doing what she loved most, hacking down a demon, she knew it wasn't only fatigue that weakened her—when the gold had been siphoned from her wings, her angelic strength had disappeared with it.

Still, she continued to stab the demon. Stab, lean forward, sink the blade in further, withdraw. Stab, sink, withdraw. She grunted each time her dagger met the carcass, low at first, but with each desperate thrust, the sounds she made grew louder and louder until she was shouting, unleashing all her frustration on the corpse.

Mid-shout, she was hit from behind and her cries turned into a scream. A second drude was on top of her, pinning her to its bony chest. Its long hands gripped her with surprising strength, and as she tried to fight her way out of its grasp, it dug its claws deep into her shoulders and collarbones. Though she screamed, she heard the demon's hiss.

"Well now, what prize do we have here? A forsaken female."

How did I not feel its presence? It was like Diniel all over again. *Idiot! You don't have the same abilities you had as an angel.*

Just because she could still kill demons and fly through the air didn't mean she was anything like her former self. The realization made her stop fighting.

The drude shushed her and sank its nails deep into her skin. It stroked her wings and cackled. "Tell me, creature, what made them cast you from the skies?"

Coryn didn't answer. The demon leaned over her shoulder and licked at the blood dripping from her wounds.

As it smacked its lips, she let out a small, dark laugh. "I wouldn't have done that if I were you."

The demon snorted and took another lick. Her skin throbbed where its tongue grazed her.

"Oh? And why is that?"

She grinned a devilish grin. "Because I am Zagan's."

As if that were a summoning, a loud roar tore through the trees. The drude's face paled, and it withdrew its claws from her body and scrambled to escape. But it was too late.

The demon knight, his face twisted with rage, landed so hard the ground shook beneath them. "She is *mine!*"

Coryn was surprised by his fury. Was he angry at the drude for hurting her? Or was it because he'd been disrespected? She didn't want to admit she wished for it to be the former.

"Pet! Come here."

As she approached Zagan, the drude made a futile attempt to run. Coryn had barely seen Zagan move before she realized he was beside the lanky demon and wrapping his tail around the creature's throat. When he lifted the drude off the ground, it kicked wildly until he shook it with his tail.

"She heals. Then I kill—no, I won't simply kill you. I will tear you apart, starting with your wings. I will make you beg for death." Zagan's speech had begun to slur. "You will pay for hunting what is mine. Now, pet, come."

Coryn shuddered, remembering the way he'd hovered over her, held her, spoke in that same slur as his mouth had filled with his antidote—and then he'd kissed her.

"I'm not doing that again," she said, unable to hide the disgust in her voice.

It was clear he wasn't pleased with her insolence, especially now that they were in the presence of a demon lesser than him.

"I am a poison, but I am also an antidote as you well know, my pet. I will negate the drude poison. Now, come to me and drink."

Coryn swallowed as the ache in her chest propelled her legs forward. As much as she wished she could refuse his antidote, she couldn't deny wanting to feel his lips on hers again.

His eyes were wide with rage and trained on the center of her chest, where she felt warm blood running from a wound caused by the drude's attack. Even through her pain, she was taken aback by how powerful Zagan was and how enraged the scene had made him, all because she'd been injured.

She looked up at him briefly, trying to convey hesitation and gratitude.

Then, Zagan took her in his arms, angled her face, and slammed his mouth against hers.

Coryn ran her tongue lightly over his at first, similar to the way the drude had sampled her bloodied skin, but when she tasted the sweet tang of his antidote, she grew desperate, drinking more than she needed and lingering just to indulge on the taste of him.

As her pain subsided, she caught herself and broke the kiss.

"Thank you," she whispered, backing away to give him enough distance to destroy the other demon.

The drude, who clearly knew he had no chance of surviving, suddenly found his voice.

"How low you've fallen, Zagan! Once a proud knight of our realm and now you're saving the life of a whore of the gods. The king will kill you when he hears of this."

Zagan's low growl was enough to make the drude flinch.

"Let him come," Zagan told him. "I'll tear him apart as well. Like this."

He pulled the drude to the ground by the horn, placed a foot firmly on the creature's back, then grabbed his arm and severed it above the elbow.

When the drude's ear-piercing screams finally subsided, Zagan spoke again. "I wanted you to witness that before I took your eyes."

Even Coryn shuddered when Zagan pierced through one and then the other with his tail. The drude howled again, though for a shorter time. Perhaps he thought that the less he screamed the quicker this process would be over.

Zagan leaned down and smirked against the drude's ear. "Apologize to her."

"Please ..."

"*Apologize!*"

With a moan, the drude looked blindly around, but Coryn made no move to let him know where she stood.

"I'm sorry, forsaken! I'm sorry."

Coryn had never heard a demon sob before. It sounded nice.

"Please, make him kill—"

Zagan slammed his foot against the back of the drude's head, smashing it against the ground. He pierced the creature through the neck and held his tail there for a while, staring blankly down at the dead demon. Withdrawing the barb, he turned from his handiwork and stalked toward Coryn.

She felt as if her heart was lodged in her throat as she prepared for Zagan to scold her, or worse. But no words were spoken between them as his red eyes pierced hers and he picked her up, holding her close to his chest, and then they were airborne.

CHAPTER 8

"Where are you taking me?"

After gathering supplies from the cave, they'd departed the Dellview area when the sun was high in the eastern sky. Now, it was low in the west and about to disappear below the horizon.

"Traveled a little too far for your liking, have we?" Zagan said, glancing at her before adding, "I'm taking you somewhere safe."

"I can fly, you know."

He knew; it was only the thousandth time she'd reminded him. The punctures in her shoulders and chest she'd received during the drude attack were almost closed, though Zagan noticed her eyes were still losing focus occasionally. Drude poison and the loss of so much blood would make anyone dizzy.

"I know you can fly," he muttered, though he made no move to release her from his hold.

He enjoyed having his angel close despite knowing he shouldn't—she was still showing weakness. He'd been treated to glimpses of her delightful intelligence and stubbornness, but he'd not yet seen any sign of the strength she'd displayed on the battlefield as an erelim. How could she have allowed a drude to sneak up on her?

"What abilities did the Heavens take from you when they made you forsaken?"

Coryn pursed her lips, clearly debating whether or not to answer him. But this was information he needed if he was going to mold her into his angel of darkness, and he would not hesitate to command her to answer.

Before he could, she answered of her own accord. "I've lost my ability to sense demons, as I'm sure you gathered."

She stared angrily into the distance, no doubt replaying the drude encounter in her mind. "Even if I had been ambushed by one of those bastards when I was erelim, I would have been able to dislodge his claws. I'm not used to this weakness. He would have been dead long before you ever had to … help me."

"Save you," he corrected.

Her ability to sense demons may be gone forever, but strength could always be improved upon. She'd need to train using different techniques than she'd used before, but with a few sparring matches, she would be good as new physically. It was her mind Zagan was worried about. Not only was she bound to him, a demon, but she was no longer an angel. She was an orphan of the Heavens, rediscovering who she was and what her capabilities were.

Zagan flew south, past miles of thick forest, an island surrounded by crystal blue water—"too obvious," he'd said when she'd asked why they couldn't stop there—and brown and yellow plains with herds of wildlife traveling over them. They were now making their way across another large body of water, and when the moon was as high as the sun had been when they'd departed, they reached the continent of Desir.

The fjords below were breathtaking in the moonlight. Coryn had been quiet for a long time after admitting her lack of abilities, so he was delighted when she came to life and looked between the cliffs. She peered over his arms at the earth below with eyes as wide as a curious child's. He swooped down suddenly, causing her to yelp and hold onto him a little tighter, then grunt in annoyance as she loosened her hold.

They descended into the trees, a few miles from where cliffs dipped into river valleys. Though he knew she couldn't see well in the dark, Coryn looked even more mystified by what she saw than she had when she'd seen the fjords.

Zagan set her down, and she took a few uneasy steps forward, gaping at the forest of gnarled roots before them, like those of mangroves with the water drained away. They were so large and rounded they reminded Zagan of a cave's tunnel system. It was hard to tell how many coniferous giants there were in this system because, over time, their trunks and branches had fused to create one gigantic life form.

Coryn placed an unsteady hand on the trunk of one of the trees, following the arc of the wood with intense curiosity.

Zagan let out an amused chuckle. "Didn't get to take in much of the human realm while you were fighting here? Welcome to Shen's Path."

She looked at him with an expression he couldn't read. Pain? Offense?

"I never had the time," she said. "But the gifts of the Supreme God are truly something to celebrate." She patted the gnarled tree like an old friend.

Zagan growled. "Your god made none of this, you know. And how can you still praise the Heavens when they cast you down to serve a demon prince?"

Looking down at her shoes, Coryn flushed. "Forget it. How did you find me, anyway? When the drude attacked?"

With a jerk of his head, he motioned for her to follow as he made his way along the tunnel of trees.

"I saw the second asshole in the tree but wasn't close enough to stop him from attacking you. I'm sorry. If only I'd been a little faster, I—"

He stopped abruptly, in speech and motion, and heard Coryn skid to a halt behind him.

I will not apologize for a situation she should have been able to handle.

He faced her with his arms crossed. "For the next few days, I want you to remain where we settle and rest. I'll hunt for us."

He turned and had taken a few more steps when Coryn answered.

"No."

Balling his hands into fists, his claws pressing into his palms, he suppressed the urge to turn around.

"I'm fine, really," she said. "Let me hunt with you. What happened today, how I let that horner sneak up and attack me, it's killing me. That never would have happened before you ... before I ..."

The muscles in Zagan's back tensed, but she said no more as they neared a smaller tunnel of shen trees. These hugged much lower to the ground, allowing for adequate cover for the night. Zagan motioned for her to enter first, and as she passed by him and into the tunnel, it took all his willpower not to spank her with his tail for her opposition. But wasn't that what he'd wanted—for her to regain her stubbornness and strength?

Careful what you wish for with this one. Smiling, he bent low and entered after her, then set their bag of supplies down and extracted a blanket.

"We will steer clear of my homes for now," he said, smoothing the blanket down on the ground. "This isn't luxury, but it's safe."

"Why wouldn't your homes be safe?"

Because now Hell will have been alerted to your presence, so it won't be long before the messenger comes for us.

"We need to lay low while you regain your strength. What little you have of it, anyway." He hoped the jab would distract her from realizing he hadn't answered her question.

He motioned for her to lie down and then looked around, growling his approval when he found a small section of trees that tapered even lower. He curled himself into a ball and tested the size of his new cubby. Lying on the ground, he bent his knees and planted his feet firmly on the trunk of one of the trees. He'd craned his neck so that his horns nearly touched his toes.

When he realized Coryn had been watching him with interest, he shrugged. "When I was young, my brethren would tease me and call me various rodent names because I liked snug spots. Always have."

Coryn laughed and settled onto her makeshift bed. "I'll admit it's a rather strange position. Did you kill everyone who called you a groundhog or shrew?"

She shrank back, scooting away as if anticipating a reprimand.

But Zagan only quirked an eyebrow in response. "Of course not. That would be savage. Now why do you look like you expect me to strike you?" Growling, he waved his hand in the air, signaling for her not to answer. "Tomorrow I will find us food. But for now, we sleep."

***

"I know humans and my kind share a love for meat, but what do angels eat?"

There was surprisingly little strain in Zagan's voice as he walked with a large buck slung over his shoulder.

Coryn, feeling wobbly on her feet and a little flushed, forced a smile. It really was an amusing question, but she was too ill to appreciate it. The only reason she was even accompanying Zagan was because she was stubborn and had insisted on going hunting with him.

70

"When we—I mean, *they*—aren't in the Heavens, they eat what humans eat, like meat. Otherwise, they feed on manna, but it's more of an energy force than food. Angels eat food for the enjoyment of it, not because they have to."

That didn't stop her mouth from watering now, however. No longer able to sustain herself on manna, she felt ravenous all the time. While Zagan hunted, she would find berries, fruit, and other small things to nibble on, and had even cooked up the wolf she'd killed so that it hadn't gone to waste. Since she'd fallen, she enjoyed the taste of food and the satisfying fullness it gave her more than ever.

The only difference is now I need to eat to survive.

For a brief, terrifying moment, everything in Coryn's vision went dark. She was unable to tell which way was up, but the sensation passed as quickly as it'd arrived. Zagan had already turned away from her to lead the way back to Shen's Path and hadn't noticed her fumble. She was relieved; the last thing she wanted was for him to get mad and force her to drink more of his antidote. Well, no—it wasn't the last thing she wanted, which was exactly why it scared her. She found herself craving the feel of Zagan's lips against hers more and more, though she pretended it was the sweet-and-spicy taste of his antidote she hungered for, not the way she felt when he kissed her.

Trying to focus on the ground and sound as normal as she could as vertigo set in, she stammered, "I-I hear a stream through the trees over there. I'm thirsty, so ... I'm just going to grab a drink."

She straightened, walking stiffly toward the sound of the rushing water and knowing he'd caught on to her lie, but he let her walk a few paces through the trees on her own before she heard him following.

As she fell to her knees beside the stream, he sighed and turned away, mumbling, "I'm going to collect wood for the fire."

Coryn splashed cold water on her face and took a few long, eager drinks from her cupped hands. While it helped her dizziness, it had no effect on her nausea. She felt as if her body was on fire, and by the time she sat back from the water's edge, her hair, clothes, and wings were dripping with a mixture of fresh water and sweat.

The next thing she knew, Zagan was leaning casually against a nearby tree, turning kebabs of buck meat over a fire.

71

"Are you feeling a bit better?" he asked when he caught her staring at him.

She tried to look away, only to find her neck stiffening. She gasped for more air, her chest heaving, and she was leaning so close to the water she was afraid she might fall in.

"I feel like I'm being ripped apart and cooked from the inside," she admitted with effort, her stomach flopping to mirror the agony she'd just described.

Zagan was suddenly hunched over the stream beside her, and she felt the heat emanating off his body.

"I was waiting for this," he said. "It's the drude poison having its way with you. I'm impressed it took so long." Gently, he steadied her wobbling form with his tail.

She turned to look up at him. "I thought you negated the poison with your antidote?"

Zagan shrugged. "You didn't die, did you?"

Before she could shoot him a sassy *I wish*, she lurched forward and began retching into the stream in forceful waves. As her eyes filled with tears and the muscles in her throat moved to purge everything from her stomach, all Coryn could think of was how incredibly fast her sickness had come on and how indifferent Zagan was to it.

When it seemed she was finally done vomiting, Zagan took her by the shoulders and gently coaxed her toward the fire he'd built. He leaned her against the tree trunk, then settled in beside her and wrapped one wing around her back like a shield.

"Stay close to the fire and underneath my wing, pet. The heat will make you sweat out some of the toxin. I know it's difficult, but you'll also need to eat and drink to absorb and purge what's left. You're welcome to my antidote, too, but I don't know how much it will help you. And if you need to vomit, go ahea—"

As soon as he'd said the word vomit, she did. It was mortifying. She would take a drink or a bite at his insistence, but moments later, she would lose that, too. As much as she craved his kiss, she was too embarrassed to ask for it— she was sure her breath and mouth were less than pleasant. Throughout the ordeal, Zagan stayed silent with his wing around her and ate his own meal.

Her muscles, stomach, and throat were all spent from retching, and she glistened with sweat and continued to pant. However, her body did seem to be purging the toxin.

For her final vomiting fits, Zagan led her to the stream. He set her on her knees and steadied her, though she half expected him to leave her to die. Inexplicably, he stayed, and she was thankful for it. She leaned against him to keep from falling over, head heavy on his side, one sleeve torn from her tunic to act as a rag that she used to clean herself up as best she could.

Several minutes passed without another attack; it seemed as if she was finally over the worst of it.

"I ... think I'm okay ... to get cleaned up at least."

She was sure that if she wanted to escape her sick area, he certainly did. She couldn't fathom how he'd been eating beside her through all of this.

Still feverish, she lifted her heavy, throbbing head from his side and moved to splash more water on her face.

And then everything went black.

CHAPTER 9

Beneath the shen trees, Zagan breathed a sigh of relief as Coryn finally stirred. She sat up slowly, chin against her chest and eyelids fluttering, though she seemed to be having a difficult time opening them.

"Zagan?" she called out blindly.

He couldn't help but smile. "Yes, good morning. I'm here."

Swinging his tail around, he caught her forehead, slowly pushing it upright while feeling for her temperature at the same time. "Your fever has finally broken. Good."

"How long was I asleep?" she asked, voice dry and raspy.

Her lids finally cracked open and he studied her gorgeous crystal blues. There was health in those eyes; a sign that her strength had overcome her sickness.

"You were out for a day. You must be ravenous." When he was sure she could support her own weight, he removed his tail from her forehead and wrapped it around a bowl of water that sat nearby. "Drink."

She grunted as his command took hold, then she leaned forward and clamped her lips on the side of the bowl. He tilted it and she drank desperately, one loud gulp after another.

When the bowl was empty, she wiped her mouth with the back of her hand. "Before you command me to eat something too, I *need* to bathe."

"The river it is," he said, helping her to her feet. "But once you are clean, you're eating."

"Yes, yes."

Zagan heard the splashing of water through the brush where Coryn had submerged herself, and he furiously scanned their surroundings. The temptation to peek through the leaves and branches made him tremble, but if any other creature happened upon her naked form, there would be hell to pay.

He caught sight of her bare shoulder and stumbled. *Get a hold of yourself, you idiot!*

Was he some kind of prepubescent fledgling? He'd seen the naked female form before—but not hers. And that made his imagination run wild. She would be so warm, so smooth to the touch. She'd be a treasure trove of pleasure, both for giving and receiving. It took all his self-control to keep standing guard.

He saw her arm extend and pull her clean clothing off a branch. Good, she was finally done and he could relax—from being on the brink of murder should anyone have seen her, and from almost short-circuiting at being only steps away from his naked angel.

She emerged, smelling fresh and clean, and let out a contented sigh. "How about that food now?"

He led her back to their lair and handed her a bowl of fruit. "Eat up."

He took an apple and bit into it.

"That sounds *so* good," Coryn said and selected an apple of her own. She took a bite, tilted her head back and moaned, causing his jaw to drop open and his mouthful of apple to nearly spill from his mouth. He wanted to elicit more moans like that from her.

She caught him staring, and he cleared his throat and looked away.

"You seem better," he said, "but you will stay here and rest today. I mean it this time. No more following me and wearing yourself out. I'll go out if we need more food or supplies, but you need to continue building up your strength."

She scoffed and shook her head. "Continue? What strength is there to *continue* building?"

Letting out an exasperated sigh, Zagan shifted so he sat beside her. She went rigid as he wound his tail around her waist, but she did not try to get out of the hold. He took another bite of his apple and chewed it slowly, letting the silence hang between them while he thought about how to word his next statement.

"I have seen high-ranking demons in their prime fall to drudes before." He recalled a number of attacks he'd witnessed in the line to Jinn's Denn alone. "Huge, hulking bastards who gave in to the poison far quicker than you. Most succumb to it. You did not."

"You helped me with that."

"I wasn't sure my antidote would work. In fact, I don't think it had anything to do with your healing at all."

"What, so you lied to me? I could have died?"

"Despite what you think about my kind, most demons do not lie, myself included. I told you my assumption, which was that my poison would counteract the drude's. I realized it hadn't when you got sick."

"It may not have counteracted it entirely, but it may have helped me survive."

"Pet, *you* beat the drude poison all on your own. I only got a pleasurable kiss out of it." He smiled, thinking about how soft her lips had felt on his. "I'm proud of you for fighting it and am happy that you are still with me."

He could feel her eyes on him as he took an orange from the bowl and bit into it. Grimacing, he swallowed. "I'll never understand oranges. The skin tastes so bad."

Coryn raised an eyebrow and fixed her gaze on him, as if trying to gauge whether or not he was serious. Then, she leaned forward and burst out laughing.

Zagan stifled a gasp as the beautiful sound escaped Coryn's lips. He'd never heard anything like it before.

Forget moans. I want to hear her laugh like that again.

But also moans, he thought with an inward chuckle.

"I'm about to rock your world, Zagan," she said, pushing off the trees.

Grabbing the last orange from the bowl, she sank her nails into it and pulled back the skin, then scooted forward. She sat on her knees in front of him, peeled a segment from the inside of the fruit and held it to his lips.

"Try it this way," she said, wiping a tear from her cheek, and Zagan noted that her tears of laughter were so much more beautiful than her tears of anguish.

When he was finally able to tear his gaze from hers, he stared at the orange slice in her hand. Leaning forward, he took the fruit between his teeth and a chill ran down his spine at the touch of her fingers against his lips. He couldn't help but give those little fingers an appreciative nip and was delighted by the small gasp it drew from her. He sat back and closed his eyes, focusing on the sweet taste of the skinless orange on his tongue.

"Holy shit." He swallowed the treat and forced himself not to jump with excitement. He was a knight, not a child, and he would control himself as such. Although, Coryn made him feel like more than a knight, like he wanted to give her anything her beautiful heart desired.

It was a strange feeling. *Love.*

His eyes widened—he hoped she'd assume his reaction was caused by his excitement over tasting the fruit—and quickly shook the thought away. He was an ashmedai demon, fully versed in the art of lust but incapable of love. Besides, that word felt far too heavy.

Affection. Yes. He had a certain affection for her, like a human would for any pet.

She watched him closely, clearly eager to hear his thoughts on the fruit.

In that moment, Zagan knew he was lying to himself. The affection he felt for her wasn't so innocent. He was certain it went much, much deeper. He wanted to understand it, what love could be, and was surprised to realize he wanted to feel that way about her.

Still lost in thought, he stared at Coryn for a while longer, then tilted his head and slowly leaned forward. He brought one hand up and pressed it gently against the side of her head, tilting it so her wide-eyed expression was at the opposite diagonal of his own. He brought her closer, closer, until their lips met. She inhaled a stilted breath, and he was surprised to find that, as he licked at her lips with the sweet taste of orange still on his tongue, she opened for him.

This kiss was different from the lustful, heady primal embraces he'd shared with female demons. It was also different from those he and Coryn had shared when his antidote had been thick on their tongues.

This ... this made his heart feel numb yet ache at the same time, like the weight of all of Manusya was sitting on his chest.

Coryn stiffened beside him, and Zagan broke the kiss and pulled back to study her features. She gazed into his eyes with equal curiosity. Was she trying to figure out how she felt just as he was? He'd certainly enjoyed their kiss; could she possibly feel the same way? He'd thought it unlikely, but he knew the blush on her cheeks hadn't been caused by the cool air surrounding them.

He leaned away, clearing his throat, and proceeded as if the moment had never happened.

"So, watermelon. Do you open that as well? Because I love the red part but hate how hard the skin is."

Casually, he picked up another orange slice from her hands and took a bite.

Coryn inhaled a shaky breath, clearly just as surprised in the change of topic as she'd been with the kiss.

Good. Do not let her grow comfortable.

A mixture of emotions—shock, happiness, and … disappointment?—played across her features in quick succession, then she let out a slow exhale and nodded.

"You open that too," she confirmed softly. She hovered a hand over the bowl of fruit, then chose a grape from the selection and popped it into her mouth. "You open any kind of melon. And grapefruit, kiwi, pineapple …"

Zagan shuddered at the mention of pineapple. *So that's how it's done.*

He was contemplating that when Coryn drew in another deep breath and asked quickly on the exhale, "So what was that kiss about?"

He smiled, appreciating that her mind still lingered on the moment. He loved the delicious way she chewed on her bottom lip and watched her teeth play, imagining giving her more of what they both craved. But he couldn't let her grow comfortable.

"It was just that. A kiss."

"It had no antidote on it this time."

"I know."

And it'd meant more to him than he'd anticipated. He'd known lust, but this was on another level. Yes, he thought about ravaging her body—and he folded his hands in his lap to keep from doing just that—but there was an additional layer to this that he'd never before experienced.

But he decided to play innocent, the ironic contradiction that a demon knight could do such a thing not getting lost on him. Cocking his head to the side, he said, "I want to do it again, yet I can't tell how you felt about the last one."

"It was … passionate."

"Is that bad?"

The beautiful pink hue on Coryn's cheeks deepened and she took a moment to respond. "No, it was just ... surprising."

"How did you expect me to kiss you?"

"I'll show you," she said, her voice taking on a sultry tone she hadn't before possessed. She set the bowl down and shifted onto her knees, pivoting so she faced him.

Goosebumps swept across Zagan's skin, but he remained frozen, his entire body going rock hard before she even began leaning forward. What was this little winged vixen doing to him?

Coryn's eyelashes brushed his cheek, making him gasp, and they were closely followed by her lips. The contact left his skin tingling.

"That would have said, I'm glad you're feeling better."

Then she gave him a sweet, close-lipped kiss on the mouth and lingered there a moment. It was everything he could do not to take her right then and there.

"That would have said, I think I like you. But," she said, "I kind of wanted you to kiss me like this." She lifted her mouth to his, but this time licked across his lips and had him open for her, reminding him of the moment right before he'd plunged his poison down her throat.

Her tongue on his was pure decadence, and as she explored his mouth, he desperately tried to hold back from returning her kiss too eagerly. He nearly cried out when she finally pulled away, breaking the kiss with a beautiful smacking of their lips. When she opened her eyes, they were dark with heat, and he was sure that seeing her that way made his body temperature raise an entire degree.

"That would have said, I want you," she finished, her voice hoarse and sexy.

Burning Hells! He hadn't expected such a wanton reaction to his curious lip-lock—but he loved it. This was a game he was very much interested in playing with her, and he could no longer deny his body's desire to claim hers. Sure, he could have commanded her to ride his cock every night since he'd bonded her, but knowing she wanted him of her own accord made this far more rewarding.

79

Without speaking, he pulled her into his lap. "I want to be your lover," he murmured, his voice gravelly, and the gasp that erupted from his little angel made him groan in approval.

He fused their mouths, massaging her tongue with his own, and drew her tighter against him. In a dizzying high of desire, he broke the kiss, releasing a low growl as he kissed down her neck, gently nipping at her skin.

"Coryn ..."

***

I want to be your lover.

What strange syntax for a demon. Coryn would have understood if he'd said he wanted *her* to be *his* lover, a more possessive claim than giving something of himself to her. Yet, as her body burned with need, she knew she didn't care how he claimed her—so long as he did.

Even more surprising, though, was that he'd said her name. The name he'd given her. It rolled off that delicious tongue of his with ease and she loved the sound.

What was he doing to her? She didn't care.

She moaned as he kissed down her neck and shivered when his growl vibrated against her flesh. She ran her fingers over his own, encouraging him to explore her body, and then put her hands on him. He was all hard, taut muscle, and she wanted to learn every rope, every groove, every curve.

"Zagan," she whimpered, hoping to hear her name leave his lips again.

She shifted, positioning herself so that his erection stood between her legs. Gods, he was so hard! Sliding up his cock with their clothes between them, she cried out in pleasure.

Groaning, Zagan trailed his hands slowly down her body, over the curve of her backside and along her thighs. Reaching the hem of her tunic, he hiked it up higher. But instead of responding with her name, he kissed her with animalistic urgency. Extending his claws, he ran them across her skin and cut away her panties, then slipped her tunic over her head in one swift movement. When all that remained was her bra, he pulled away from her lips and admired her nearly naked form.

"I always knew you'd be beautiful, but this …" He kissed her again, moaning as he bit her lower lip. His claw tip grazed her bra, ripping the fabric, and he pulled the garment away. "Coryn. My Coryn."

"Yours," she breathed with a shudder.

She would never grow tired of hearing her name escape his lips. Panting and flushed from his touch, his regard for her body, and his sexy words, she leaned forward and pressed her bare breasts against his warm skin. His hands came up to stroke her feathered wings, and she ran hers through his hair, over his shoulders and back. She dragged her nails against his skin, making soft noises as she kissed, nipped and sucked down his chest.

When Zagan retracted his claws and slid his hand between her legs and found her center, she almost exploded with release. Though he was naive when it came to romance, he was an expert in handling her body.

He smirked, applying pressure to her exposed bud with his palm as he brushed along her slit with skilled fingers. Digging her nails into his back beneath his wings, she bucked and cried out for him, already so sensitive to his touch. He groaned and arched into her, lifting her legs off the ground as he greedily sucked one of her nipples into his mouth. He sought her other breast with his free hand and squeezed roughly, making her cry out in delicious pleasure-pain.

"Coryn," he growled, "I must have you. Now."

He'd reduced her to an animal in heat, and she wanted to give him every part of her as they sought sweet release together. She wrapped an arm around him and, breathing heavily in his ear, trailed a hand down to his arousal, pressing against it through the fabric of his pants. Feeling him stiffen even further under her grasp, she purred, tore wildly at the fly of his pants and freed him. She took him in her hand and gripped tightly, stroking up and down.

"Take me," she groaned, her voice husky. Whimpering, she bit his earlobe and pressed herself closer to him. "Gods, Zagan, please have me."

She felt him smirk against her skin, and he bit down, hard enough to make her gasp but not to draw blood.

"My Coryn, I shall make you mine in the most primal way. I want you to *always* crave me."

She noted his choice of words—a desire, not a command—as he brought his free hand to her waist and slowly lowered her onto his erection. They groaned in harmony as she slid down, sheathing him within her tight walls. It was like her sex was made for his, and his desire was as much her own. She would always crave this, the way he filled her.

Zagan held her tightly, rubbing her clit while buried to the hilt inside her. He groaned, her name the only word he spoke as he rocked his hips, making her move with him. His lips sought her hardened nipples, and she lost her hands in his hair, pulling him closer to her as she bounced in his lap, matching his thrusts.

Desperate, she moaned, deep in the back of her throat, her skin coated with sweat. His hair grazed her skin, tantalizing her. Her moans became louder and more passionate the harder he pounded into her, and she felt herself climbing closer and closer to orgasm.

Zagan stood, leaving himself buried inside her, and pressed her against the wall of trees. She opened her wings to brace for the impact, exposing more of her back to the bark. She reveled in the feel of it grinding against her skin.

Zagan held her thighs wide as he thrust into her, moaning her name, his eyes closed. A light gleam of sweat coated his skin as he pumped his length inside her, his lips and tongue still busy with her breasts.

"Zagan ..." she pleaded, asking for permission to release.

His red eyes opened and stared into hers. "Hold it," he commanded.

She roared loudly, her body forced to obey.

Moving one hand from her thigh, he massaged her clit roughly with his thumb, only furthering his game of pleasure torture. When her moans turned to whimpers, he slipped his tongue into her mouth and his movements against her clit became more feverish.

"Do you want to feel it?" he growled. "My seed inside you?"

She threw her head back as if begging the Heavens for it. "Yes!"

"I will come deep within you, Coryn."

Even through her lustful haze, she realized he was making sure it was what she wanted. "Yes. Please, yes."

"Then I will give you what you want." He thrust hard, forcefully, a few more times before he whispered breathlessly into her ear, "Come for me."

As soon as he commanded it, her eyes flashed and her entire body detonated with the most intense climax she'd ever experienced. On her scream, he slammed his full length into her and came, releasing jet after jet of his seed deep inside as her walls milked him of everything he had.

Zagan held her in that position, kissing and nipping along her neck and jawline as he pushed his length back inside and continued to convulse.

"Coryn …"

Still bracing her against the wall as they came down from their high, Zagan nuzzled and kissed along her neck and up to her lips. He smiled against her mouth before kissing her deeply, still slowly thrusting until he fully softened and her breathing returned to normal. He pulled out, moaning softly, and sat down with her in his lap, holding her tightly against him.

She pushed away the hair that was plastered to his cheek as she stared into his eyes.

"Gods," she whispered, "that was …"

She didn't know what it was, though it had been incredible. But as they caught their breath and her hormones calmed, the magnitude of what had just happened hit her full force. She was his now. Entirely his.

I was a powerful erelim, and I just fucked a demon.

It had to be the bond drawing her to him. A demon, a horner. Her sworn enemy. The one who had destroyed her existence and had now reduced her to … his fallen sex angel? Her heart pleaded with her mind to believe otherwise, but there was no denying it. Giving in to her lust had been a mistake.

Zagan ran his fingertip against her skin, over her bare collarbone. "I almost want to demand you remain like this from now on. But no, this body is for my eyes only."

He nipped at her lower lip, then seemed surprised when she turned her head and her lip fell away from between his teeth. He shifted, and she could tell he was trying to catch her gaze.

"Was that not enjoyable, sweet one?"

She stayed silent, unsure of what to say.

With a curt grunt, he took her chin between his fingers and forced her to look at him. The air around them smelled of sex and sweat; it was intoxicating. With her head tilted, she caught a brief glimpse of her sex spread over his and noted both glistening with his spend. When his cock twitched, evidently ramping up for another round, she looked away.

No, she thought, even as her body burned with a resounding yes.

Coryn spoke, ignoring his question. "What's gotten into you?"

Whether she was asking him or herself, she wasn't sure. The situation felt so surreal; she got sick, and he was suddenly infatuated with her when just yesterday he was calling her his forsaken pet and threatening to have his brethren corrupt her in any way they saw fit.

Oblivious to her inner turmoil, Zagan gave her a smug smile and pulled her up to straddle him again. "I do not know exactly. I just know I like it."

Hovering over his lap, she gasped when she felt his erection positioned at her entrance.

"Want to go again?"

Coryn shivered in his hold. The temptation to nod and sink onto him so he could fill her once more was far too enticing. Was this the true power of the bond, making her completely submissive to this demon?

Shaking her head violently, she pushed off his shoulders and wriggled out of his grasp until she stood before him, then collected her tunic—he'd torn all of her undergarments, the bastard—and pulled it quickly over her head.

Zagan looked dumbstruck and hurt. "Was it something I did, Coryn?"

She hadn't anticipated such a reaction from him, one of genuine confusion and concern. But that didn't change her abhorrence for what she'd just allowed to transpire. He was a demon, and he was corrupting her. He wasn't concerned about how much she may or may not have liked it. All he cared about was possessing her, claiming her in every way he could. For the gods' sakes, she hadn't even fully removed his clothing. He sat there with his pants on and undone. In any other circumstance, she would have quite liked that look, erection hard and waiting for her, but not with this creature. Never again.

"I need to make my kill," she said, avoiding his question, and before he could protest, she spread her wings and flew out of the trees.

CHAPTER 10

The village near Shen's Path was different from Dellview. The white roof she sat upon was a design iconic to the Lochmont region of Desir, built like steps to catch any of the brief rain showers that fell. She tried not to reminisce about the dozens of demons she'd killed here as an erelim and focused instead on finding her daily prey.

Sighing, she watched the bustle of people go about their day, blissfully unaware of the gray-winged killer above them. Worse, a demon fucker.

She pressed a hand against her stomach, unsure if it was the drude poison still in her system or the idea of Zagan's seed inside her that had tied her in knots.

"Ama'arhus, Goddess of Fertility, I beseech You." Would the gods still listen to her prayers? "I have committed a most egregious sin, for the demon knight and I shared a lustful exchange. I beg of you, do not grant the demon and I with spawn."

Coryn wasn't sure such a conception would even be possible, but it felt better to petition the goddess no matter how far removed from the Heavens she'd gotten.

The urge to take her frustration out on something—or some*one*—was even more alarming than what she'd allowed to transpire with Zagan.

Perhaps I really am becoming his angel of darkness.

But as she scanned the shadows and alleyways of the town, she found no demons lurking. Sightings of manifestations were even more rare—even those that looked different from humans. It took most of the day, but she finally found someone worthy of her blade. In the market down the street were two small children—disheveled, dirty, and dressed in tatters—hungrily eyeing a fruit cart. Coryn watched them circle the fabric-covered shop, clearly longing for one small apple or orange to ease their hunger.

It was almost too much for Coryn to bear, and she'd been close to making a break for another rooftop when the little girl finally moved to take a banana dangling off the side of the cart while the shop owner wasn't looking. But it was as if he had baited them, waiting for and expecting them to take the fruit. He turned around and pulled the girl by the arm so hard she wailed. Coryn felt the pull in her own shoulder and rubbed at it as the man screamed at the girl.

"Do you know what happens to thieves where I'm from?" the merchant snarled, and he unhooked a hidden, rusty sword from his belt. He smirked evilly at the squirming girl.

People nearby screamed and backed away from the mad merchant as the little boy went running toward him, pleading with him to let his sister go.

Before Coryn could scramble to her feet and fly from the roof, the man hacked the girl's hand from her wrist. The girl pulled her arm to her chest and her ragged clothing soaked with blood. Her hand, still gripping the banana, rolled across the sandy street.

In that moment, Coryn considered Zagan's command a blessing.

Darkness shrouded her vision as she spread her wings, and the loud *whoosh* caused people nearby to turn and look up. Shrieks of horror for the girl's fate turned to shrieks of fear when Coryn soared from the roof and landed before the merchant, slamming him into a concrete wall, and pressed her blade to his throat.

"Your name," she growled through clenched teeth. "Tell me your name."

He panted as his eyes snapped to her wings, then to her hand holding the dagger beneath his chin. He began to tremble when he met her gaze again.

"Tell me your name!" she roared.

He opened his mouth and stammered, but another burst of shrieking behind her interrupted his response. With her blade still pressed to his throat, she turned, half-expecting to see the girl had died. But what she saw was even more shocking—an erelim, golden-winged and beautifully armored, pointing a long blade right at her.

"Forsaken!" the female boomed.

She must be a new creation; Coryn had known the names of every angel among the erelim and taqaphim ranks before she'd been cast from the Heavens. Had she still been an angel, she would have known this new female's name instantly through the telepathic bond they all shared. But now, she could only identify this female as a beautiful warrior angel, while she was a simple forsaken.

"What are you doing?" Coryn growled.

"By order of the archangels and the seven gods of war, I, Israfel, have been sent here to carry out your judgment for the attempted murder of this man, Fadel Malloy."

Coryn smirked before letting out a dry laugh. *Fadel Malloy.* His name was all she needed to know in order to fill her quota.

Without turning to look back at the trembling man in her grasp, she swiped her blade across his throat and warm blood sprayed onto her hand and cheek.

"I don't think that's *attempted* murder."

Coryn dropped the merchant's body and, glancing over Israfel's shoulder, was pleased to see that a woman had tended to the small girl's wounds and they, like the rest of the villagers, were both trying to get out of the way.

Taking a few steps forward, Coryn wiped her bloodied blade on her equally bloodied clothing. Who did this new angel think she was? Did she not know which former erelim she was dealing with?

"Your judgment is invalid. I am not a demon."

"You are a bonded forsaken. You're about as close to a demon as any beast not born from Hell can get. In the eyes of the gods, you are the same."

It was like a stab to the gut.

Coryn bit the inside of her cheek to keep from snarling and narrowed her eyes at the angel. "So that's it, then? The rules of the Heavens forbid me to end my own life, but now I am fair game for a hunt?"

"You were fair game as soon as you, a bonded forsaken, endangered the lives of humans."

Coryn barked out a single, humorless laugh. "More human lives were taken by my command when I was erelim."

The logic of the gods hadn't made sense when she was an angel, and it made even less sense now. How could the all-powerful leaders of the Heavens have rules that shifted like the wind?

Well, she wasn't some abandoned feral dog that needed to be put down. Maybe in the eyes of the gods her soul could never be cleansed in this life, but she was done with worrying about what they thought.

Spinning her blade in her hand, she begged the erelim to come at her.

"That little girl was hungry," Coryn said. "Fadel baited her to take that fruit. Did the gods not see the pleasure in his eyes as his blade severed through her wrist?"

"She stole that fruit and paid the price for her sin. Fadel taught her a lesson and her soul is lighter as a result."

How did so many angels think this way? It was like the humans with the pentagram—to the gods, every human soul could be salvaged. What Fadel had done was a crime to humans, but to the gods, he had cleansed the soul of his victim. By their reasoning, his soul would also have been salvageable had Coryn not killed him.

But Fadel Malloy was dead now, his dark soul had gone to the demons, and Coryn was all too happy that he would spend his days in Hell. With a loud roar, she launched herself at Israfel, her dagger drawn. But the angel had been prepared to parry, and she took a step back, bracing herself before a voice growled from behind Coryn.

"Stop."

Halting in mid-attack, as if time itself had frozen, Coryn sucked in a breath as her entire body burned. She kept her eyes on Israfel, though, who stared over Coryn's shoulder and took one step back, then another.

"Let me fight her!" Coryn pleaded, her body loosening as Zagan came into her periphery. Even still, she advanced as the erelim continued to put distance between them.

"No," Zagan replied.

Bloodlust filled his dark red eyes and, as he approached Israfel, he licked his lips, sending a barrage of emotions through Coryn that she didn't want to analyze. All she knew was that she wanted to battle this erelim, to show the Heavens that she was no longer one of them.

She took up a fighting stance, feeling stupid that she couldn't do much else.

Zagan swiped a clawed hand at Israfel, and she jumped back a few more feet, her golden wings kissing the wall of a house. She sprang forward, swinging her blade up in an attempt to cut him down. He leaned back and fell to his knees to avoid the attack, then swiped at the female with his tail. She managed to escape its barbed tip as she jumped, but as Zagan spun, he thrust his left arm forward and impaled the angel through the chest with his claws.

He began to twist his hand, but at that point, Coryn quickly looked away and closed her eyes. Sounds of cracking ribs and wet coughs filled her ears as Zagan brought an end to the fight, and when Coryn opened her eyes, she saw Israfel slumped on the ground across from Fadel's corpse.

Zagan turned, scanning the area as he strode toward Coryn and took her by the arm. "Let's go."

***

It was time to move again. Zagan cradled Coryn in his arms and headed toward another of his homes, and his little angel began to get irritable.

"Put me down. I'm not a child," Coryn snarled.

Her wriggling only made him hold her tighter against him. "I will not," he responded, "and you will stop struggling."

She slumped back with a growl, now a dead weight in his arms.

Great; he wouldn't allow her to fight, so now she was punishing him by obeying his command in a way that made it difficult for him to carry her. Well, at least her actions put his mind at ease—he'd been worried she'd be traumatized at seeing the erelim and lose her stubborn streak. Plus, any excuse to hold her was good enough for him. Her body was far too warm, her scent far too intoxicating ...

Zagan shook the thoughts from his head.

"What were you doing in that village?" he asked, soaring higher with a violent flap of his wings.

Coryn narrowed her eyes. "What do you think I was doing? Following your orders. Making my kill of the day. Fadel Malloy, may his soul rot in Hell for all eternity."

She stiffened in his arms, clearly realizing what she'd said.

He grinned widely, exposing his sharp fangs.

"How very unangelic of you to say," he replied with amusement. "Weren't you to cleanse the Lake of Souls from all darkness and purge the world of evil? Eternally condemning a soul to Hell ... well, it would be black as night forever and its corruption would live in infamy."

Coryn shuddered in his grasp and he laughed darkly.

Instead of going back to Shen's Path, he landed by the lake outside the village and, setting Coryn down, frowned when she shoved her way out of his hold. He growled low in his throat, his ideas for winning her over nicely completely dissipating. She needed to understand that no being was completely good or evil. They could find a balance and be together, and damn it all, he wanted that.

Before he fully comprehended his actions, he had his tail around her throat, forcing her nose to touch his. Looking into those endlessly blue, defiant orbs, he wanted nothing more than to take her again. He wrapped his arm around her and, pressing his hand to her ass, pulled her against his body. He was rock hard for her already. She gasped, a gorgeous pink blush surfacing on her cheeks as his sex met her stomach between their clothing. He smirked, his mind spinning with the knowledge that she still wore no panties beneath her tunic.

"You hold onto the ideals of the Heavens, yet you know they are illogical," he murmured against her lips, wanting so desperately to bite them.

But her eyes were cast down, her thick lashes making it difficult for him to get a read on her. Did she want him as much as he wanted her but was too damned proud to admit it?

"Look at me. Good. Now, you say you went to that town to make your commanded kill"—his smile widened against her lips, but he willed himself to pull away, wanting to see her reaction to his next words—"but I did not command you to take a life this day."

And there it was—his beautiful creature on the cusp of revelation.

"I had relieved you of your daily hunt while you healed. I did not command you to resume, did I?"

He brought his hand up to stroke her cheek, her skin taut as her mouth gaped with realization.

"You'd better seal those lips before I claim your mouth again, my sweet angel of darkness. Keep looking at me like that, and I will not be able to control myself."

Her eyes flashed, and Zagan would have sacrificed brethren in order to read her expression. Was it intrigue? Acceptance? Disgust? If she was tempted, she didn't give in. Instead, she took a few steps back, increasing the distance between them.

"No ..." she said, bewildered, and looked down at her clothes that were covered in Fadel Malloy's blood.

Zagan smirked. "Oh yes, my darling forsaken. One more dark soul to tip the Lake further in favor of the demons, all by your voluntary hand. And then you wanted to fight one of your precious erelim!"

Coryn narrowed her eyes and ran her tongue across her teeth. "That soul was beyond saving in this life. The gods preach that any human soul can be cleansed, but I never truly believed it. In its next iteration of life, perhaps ... but there was no leading that man to salvation."

"That does not tell me why you wished to kill your erelim."

She regretted her intimacy with him, that much was obvious, but he would not allow her to regret killing what she used to be. He would never force angel blood on her hands.

"You will never kill an angel of the Heavens. That is an order."

Her anger at this command caught him off-guard.

"I could have taken her down!" she spat, her fists so tight her knuckles were void of color. She bared her teeth like a wild animal, lips folded back and jaw so rigid Zagan was sure it must hurt.

He could feel his anger rising. Couldn't she see he was only trying to protect her? But she was a creature of pure bloodlust—which was exactly what he wanted in her when she faced demons and humans, but not when it came to angels. If she were to spill an angel's sparkling silver blood, she would regret it forever. Despise him forever. And he couldn't live with that.

91

He smiled despite himself. "My forsaken, did you wish to kill the angel because you are one no longer? Because you were jealous? Or because you thought it would please me?"

"Absolutely not!" she ground out between clenched teeth.

How he would have liked to coax her to relax with his tongue.

"I'm not one of them. I see that now." Her shoulders dipped. "The gods must have made a mistake when they created me."

Zagan wanted to howl in agony. If he'd hated the gods before, he wanted to tear them limb from limb for making her feel that way.

She stared at the ground as if it would provide the answers to all her questions. "Maybe I just wanted to take a piece of what they took from me."

Zagan's mouth twitched as he watched her. The pitiful way she spoke would normally enrage him, but now all he wanted to do was take her in his arms and tell her everything would be okay.

And so he would.

Before she could protest, Zagan closed the gap between them and wrapped his arms around her protectively, possessively.

"I will not allow you to suffer the pain of taking the soul from an erelim as they did with you," he murmured, his breath bouncing off her ear.

She shivered in his arms and let out a sexy little gasp that nearly undid him.

"You will never kill an angel. Am I clear?"

She hesitated, and Zagan wasn't sure if it was because she still wanted to argue the point or because she was paralyzed by their closeness. He preferred to think the latter.

"Crystal." She whispered it so quietly that he wouldn't have heard her had he not been standing so close.

"Excellent," he said, and before he pushed too far, he pulled away.

She wrapped her arms around her waist, her expression enigmatic as she continued staring at the ground.

Should he warm her? Did she miss having him close?

Don't push it.

Despite his arousal straining against the fabric of his pants, he resolved to do this right. For Coryn, he would wait forever … well, his heart would, anyway. He wasn't so sure he could control his body for that long.

Let her come to you.

Zagan stepped back, sensing Coryn's longing for him from the look in her eyes and the tightness of her exquisite lips. Her lust was palpable, and how he wished he could nurture the curious dark spark within her soul—but he was unable to corrupt beings from the Heavens in the same way he could humans. Maybe that was for the best; this relationship would have to come honestly.

Her lust only emanated stronger as he increased the distance between them.

CHAPTER 11

Coryn was silent and brooding as Zagan swooped into another cave with her in his arms. As soon as her feet hit the ground, she spoke, as if she'd been protesting by not speaking while he held her.

"How did you know to find me in town?"

Zagan shook his head as he strode further into the cavern. "I had not been expecting to see you there."

Coryn raised an eyebrow. "Sure you weren't. What were you up to, then? Attempting to set up one of your meals of corruption?"

"Not this time."

"Okaaaay." She tapped a finger against her chin. "You went to get more fruit?"

"It had nothing to do with food."

"You wanted to terrorize more humans?"

"How simple do you think I am?"

"Do you really want me to answer that?"

Zagan rolled his eyes and considered how to phrase what he'd actually been doing in the village. Clearing his throat, he broke the silence.

"I wished to get you more things," he said. "Imagine my surprise when I found you there. My forsaken, on the verge of death."

Coryn snorted. "On the verge of death? Not quite! Surely you have more faith in your forsaken than that."

A furious blush rushed into Coryn's cheeks as soon as the words left her mouth. Of course, Zagan hadn't missed it—he hung on her every word— and he couldn't help but smile.

"Yes, *my* forsaken." Before she could avert her gaze, he'd closed the gap between them and slid a clawed finger beneath her chin, angling her stare to meet his. "My *everything*."

What am I saying!

Flustered at his own slip-up, Zagan snarled, dropped her chin and walked away. He couldn't believe he'd said those words aloud. Wasn't even sure he meant them. He didn't *want* to mean them at least, but he knew all too well the truths one's self-conscious could reveal in times of vulnerability.

"Zagan …" Coryn began, and his knees buckled with the way his name sounded coming from her lips.

But, all at once, the hair on his arms stood up and his stomach lurched. *No. No, not now!*

"Coryn! Avert your gaze from the cave's entrance!" he commanded, thankful that she would have no other choice but to obey him.

Instantly, she twisted, her face awash with confusion and betrayal as he walked past her.

"Good, Coryn, good. Now go to your chamber, the first on the right, and wait for me," he said, raising his hand to ignite the lanterns that would guide the way.

He glanced over his shoulder and watched her disappear obediently, knowing she'd ask questions later. If they got too difficult for him to answer, he could always command her to ask no more. But he couldn't get too comfortable with forcing her to obey him. If he wanted her to care for him, ordering her around without giving anything in return wouldn't help his cause.

The messenger, with his two pairs of feathered white wings, appeared at the mouth of the cave, but before he could speak, Zagan had his hands around his neck and slammed him into the stone wall outside.

"A warning would have been nice," he growled.

As close as their faces were, he couldn't see the messenger's features beneath his hood; it was as though the darkness went on for miles.

"A thousand apologies, my deliverer," came the messenger's raspy voice.

As he was the only being with direct daily access to the demon king, Zagan knew he was hardly sorry, and his desire to slam him into the stone once more was overwhelming. Having learned so much about this servant recently, Zagan was desperate to keep him away from Coryn. He'd be happy to behead him right now. That he was protected by the king was the only thing keeping him alive.

"Speak and make it quick."

"Yes, gracious deliverer."

Though he couldn't see it, Zagan pictured the messenger's scarred face as he nervously searched for his message in the shadows of his cloak.

"The king commands you direct the army west. It appears there is a priest on the Wahein peninsula cleansing souls for their ascent Heavensward. Angels will surely intercept before you arrive, so be prepared."

He hesitated as if considering whether delivering his next message was worth the pain he knew Zagan would inflict upon hearing it.

"His Excellency also wishes for me to convey his displeasure at your blatant unwillingness to train the lessers for battle. Demon Knight Lamia has also expressed her concern in the matter."

Zagan grit his teeth. What he had with Coryn was a hundred times more powerful than any lesser army, but neither the messenger nor the king needed to know that.

"Consider the attack on Wahein done and tell the king that his message regarding the army was delivered loud and clear." He spun the hooded messenger and shoved him closer to the cliff's edge as a gust of wind blew up from the canyon. "Now get the fuck out of here."

"Yes, my deliverer." The messenger spread his snowy wings and, falling forward, disappeared over the cliff.

Zagan exhaled, waiting a few moments before turning his attention back to the cave. Coryn would be outraged that he'd sent her away. He walked in with a sigh and prepared to face his angry angel of darkness.

He entered her chamber and there was his feisty forsaken in all her glory.

"What was that about?" she snapped.

Zagan took in her exasperated expression and the new clothes she wore. She'd decided on a dark blue tunic, and though it brought out the ethereal blue of her eyes, she'd selected a color that kept her tied to the Heavens. Purple or red would have shown she'd relinquished their hold on her.

"Why are you wearing that?" he asked, avoiding her question. "I am going into battle, but you are not."

"You're going into battle? Why can't I come?"

"Because I want you to remain here and rest. I am not convinced you are fully healed. I have yet to see your strength, and you continue to make inconsistent choices."

Coryn put her hands on her hips and narrowed those beautiful eyes at him. "Like what?"

He motioned to her outfit. "You choose to wear this stupid Heavens-colored tunic, yet you wanted to kill an erelim. You are being insolent toward me, yet you allowed me to taste you. To take you."

A shiver tore through her like a tsunami, and it gave him hope that there would be more tasting, more taking. He took a step closer, then another, until he was sure she wouldn't back away. He lifted his hand, claws retracted, cupped her chin and dragged his thumb across her lips.

"I hunger for that again, Coryn."

Her eyes rolled back and fell closed at his touch, but with a quick breath, she forced them open, put her hands to his chest and shoved him.

"Well I don't!" she snarled. "Especially since you're hiding something from me. And now you won't let me into battle? Fuck off, Zagan!"

"I am trying to *protect* you," he rasped, keeping his voice low as he closed the distance between them.

For every step forward he took, she took one back, until he had her pinned against the wall. He needed to put this former angel back in her place.

"Consider who you are speaking to, dear forsaken"—he braced one hand beside her head and, leaning forward, whispered into her ear—"and the things I can command you to do when you misbehave."

Before she could respond, he pushed off the wall and trailed his tail up her stockinged thigh before making his way out of the room. "I will be back soon. Be good."

***

Infuriating demon! He made her feel wanton and rageful all at once.

When Coryn could no longer hear Zagan's footsteps, she let out a long, deep breath and her lungs deflated with gratitude. She was relieved that it had been the oxygen making her chest burn rather than one of Zagan's commands.

Wait ...

She moved along the path toward the mouth of the cave, the same one Zagan had taken, and her body didn't freeze. Her heart wasn't threatening to explode in her chest unless she turned back to her room.

Zagan said he wanted me to stay, but he did not command it.

She let out a celebratory whoop before sprinting to the cliff's edge. Looking over, she caught a glimpse of Zagan in the distance, banking east out of the canyon like a bird of prey. She was far too curious to sit around and ponder who, or what, had given Zagan the order to head into battle, and she refused to wait until he returned. Plus, with his attitude, it was unlikely he would ever tell her anything.

Stubborn ass!

Fresh air filled her lungs as she tilted her body and free-fell from the platform, enjoying the plummet before she stiffened her wings and straightened out. With a few flaps, she made her ascent.

She made sure to keep her distance from Zagan, but the farther she pursued him, the more she realized he'd been right—she wasn't healthy enough to join him in battle. She hadn't anticipated the distance, nor had she flown for this length of time since she'd been cast from the Heavens. Being forsaken sucked—she just didn't have the stamina or power she'd had as an angel.

Giving her wings another violent flap, she grimaced, feeling as if she'd pulled a muscle.

"Stupid, stupid Zagan," she whispered to the wind.

Closing her eyes, she forced herself higher into the sky but winced again when the wing she'd pulled burned at the base of her back. Heavens above, it hurt! She must have really done some damage.

Panting, she slowed her pace, taking it easy on her wing. Sweat began to bead on her face, and her muscles ached with the effort it took to keep herself in the air. She considered revealing herself or calling out to Zagan but knew it would send him into a tirade.

Realizing she was losing altitude, Coryn gave her wings another flap, then another, sucking in air through her teeth as her back screamed in protest. Her left wing seized, the cramp so bad she cried out in pain, and she began spinning wildly through the air. No matter what position she forced her right wing into, her left stayed up and extended, making it impossible to control her trajectory.

As she plummeted toward the ground, Coryn closed her eyes, unable to tell which way was up. Even the darkness felt like it was spinning, and the hair whipping at her face was no longer a joy. She groaned as she tried to gain control, flapping her good wing as hard as possible to at least slow her descent.

Plummeting. This is how every chapter in my life comes to an end.

She stilled, allowing herself a moment of calm as she anticipated slamming into Manusya one last time. But she bounced off the ground with a thud, then rolled until she crashed against a tree with a groan. She'd survived, but at what cost?

Strange … I feel no pain.

She went to push off her side but found she couldn't. Panic set in. She was paralyzed.

Could it be a result of the drude poison still in her system? The alternative—that she might be irreparably damaged from the fall—was much worse, but still, she would kill every last drude in the realms if given the chance.

Peeking through the brush, she spotted a white church with an impossibly high steeple extending into the sky. The point was nearly lost to the clouds, and beside it, Zagan hovered.

Coryn knew this place; she'd fought demons here once. It had been so overrun with the corrupted beasts that the entire area had been abandoned by humans, but now, a dozen of them, peering anxiously at one another, formed a line before a dark-skinned man in robes of white feathers.

Without warning, Zagan slammed into the feather-donned man, knocking him to the ground, the humans' screams ringing the air. As if that were a call to charge, lesser demons began pouring from a red circle set on the wall of the church. They slithered around, scaling up their victims as Zagan grabbed the leader by his robes and roared into his face.

Coryn was surprised it took the angels as long as it did to arrive, but she was impressed by the numbers that eventually fell from the Heavens. They were slicing through the horners before their feet had even touched the ground.

The sweet sound of dying lessers' screams filled the air as black blood poured from wounds ripped open by the Heavenly army, and lifeless demon bodies hit the earth, one after the other. Coryn imagined their souls continued to scream as they crashed into the Lake, hopefully to be reborn as humans so her brethren could cleanse them.

The angels were having a difficult time cutting through the thick crowd of lessers to get to Zagan. Even though it brought Coryn relief to see the heads and limbs of other demons roll, her stomach lurched each time an angel got close to the knight.

It wasn't long before the angels began gaining the upper hand in the battle. One erelim, reminiscent of Coryn's old self, eagerly hacked and slashed her way through the circle of demons toward Zagan. She was lithe and skilled, and while Zagan had his back to her, she cut through lessers as easily as Coryn once had, sneaking up on Zagan all too quickly. Coryn sucked in a breath as the angel prepared to attack, but a loud screech sounded over the battlefield, stopping angel and demon alike. Coryn's ears were ringing, and she desperately wanted to cover them with her hands, but it was as if time itself had frozen.

Another demon had emerged from the pond before the church. Zagan, unaffected by the new demon's immobilizing screech, stabbed his claws through his attacker.

"Thanks, Lamia," he called, giving the other demon a nod of appreciation.

Screeching again and causing Coryn's paralyzed body to shudder, the demon called Lamia manipulated the water from the pond to launch herself forward. Her dark skin had patches of shining blue-and-green scales, and her thick serpentine tail swept behind her, knocking over an angel before the effects of her screech wore off. The lessers and angels on the battlefield regained control of their bodies and resumed their fight.

With their backs to one another, Zagan and Lamia, together with their demon army, overtook the humans and angels, sending countless souls to the Lake. How many of them would be reborn on the side of the light? A third, Coryn guessed, maybe less; with each swipe of a demon's claws the souls became more tainted before they passed on.

But Zagan is safe.

The thought shouldn't have brought her as much comfort as it did. In fact, it should not have brought her comfort at all. What would happen if he fell? Would their bond be broken? Or would she die alongside him?

Lamia turned toward Zagan. "Looks like you owe me yet again, Zag."

Zag?

"Hmph. As if my gracing your presence is not thanks enough," he chided, a sly smirk on his lips as he brought Lamia in for a hug.

Coryn had watched an entire battle, had witnessed angels and demons get slaughtered, and yet it was Zagan embracing another female that broke her paralysis.

Lamia spotted Coryn before Zagan did. Her eyes seemed to pierce Coryn's soul, their bright yellow hue nearly as bright as the sun and just as painful to stare at directly.

Zagan followed Lamia's gaze and growled.

"Coryn?" he demanded, dropping his arms from Lamia.

"You *know* this female?" Lamia asked, giving Zagan an odd look as he approached Coryn.

His voice was thick with anger yet laced with confusion. "I commanded you to stay in your chamber."

"That you did not," Coryn countered, raising her chin. "You said you *wanted* me to stay home."

Zagan's eyes flashed with amusement and he grinned, surprising Coryn. "Is that so? Well, rest assured I will not make that mistake again."

"Zagan?" Lamia asked, her tone demanding an explanation.

Zagan closed his eyes briefly, bracing himself before turning to face the other demon.

"This is my bonded forsaken," he said, motioning toward Coryn. "Coryn, this is Demon Knight Lamia."

Coryn narrowed her eyes at the female. "Pleasure."

Lamia's condescending laugh wasn't the response Coryn wanted.

"A bonded forsaken? Z, surely you're joking!" Lamia circled Coryn, inspecting her, hands on her swaying hips. She scrutinized Coryn's breasts, the curves of her hips, her flat stomach. Coryn hadn't even blushed this deeply when Zagan studied her body, but she resisted the urge to cave in on herself and cover her chest with her arms.

"She's a puny little thing."

Coryn scoffed, and Zagan growled deep in his throat. "Do not question my decision or the state of the female, Lamia."

Still circling Coryn like a cat about to pounce, Lamia shrugged. "I'm just surprised. The boys have been pestering you to find a female. I'd like to be there when they discover you have one."

Zagan clenched his jaw. "She was a powerful erelim when I found her. Now, she is my angel of darkness."

Lamia barked out a laugh that reverberated so loudly Coryn thought it might have shaken the very stars above. "So you neglect your army but spend your days training this little bird?"

Coryn averted her eyes from Lamia's when she leaned in and pressed her extended claws against her throat.

"Show me how you fight, then, little one."

"Gladly." Coryn shoved out of Lamia's hold and backed up a few paces. Even though she wasn't at her best, she would not give up the chance to fight a demon knight. She was surprised when Zagan agreed.

"Yes, Coryn, fight Lamia. Show her why I have chosen you."

CHAPTER 12

He hadn't meant to give her a command, but Zagan saw it register in Coryn's beautiful yet infuriated features.

Lamia laughed loudly. "I'm sorry if I break her, Z."

Before he could insist otherwise, Coryn was propelled forward by his command. Gray feathers exploded from her wings as she spread them, descending on Lamia like a hawk, her fingers as talons. Lamia sidestepped the attack, but Zagan could tell she was caught off guard by the sudden advance, and he had to grin.

With a grunt and light beaming from her eyes, Lamia launched a counterattack, and soon the two females were a blur of feathers and scales.

It was clear that Lamia had severely underestimated Coryn, which made Zagan both amused and angry. As she was the knight training the lesser army, he was disappointed that she would play down any foe, particularly one Zagan believed was strong enough to serve him and their kingdom.

Lamia managed to grab Coryn by the shoulders, trying to force her to look into her blinding eyes. But Coryn slammed her own eyes shut, then reared her head back and slammed it into Lamia's face. Roaring in pain, Lamia let go of Coryn and staggered backwards. The light in her eyes dimmed as she brought her hand to her forehead.

Blinking furiously, Coryn took a few steps back, increasing the distance between her and Lamia, then reached into the sash of her tunic and extracted her dagger. As Coryn's blinking slowed, Lamia whipped her tail against the ground, taunting her.

Coryn took the bait but didn't fall into Lamia's trap. She ran at full speed toward Lamia, her blade tucked against her side. As Lamia turned and whipped her serpent tail forward, Coryn dodged it and leaped. Landing, one-footed, on the arch of Lamia's tail, Coryn launched off it and slammed both feet into Lamia's spine, sending the demon to the ground.

Lamia rolled quickly onto her back, but Coryn was on her in an instant and pressed her blade against her throat. Lamia struggled, but Coryn gave a warning shout and planted both knees against her shoulders, pinning her down. Panting, Coryn dug her dagger into Lamia's skin, drawing blood.

"Now, now, forsaken," Zagan said, pleased with the brawl and how Coryn had handled herself, "I said fight her, not behead her."

"She wouldn't," Lamia hissed, glaring up at Coryn. "She couldn't bring herself to do it."

"Don't tempt her, dear sister." But Zagan's eyes were still on Coryn, who remained wide-eyed and manic from the fight—being so close to killing a demon knight must have been incredibly tempting. "Enough, Coryn. Do not kill her."

Coryn snarled like a wild beast deprived of her meal, but she pushed off Lamia, who returned the snarl in kind and shoved Coryn back further as she stood.

Zagan was proud of his angel, but as he smiled over at her, he caught her waver. She seemed to be having a hard time focusing for even the briefest of moments. He pushed past Lamia and gripped Coryn by the chin, angling her head up so he could look into her eyes.

"You are still not fully healed. How is that possible?" He turned to Lamia. "Drude poison. I have given her my antidote, yet it still takes hold in her body. Why?"

Lamia pushed Zagan's hands away from Coryn's chin and forced Coryn to meet her own blinding gaze. Coryn thrashed in Lamia's hold, and when Lamia's claws nicked the side of her face, she gasped.

"Coryn, hold still!" Zagan snapped, and she cried out when her body froze in place. "Lamia can heal you, but if she harms you again in the process, she will have hell to pay."

"Dragon-like features, an affinity for water, healing abilities—you're a gorgon," Coryn said, head bouncing in Lamia's grasp.

Tears flowed freely from her eyes as Lamia continued to stare into them, but she was able to stare right back without blinking as time went on. In time, her eyelids drooped, and she seemed at peace. Both females snapped out of the trance at the same time.

Lamia grunted and let go of Coryn's face. "It's not drude poison."

Her lack of effort to expand on the thought made Zagan's blood boil.

"Then what the fuck is it?"

"She's a forsaken." Lamia spun Coryn around and pointed at the blackening base of Coryn's left wing. "Her wings are dying."

Zagan panted as he stared at the deadening appendage. She would never learn to care for him if those wings fell from her back.

Coryn gasped and wobbled on her feet, but whether it was from hearing Lamia's news or from the effects of her wings dying, he wasn't sure.

"Wh-what is it?" Coryn asked, her speech slurred as if her tongue had seized. She tried to look over her shoulder but couldn't crane her neck far enough. "What's happening?"

"Your wing is blackening, like a limb with gangrene," Lamia explained. "I can probably stop the progression—or at least slow it down—but the problem will never fully go away. A forsaken is not quite angel, not quite demon, but something in between. You're essentially human now, and humans are undeserving of wings."

The panicked look Coryn gave Zagan made him shudder.

"You can't become human," he said softly, eyes as wide as hers. "You'd never forgive me."

Lamia glared at him. "How can you care for this creature from the Heavens?" Her gaze dropped to where Zagan cradled Coryn's hands with his own.

He bristled, wanting to deny his affections for the angel—but he never lied and was not about to start now.

"Just help her," he said, and they held each other's gaze for a long while.

"Fine," said Lamia, "but this is only because she won that fight."

When she put her hands on the black base of Coryn's wing, Zagan could finally breathe.

The two females illuminated, brightened by the healing powers emanating from Lamia's eyes. Zagan braced himself, expecting the healing not to have worked, but he breathed a sigh of relief when the light faded and Coryn's wings looked perfectly gray.

Perfectly gray. How he wished they could have been healed back to gold.

"Lamia," he said, pulling her into a tight hug.

She patted his arm. "All I've done is buy you time. Extreme negative emotions, like hopelessness, discouragement, and other stresses will speed up the process. I'll be honest—I don't expect she'll keep her wings longer than another month."

"So I will bring her to you, and you will heal her again."

"Maybe once or twice more, but eventually the infection will adapt. It will no longer respond to my powers, and there will be nothing we can do."

He would remove his own wings and fuse them to her back if it came to that.

"Research other ways to fix this," he said. "Leave us now. I will take her to your waterfall. It's the closest place of refuge."

Lamia laughed incredulously. "But that's *my* home."

"I found it first," he said, feeling like an older brother arguing with a sibling. "After we are gone, it's yours again. You need to research this infection anyway."

Lamia pinched the bridge of her nose and sighed. "You need to be out by tomorrow."

"Deal."

"Good luck. Do Jinn and O know about her?"

Zagan's expression hardened. "Not yet."

Lamia's glowing eyes were fixed on Coryn as she spoke. "Hmm, and how do you think they will take this news?"

"About as well as you did. Now go, and report back to me with your findings."

With a sigh, Lamia dove back into the pond. The water glowed red, and then she was gone.

Zagan turned to find Coryn staring at the place where Lamia's hell portal had just disappeared as if it could answer all of life's mysteries. His forsaken always had something to say whether he liked it or not; but now, he only wished she would say something. Anything was better than nothing at all.

"Coryn, I'm sorry about your wings. I had no idea something like that could happen."

She kept staring at the pond's surface. "Yeah, sure."

"You have to believe me." He caught himself just as he'd issued the final word of his command.

Coryn's entire body trembled and she roared into the sky. "I believe you. Are you happy now?"

Zagan sighed. "No, I didn't mean to do that. I am sorry. Just know that when I bound you to me, it didn't feel like a choice—it felt like the only right thing I would ever do. And I want to do right by you, always. You will always be my angel."

When he looked down, he saw she was losing her battle for consciousness. Perhaps it was best, for now. "Sleep, Coryn."

Her body seized, and as she began falling to the ground like a tree, Zagan cursed and caught her. *I have to get better with my words.*

He hadn't meant to issue her with commands, but in doing so, he'd taken away what little control she now had over her body. She gave in to sleep, though, and he was able to focus on the most important thing—how to take care of her.

***

Lamia would have returned here to lick her own wounds if he hadn't borrowed the place from her, but he quickly dismissed his guilt. Coryn's needs would always come first, no matter the circumstances or whom he needed to take things from in order to make her feel safe and comfortable. He shook his head and smiled—if only she knew the power she had over him.

Hard surfaces were abundant in Lamia's home, from towering bookshelves to writing desks and a large dining room table. There were no couches or softer, more comfortable pieces anywhere, spare her large bed in the back of the cavern. Zagan ran toward it, careful not to jostle Coryn in his arms as he carefully placed her on top of the comforter and climbed on to lay beside her.

Though she took great pride in her strength as an erelim, Coryn was stronger as a forsaken—even if she didn't realize it. Any other angel would have surrendered fully to his curse by now, yet she challenged him at every turn. She'd refused to succumb to the drude poisoning, and now? She'd fought through her pain once again and won a battle against a demon knight. To know that she was losing her wings and to have had Lamia heal them must have been devastating, yet even as she slept, her face gave no hint of her suffering. But he knew that losing her wings would be the final straw—it would break her. He couldn't let them fall.

Could he command them to stay on her back? He opened his mouth to try the order, but an image of her with dead black wings and an inability to remove them made him stop.

My commands are already a curse. Best not make this worse for her.

"Please be all right," he murmured instead.

Lifting her gently, he slid his legs beneath her and pulled her onto his lap. He was careful not to disturb her wings, afraid they would fall off or disintegrate with the slightest touch. Resting the tips of his horns against the stone wall and angling his face upward, he closed his eyes and spoke Heavensward, admitting to the gods who created her, "I love her. I love Coryn."

It felt good to get the words out. Based on the warmth inside his chest he knew he'd never been more sure of anything in his life. He could no longer deny it or claim he only felt affection for her. He loved her, his beautiful, strong, brave forsaken angel. Perhaps he should pray to the gods and thank them for such a perfect gift.

Now, let's not get too carried away.

He smiled gently, and as he cradled Coryn's head in his hands, he could no longer resist her. He was a demon, after all; a knight—and knights never resisted temptation for long.

"Coryn," he whispered, recalling how that same husky tone had made her shiver during their last intimate encounter.

He gently lifted her head. Even while sleeping she was a sensual creature, fragile yet capable of taking his breath away. He would hand her the stars, if that's what she wanted.

He checked her wings again and breathed a heavy sigh of relief when he saw the infection hadn't yet returned.

"I swear, I will take better care of you, Coryn. I am so sorry I wronged you." He gently placed a kiss on her forehead. She didn't have a fever or signs of pain any longer and he was glad for it.

He moved her auburn hair from her face and sighed. "You make me crazy, angel."

She'd reduced him to a sap. If Oriax heard him, he'd have hell to pay.

CHAPTER 13

When Coryn regained consciousness it didn't take her long to recall what had happened with Lamia and her wing. She remembered the pain but realized it was only that—a memory. She felt normal now. As she willed her eyes open, she felt a dampness in the air, heard the powerful sound of rushing water, and smelled ...

Oh.

Her eyes flew open and she inhaled slowly, taking in the delicious aroma of pork cooking over a fire. She was lying on her back, and though the air was a little chilly, the heat from the fire by her right leg warmed her.

With effort, she braced her elbows beneath her and propped herself up to get a better look around. The light of the fire blinded her newly opened eyes temporarily, but she saw the distinct curvature of Zagan's horns in silhouette. Before she could try to call for him with her dry throat, the demon glanced over his shoulder at her.

"You're awake!" he said, quickly grabbing a small bowl of water and closing the distance between them. Placing one hand on her back beneath her wings, he helped her to sit so she could drink from it. As she took a few refreshing gulps, he craned his neck to look at her wings.

"Tell me. How are you feeling?"

She lurched and almost spit out her mouthful of water with the burning in her chest she felt at the command. She nodded and swallowed quickly.

"Much better," she said and took in a comforting lungful of air as the burning ceased.

She held up a hand, signaling that Zagan should give her space—she was surprised when he took the hint—then shifted so she was supporting her own body weight. She was upset by what they'd learned from Lamia about the

110

infection, but she didn't have the energy to process her words right now. More immediate issues were at hand; she was glad the sound of the waterfall at the cavern's entrance masked the loud rumble of her stomach.

"Are you cooking a pig?" she asked, squinting to see what was mounted over the fire a short distance away.

"A boar," Zagan corrected. "I thought you would be hungry when you woke."

"You thought correctly," she said, unable to keep from smiling as she set the bowl down. "Thank you."

"Don't thank me," he said casually, but they both winced at the command. "Are you well enough to stand? Here, let me help you."

He was being sweet again.

"I'm fine," she said, shaking her head as he moved to assist her. The last time he'd behaved sweetly towards her they had an even sweeter joining, and she wasn't about to let that happen again.

She stretched every muscle as she stood, then smiled a thank you at Zagan before making her way closer to the fire.

"Where are we?" she asked.

The chamber, with its entrance hidden by the waterfall, reminded her of the first cave Zagan had ever taken her to, but she knew it wasn't the same one. This cavern was much smaller, more intimate. The thought made her blush.

"Not too far east of where you fell," he explained as he joined her by the fire.

Much to Coryn's appreciation, he sat with the fire and boar between them. She took a moment to enjoy the warmth of the flames before speaking again. "And when can we dig into this delicious-smelling meal?"

Zagan smirked, exposing one fang to gleam in the firelight. "It should only be a few more minutes. By the time you are warmed we can take a seat at the table and begin."

She raised an eyebrow and glanced around. "The table?"

He gestured behind him and so she leaned to the side to get a better look. The cavern curved to his right where a large table was already set with two plates, utensils, candles, and even two glasses and a bottle of wine.

She swallowed. "How long was I asleep for *this* time?"

Zagan's smile fell and his face hardened. "Too long for my liking. If you have to follow my commands so closely, you are not to sleep for so long after being hurt again. I was worried about you."

She felt the command take hold and rubbed her collarbone. "Got it," she said flatly, despising that he possessed the power to tell her how long she was allowed to remain unconscious.

His blood-red eyes stayed fixated on her for a few moments more before he coughed, cleared his throat, and looked away.

"I would like you to take a seat ... if it pleases you," he added, but when she stayed in front of the fire, he waved his arm toward the table again. "Please."

She regarded him a moment longer, then stood and did as he requested. *Requested,* this time, not commanded. It was a small victory, but it made her smile inwardly.

As Coryn made her way to the table, she noticed a smaller table beside it, which held apple sauce, fresh salad, and rice. Perhaps she *had* been asleep for far too long if he'd had time to prepare all of this. Maybe his command not to sleep for so long was a good idea.

"Can I ... help you with anything?" she asked.

"No, you do not need to assist me with serving a boar."

She turned the bottle of wine toward her, then laughed. She hadn't even known apple wine existed. "You really like apples, huh?"

"And what's wrong with being partial to apples?"

She shook her head. "Nothing's wrong with it," she said quickly. "In fact, it's sort of ... endearing." She blushed.

"Um ... thank you." Zagan had his back to her, so it was difficult for her to detect his reaction.

She let out a short laugh. "Do not thank me if I'm not allowed to thank you." Though she'd meant it as a joke, it came out more accusatory than intended. She felt her cheeks heat as she scrambled for a way to explain. "I didn't mean—"

"Let's just eat," he said.

She closed her eyes and nodded, cursing herself. "Sure."

Zagan walked to the table with two large plates, each with a few pieces of boar meat on them. She wanted to thank him, but his previous command made the words die in her throat.

Zagan frowned. "You are free to thank me whenever you wish."

The words bubbled up again. "Thank you."

She served herself portions of the side dishes, then passed them to him. She thought it would be a good idea to keep quiet and let him be the next to speak. They sat there, the rushing water and clinking of utensils the only sounds as they ate. After she'd finished one slice of meat it became evident that Zagan was going to make no effort to converse.

"Everything is excellent," she offered hopefully, in an attempt to lighten his mood. She uncorked the apple wine and topped up her glass, then did the same with his. "The apples go particularly well with the boar." When he still gave no answer she let out a soft sigh. "Weren't you hosting a dinner before I descended that night in Dellview? Is this what was eaten?"

That finally got his attention. His eyes flicked up from his food, measuring her.

"No. Steak. And cheese." He shuddered.

She had to chuckle. "Not a fan of cheese. Got it." She took a few more bites, then asked, "What was the purpose of that dinner?"

"It was for Alexander," he answered. "He was the conduit to corrupting souls in that town. Feasts gain the attention of humans, and their own curiosity becomes their downfall to Hell. I speak with them, relate to them ... encourage the sins of their souls to darken them."

It was a brilliant, subtle way to turn souls to the dark, and even Coryn was impressed. She was humbled that Zagan offered so much detail—to her, a former Heavenly being. He picked up on that too.

"You are not to share that information with any of your friends from the Heavens ... that is an order."

She trembled as the command took hold and her humble attitude quickly morphed to resentment. Just what friends did she even have in the Heavens?

"Yes, *Master*," she spat, then let the angry silence between them linger. But she soon felt the need to lash out. "Is that what you're doing with me? Tainting my soul? It's already obliterated. You crushed it, tore it apart, and stepped on it."

Zagan shook at her words, just as she'd done to his deliberate commands. *Good, I hope he feels guilty for what he's done to me.*

"That is not the intention of this dinner," he ground out between clenched teeth. He seemed so disgusted with the accusation that he couldn't even look at her. "Is it so impossible to believe that I was trying to do something nice for you? You were sick. You fought valiantly against Lamia. Then you got sick again and fell. After all that, I thought you would enjoy a good meal."

Stunned, Coryn couldn't even open her mouth to speak. She didn't think demons were capable of doing things for no personal gain, yet he seemed truly offended by her accusation and angry that he had to explain himself.

"If it is the command about confiding in your angel friends that has you so angry with me," he continued, "know that it was something I had to say. That, I would hope you would understand. I trust you, Coryn, but not your brethren in the Heavens."

She swallowed, feeling her cheeks heat at his words.

"I guess I'm sorry too," she managed to say, then took another generous bite of boar.

He offered a small smile as he watched her. "I want to prove to you that I have a heart, Coryn. Not just the thing that beats in my chest, but ... I want to prove I can care. For you."

She coughed to stop some food from going down the wrong pipe. Was this some sort of hallucination, a side effect of her wing dying or the drude poison lingering in her system? Was she still unconscious, dreaming?

He reached out, took her hand that held her fork, and guided it to the table where he encouraged her to drop the utensil, then he enveloped her hand with his own.

"Coryn," he said, squeezing her hand gently, "this bond may be one-sided in your eyes, but believe me when I tell you, you are the one in control. I do not know what you have done to me, but ... I want you, my angel. I need you. And whatever I need to do to prove that, I will."

The rest of the meal was a blur to Coryn.

As soon as Zagan had made his confession, he quickly dropped her hand, picked up his fork, and resumed eating—it was the first time she'd ever seen him do so with more than just his claws. She stared, trying to comprehend what this meant for them. For her.

"Finish eating, Coryn," Zagan said.

It was a command, though she didn't think he realized that and she was too stunned to retort. She slumped in her seat, picked up her fork, and joined him in finishing the meal.

Soon, the time came to clean up and head back to Zagan's home; aside from telling her to finish eating, he'd stayed silent for the rest of the meal and the flight home—for which he'd carried her, and she had let him. Now that they were back in their original cave, she wasn't sure what to say to break the silence. If she even *should* break the silence.

The more she thought about Zagan's words, the more she realized how much she'd enjoyed hearing them—and that scared her. This was Zagan, the demon knight; as an angel she'd made it her life's goal to kill him. Now, having him tell her he wanted her, needed her even …

He sat on the other side of the cave, had extracted his claws and was cleaning them meticulously, one by one. He was busying himself, she realized, in an attempt to avoid her. Did he regret what he'd said? He must, otherwise he would have demanded a response or commanded her to forget the whole thing ever happened.

She almost wished he would.

Eventually, and without a word, Zagan retired to his bed. She lay in hers, and even though he had his back to her, Coryn knew he wasn't asleep. With her heart thumping in her chest, she studied his folded wings, his broad shoulders curled inward, and his tail moving lazily back and forth. She wouldn't be able to sleep, either, she knew. Her feelings would keep her from dreaming.

Gods … I think I love him. How can I love him?

She wondered if he heard the soft groan that escaped her lips as she rolled onto her back. Despite everything—the way he'd bound them together, constantly commanded her and took pleasure in her fights against him—he treated her well. He was suffering through the consequences of this bond as much as she was. She could see the hurt in his eyes every time he accidentally commanded her to do something. His words weren't empty; he cared for her. And maybe it was the bond, but she'd always been inexplicably drawn to him.

She squeezed her eyes shut as she absently stroked the soft down of her wings, which padded her as she rolled. *A former angel ... in love with a demon knight. I deserve to be forsaken.*

Was now the time to break the silence between them and tell him how she felt?

"Zagan? Are you still awake?"

CHAPTER 14

Zagan's heart lurched at Coryn's words and he sat up facing her. Was she still feeling ill? "Yes, I'm awake. Are you all right?"

"Yes. But, Zagan, I ..." She sat up as well, her eyes bouncing back and forth as she studied the blanket covering her legs. "Zagan, I ..."

Not long ago, Zagan wanted nothing more than for his name be the only word that left her lips. He also would have accepted, 'Yes, Master,' right before she spread her forsaken wings to go do his bidding, or her legs so he could ravage her. Now, he wished she would stop repeating his own damn name—she was stalling, that much was clear—and tell him what was on her mind. He couldn't command her to; doing so would undo everything that had led up to this.

He stilled. A command and one other thing would prevent them from moving forward. "No. No, no, no!"

Turning away from her, every nerve in his body tingling, he dashed toward the mouth of the cave.

"Turn away!" he shouted back at Coryn. "Do not listen!"

He was outside the cave in a flash. "It's like the king knows when to send you to make things most inconvenient for me," he hissed, grabbing the winged fool by his robes. "Now talk, and you'd better make it quick."

The messenger didn't bother with formalities. "You are to return to Hell," he said, his pale human-like hands coming to rest over Zagan's.

"For. What. Purpose?"

"I am not at liberty to discuss it." The messenger tilted his chin up a little too high for Zagan's liking. "But you must return now."

Zagan growled. "I will wrap up my business here, and then I will return."

"Fine. You have twenty minutes."

117

"You do not tell me how long I have." He released the messenger, who spread his snow-white wings and took to the skies.

"Damn this!" Zagan shouted. He punched the hard stone at the entrance of the cave.

Back inside he frowned when he saw that Coryn was kneeling and facing the rear wall with her hands over her ears. He moved into her view. "I am sorry. Look at me, Coryn."

If looks could kill, he would have been dead a thousand times over.

"Fuck you!"

"Tempting me, are you?" If only he had time to play this game with her now. "I must return to Hell, but I will be back soon."

Her shocked expression warmed him. Did she not want him to leave?

"Why? And who was that? You can't just make me run and hide every time you have company."

Zagan spat on the ground. "He is nothing. I will do what I can to keep you and your wings safe, but that includes ordering you to do anything I need you to do, at any time, to ensure that safety. I do not want you *exposed* to that monstrosity."

He lifted her from her kneeling position and dusted off her clothing.

She shoved his hand away and finished cleaning her tunic. "Was that the same demon who told you to go to battle at the church?"

He supposed giving her some detail wouldn't be harmful. Perhaps it would ease her anger with him.

"He is known as the messenger, and he delivers orders on behalf of the king. He was indeed the one who delivered the message about the church yesterday and has now requested I return to Hell for a time. He's an ugly fucker and a poor fighter with a bad attitude. He's worth no one's time, especially yours."

"So you're afraid he'll find out about me and report it back to the king."

Zagan looked up at the ceiling of the cavern, half-expecting to see the gods shrug and say, "We don't know how to handle her either."

"That is *not* what I am saying. I would shout from every rooftop on Manusya and in Hell that you are my angel of darkness. But he is not worthy of laying eyes on you. Now, I will return shortly, and you will wait for me here until that time."

He couldn't look at her as he turned away; if she retorted with another clever comment, he wasn't sure he could keep making excuses. He didn't want to return to Hell and preferred to stay with her always, but while Zagan was a powerful knight and could do almost anything he damn well pleased, the king needed to be obeyed—to an extent.

"Return to Hell," the messenger had said, and that was it.

When it came to following orders just enough to be in compliance, maybe his stubborn little angel was on to something.

***

There was something different in the energy of the club, and whatever it was, it was making Jinn a shitload of money. But despite the crowds and chaos, demons of every shape, size, and rank parted when Zagan returned to Jinn's Denn.

It had been a week since Zagan had last visited Hell. Usually he stayed on the surface of Manusya for months at a time, which made it difficult to train the lessers. He was grateful that Lamia always picked up his slack. They fought better under her tutelage, anyway. Zagan usually ended up beheading most of them in frustration. He thought about how satisfying Coryn would find that and smiled to himself.

"What the Hell, man!" said the familiar voice of the tall demon who fell in step beside him. "I own this damn place and these fuckers won't move for me."

That was indeed surprising. Not only was Jinn also a demon knight, but he was filthy rich from his various business ventures and the most sought-after incubus in Hell.

"Maybe all these lessers slept with you already and realized you're nothing special," Zagan offered with a shrug.

"Y'know, I thought I was disappointed when you left here so quickly last time. I don't know what the fuck I was thinking," Jinn said, giving Zagan a forceful slap on the shoulder.

"Oh, please," Zagan retorted. "I know you cried for days."

Jinn shrugged. "Only three." They both shook their heads and smiled.

Shoving his way through a horde of entangled, gyrating demons, Oriax intercepted Jinn and Zagan on their way to their corner booth. He flashed them a sinister grin.

"The line out there is insane, brother!" he shouted excitedly over the booming bass of the sexy club beat. "Dude, I watched two dretches duke it out and eat each other alive when they were trying to get in. I won fifty brym betting the fat one would lose."

Jinn smirked and gave O a fist bump before throwing his arm around the first female that passed him by—a striking demoness with shocking yellow eyes and wearing a tight red dress. She seemed alarmed at first and flashed her poison-tipped fangs at Jinn before realization of who he was settled over her features.

"What's your name, sweetheart?" Jinn asked, leaning down to get close to the female's long, pointed ear.

She shuddered and smiled, practically melting into Jinn's hold as she lifted her lips to his ear and responded. Jinn winked at her, smacked her on the ass and waved as she got carried into the undulating crowd.

He shrugged as he looked at Zagan and O. "Don't like girls named Dryda. Seriously, though, what brings you back here so soon? Not that you're not always welcome, of course."

"King's orders," Zagan said as the knights' usual table came into view with Lamia already sitting there.

"The king told you to come here? To my club?"

"Hardly. The white-winger came knocking, told me the king had ordered my return to Hell. He didn't mention I had to visit him."

Jinn rolled his eyes as he shook Zagan by the shoulder. "You're going to piss him off, and we're all gonna pay for it." He glanced behind Zagan and sighed. "Speaking of people that are pissed at you …"

He gestured with his chin toward Lamia, who was nodding to Oriax as he joined her at their corner table.

Zagan sighed. *I would have been better off going directly to the king.*

"Go on," Jinn encouraged, pushing him forward. Zagan snarled at him, but Jinn just gestured toward the table again.

"I'm going, I'm going," Zagan spat. "Ass." He felt like a fledgling being sent to his elders for a scolding.

There were few things between Manusya and Hell that made Zagan nervous. One of those things was losing Coryn. Another was Lamia's wrath.

"Oh, hi," she said to Zagan. "We were just talking about how you're a fucking moron."

Lamia turned her attention to the empty bottle of hellsglory, sighed, and knocked it away. "The service in here can be real shit sometimes, can't it?" she asked O, knowing full well Jinn was beside Zagan.

Oriax had never looked so uncomfortable to be in the middle of a situation before, and they'd been in some harrowing scenarios with angels and gods. He mouthed *run!* to Zagan, and Zagan was tempted, but they needed to talk about Coryn. They all needed to know what was going on.

"Seven Hells, all right!" Jinn snapped at her. "I'll go grab another bottle ... or three." Despite his air of frustration, he seemed relieved to be escaping the scene.

"I'll help you carry them," O offered and moved to stand, but Lamia gripped him by one of the small horns atop his head.

"You'll do nothing of the sort, Oriax." She waved Jinn away as O deflated back into his seat.

Deciding O had already taken enough of Lamia's misdirected lashings, Zagan sat down.

"What's your plan with the angel, Zagan?" She motioned toward the crowd of demons before them. "The change has begun. Everything we've been working toward, it's almost here. But instead of preparing to challenge the king, you're screwing around with an erelim?"

"A forsaken," Zagan corrected. "She is no longer an angel of the Heavens, but my angel of darkness. My bonded servant." Coryn would kill him if she knew he'd referred to her like that, but he needed his fellow knights to accept that she was now part of his life.

Lamia barked out a laugh. "Servant? Right. After what I saw, I can't help but wonder who is serving whom."

Zagan snarled. "Look around you, Lamia. As you said, the change has begun. The lessers all sense it, and I have grown much stronger now that I have Coryn. She has triggered the change."

The changing of the king had never happened in Zagan's two hundred years of life, but Jinn had been a knight during the last king's regime. They

121

all knew what signs to look for—uprising, unsettlement among the demons, and the lessers acting far dumber than usual. It was as if the king's clock, despite having never wronged his subjects, was running out, and the demons were getting restless. The lessers, simple though they were, felt his power shift in the same way Manusyan animals sense an impending earthquake.

"For years you've said you're not interested in taking the throne yet," Lamia said.

"Yes, well, things change." What made taking the throne feel right was having someone to share it with—but again, he needed to ease the rest of them into that idea.

Lamia chewed on his words as Jinn reappeared, set down four bottles of pure angel's blood and took the last empty seat at their table. Mal was behind him with an armful of mixers and glasses, but she didn't stay to chat like usual. Jinn must have warned her, and the scowl Zagan wore no doubt confirmed whatever Jinn had said.

"Thanks, Jinn," O said, reaching hastily for a glass and one of the bottles.

As soon as he popped it open the scent of angel blood wafted to Zagan's nose, both enticing and repulsing him in one whiff. Oriax poured each of them a shot, no mixers. The glow was nearly blinding in their dark corner of the club.

"Let's not argue with one another tonight, yeah?" He slid a glass before each of them, then held his up. "The change is upon us, and Zagan will soon take his rightful place as king."

Jinn held up his glass. "To the brotherhood, and to King Zagan."

Oriax leaned back in his seat and drained his hellsglory. He slammed the glass on the table and flashed his bright eyes and wicked grin up at Lamia. "To King Zagan! This is going to be a damn fine upheaval."

Zagan felt Lamia's eyes on him as he tentatively lifted his own shot. Images of Coryn flashed before him, and Lamia knew it. He met her gaze and hardened his resolve.

"To the brotherhood ... and soon, my throne." He held his breath as he put the glass to his lips and knocked it back.

His eyes rolled back and he moaned in ecstasy when the liquid first hit his tongue. Pure distilled angel blood was difficult to come by; Zagan was surprised his brother had this much of it on hand. Hellsglory, a less potent version, gave him a decent buzz after a while, but his head was already growing fuzzy with just one shot of the pure stuff. He tried not to think about what he was actually consuming, yet he was conscious of how right Lamia had been—he should not be repulsed by drinking angel blood. He was to be the demon king, for fuck's sake!

He slammed the glass onto the table. It was already difficult to focus on Oriax as he shoved the glass toward him.

"Another."

CHAPTER 15

Zagan was a good-for-nothing, infuriating son of a bitch! An animal that, despite everything, made Coryn's heart race and her body heat.

His refusal to unveil her to the messenger bothered her. He hadn't hidden or shielded her from Lamia, despite her obvious disapproval of their bond. Instead, he'd made her fight Lamia to prove her strength. If the messenger was as lowly as Zagan made him out to be, why did he panic and send her away any time he came near?

She busied herself as she pondered by cleaning Zagan's already immaculate dwelling. For a demon, he was disturbingly clean; his servants wouldn't have to do much tidying when he became king. It was one of his cute quirks, along with liking apples and small spaces.

If it weren't for the bond, I wouldn't have ever fallen in love with him ... right?

And when he became king, he would take a queen.

She froze. Her face grew cold as her blood retreated. She hadn't thought of that before, but the reality of her future now hit her full force. There was no way the demons in Hell would support her as their queen, especially after she eventually lost her wings. Everything—her wings, her demon knight— would be taken away.

She knelt and scrubbed angrily at the stone floor, haunted by thoughts of the myriad of demon females Zagan would have to choose from, all wicked and tempting in their own right. She imagined Zagan atop a huge throne with a succubus on his lap, surrounded by flames, while she stood in the corner and awaited her next command. Maybe, since he cared for her so much, he'd allow her to behead his lesser subjects who acted out of line. Or maybe his command would be for her to feed him and his succubus queen apple slices while they fucked.

Gods, the solitude made her think too much!

He'd already told her he had no plans to take the throne just yet, so it was stupid to worry about his queen selection now. It was her fault she hadn't followed orders in the Heavens, and he was the oasis in an otherwise shitty situation. Even if the only reason they cared for each other was because of the bond, she could at least enjoy her time with him.

Had he known his curse would make him care for me, too?

Her thoughts were interrupted by the familiar *whoosh* of Zagan's wings at the cave's entrance. She turned, her stomach tying in knots.

A crash sounded, and Coryn froze in place, her spine straight, and listened. It was dark in the cave—damn her poor eyesight after sunset! She listened for another crash, more footsteps, or evidence of a struggle. Had someone followed Zagan home? She shuffled one foot forward, then the other, and bit her lip when she heard a low groan.

When she didn't hear any more commotion, Coryn grabbed a candle from her nightstand in one hand and her dagger in the other. She left the lighted bedroom area for the dark abyss of the cavern with her ears still pricked.

"Zagan?" she whispered, squinting, desperately trying to make out shapes in the candlelight.

She nearly dropped the candle altogether when her whispered call was met with a grunt of surprise and a flurry of more objects crashing to the ground. But instead of retreating, Coryn's battle instincts kicked in. She set her only light source down a safe distance away and hurled herself toward the flailing shadow with a cry.

Still gripping the dagger, she grabbed for the shadow and flipped the intruder onto his back, pinning him to the ground with her knees on his chest, reveling in the sweet sound of panicked gasps for air. It wasn't until her dagger was pressed against her victim's soft, warm throat that her head began to clear. She'd only spent a brief time pressed up against this body before, but she'd know it anywhere.

Zagan let out a weak laugh beneath her. "There's my beautiful angel of darkness."

125

Coryn cursed under her breath before pushing off the demon. "Who else is here?" she asked, squinting into the darkness again. "Did someone follow you?"

Zagan coughed a few times before he answered. Why was he still lying there?

"No one followed me, darling. Why did you think that? Because of all the shit I knocked over?" He laughed. "Eh, we needed to redecorate anyway."

Coryn noted the slight slur in his speech.

"Are you drunk?" she asked incredulously, then remembered the candle a few feet away. The flames danced as she picked it up and brought it closer to the demon that seemed plastered to the ground.

"Gah!" Zagan whined, turning his head the other way and shielding his eyes from the light with his arms.

"You *are* drunk!" Coryn said, half-amused and half-surprised. She set the candle down and grabbed Zagan's forearms, gently trying to coax them away from his face. She wasn't sure she'd ever get used to the incredible warmth of his skin, let alone the heat that coursed through her body whenever she touched him.

"Oh, come on, you baby! It's not that bright."

"Not for you, maybe. But for me, the darkest of demons, I may as well be staring at the surface of the sun."

Coryn rolled her eyes. "Whatever you say, oh darkest of demons. So let me get this straight, you left me here to go to a bar? With a ... a what? Demon, beast, creature, some other thing I'm not allowed to see?"

When he shook his head, denying the options but offering no alternative answer, her mood quickly soured. Drunk Zagan was cute, but only when he wasn't trying to hide something.

She pressed on. "Then who were you with?" If he'd been with other women, demon or otherwise, then what?

Maybe he'd been selecting his queen. Dagger or no dagger, she couldn't hurt him. *Damn this curse!*

She widened her eyes in anticipation of his answer when he turned to face her. No wonder he'd complained about the light from the candle's flames—his pupils were noticeably dilated. What kind of alcohol did that? Her worried

126

expression must have amused him because he smiled, and that made her want to stab him all over again.

"I was with the knights, at Jinn's club in Hell. We had a … strategy meeting."

Clumsily, he brought a hand up to stroke her cheek, brushing past her breast in the process. His pupils dilated further and a sinister grin played across his lips.

"Why? Were you worried I was with another female?" He struggled to sit up.

Coryn couldn't tell if it was his hand or his question that warmed her cheek. "No," was all she managed to croak out.

Zagan's pleasured smile only grew, and in that moment, he was Coryn's entire world. He was all she could see in the darkness, all she could feel as his hand lost its place at her cheek and pressed against the small of her back, coaxing her into his lap. He was all she could smell, his ember-and-sandalwood scent an instant aphrodisiac that made every one of her nerve endings ache. His raspy breaths were all she could hear as her own grew more desperate. She trembled in his strong hold as he leaned into her neck. She shivered, and goosebumps formed over every inch of her.

He held her tighter and growled against her throat. "Coryn."

She looked up at the ceiling, neck muscles straining, giving him as much access to her tender flesh as he wanted. She moaned in anticipation as he breathed one heady exhale, then another, against her skin.

"My angel."

She'd told him not to call her that, and yet enjoyed the claim he had on her. She wrapped her arms around his neck, cradled his head, and eagerly pressed him to her. His fangs grazed her skin. His tongue flicked out, running along the path his teeth had taken.

"So delicious."

Coryn gasped, another chill rocking her to her core. He got more ravenous in response, his clawed fingers roughly raking down her back, and he took a greedy inhale of her skin. His fangs struck her neck again, and she cried out in delicious pleasure-pain. Spreading her legs, she straddled him, desperate to grind her sex against his arousal.

Only she found he wasn't hard—though the bite that broke her skin was.

127

She cried out, his hands bracing her as she arched her back. As he sank his teeth into her neck, she tried to decide whether or not she was still enjoying the ride.

Holding her breath, she froze as his teeth retreated from her flesh. Her blood—warm, thick, and smelling of copper—dripped down her neck. Zagan let out a low, delighted moan right before his lips closed around the wound.

She cried louder when Zagan sucked on her neck as if he was a starving vampire after centuries without blood. Her fingers, wrapped tightly in his hair, began to cramp. Every part of her brain screamed that this was wrong— something was so very wrong—yet her body wanted to ride him to oblivion.

She sat there, still frozen, waiting until he relented or sucked her dry. The tiniest of squeaks left her lips as she stared blankly into the darkness.

Finally, his breathing slowed. He stopped sucking and licked weakly at her skin.

"It's blood ..." he whispered on a deep exhale, seemingly to himself, his lips still against her skin. "It's just ... human blood."

He pulled away, his eyes wide, her blood trickling down one side of his mouth.

A combined wave of confusion, shame, and betrayal flooded Coryn as everything became clear—angel blood had reduced him to this state before he'd returned to the cave, and though he craved more of it from her, she had none to give.

He rolled onto his back and groaned.

Coryn pushed off from his lap and, pressing a hand to the wounds in her neck, stared down at him in disbelief. He'd been lucid the instant after he realized what he'd done, but he was lost to the blood high again all too quickly. His dilated pupils stared up at the ceiling of the cave, his eyelids at half-mast as his breathing slowed.

"My angel ..." he said, but Coryn didn't think he realized she was still there.

His eyes closed, and he was soon fast asleep, right there at the cave's entrance.

Coryn had never before paid attention to a demon that was high on angel blood. She was shocked to see the effect it could have on such a controlled and disciplined creature.

She felt the searing pang of hurt and betrayal hit her—after all, Zagan must have known she would be upset when he came back in that state after consuming the blood of angels—and then he'd tried to use her as a vessel to continue his high! She was furious, and mortified, but as she cleaned her wounds, she thought about what Zagan had done. He was too calculated to pull a stunt like this at random; he must have had a good reason for letting this happen. At least, she would give him the opportunity to come up with one before she returned the puncture wounds tenfold—with spikes instead of teeth. She couldn't harm him without his permission, but after he suffered her wrath he would be begging to be stabbed over any other alternative she would offer him.

As the night wore on she watched his peaceful, ignorant sleep turn restless. He grumbled and tossed and turned, and Coryn knew he'd likely slipped into that awful place between sleep and consciousness, where his fevered mind worked overtime. She gripped his shoulder and shook him. His skin was sweatier than she'd realized in the dim light.

"Zagan," she urged in a soft voice. But when that didn't rouse him, she said it louder and spoke directly into his ear. "*Zagan!*"

"Angel," he grumbled back.

Coryn wasn't sure if he was calling out to her or for the blood he craved. Either way, he'd no longer be calling her that—it brought up too many mixed emotions.

As she coaxed him to his feet with grumbled curses and a lot of shoving, she imagined this was how she must have been when she was sick from the drude poison.

She got Zagan into bed and made him drink some fresh water. When he lay down, the back of his head rested against the headboard, forcing his neck to bend at a strange angle.

"Scoot down, Zagan," she said, tapping him gently on the chest in an attempt to rouse him again. She was amazed at how quickly he gave in to sleep.

Coryn sighed and, with a deep breath, grabbed Zagan's legs and tugged him down the bed. He was heavier than he looked. His long horns left deep grooves in the wooden headboard as she dragged him down, but other than that, her efforts only resulted in his head tilting at an even less comfortable angle.

"Come on, Zagan!" she growled. Climbing onto his bed, she straddled him and used her own weight to shimmy him down. The act reminded her of the desperate way she'd ground into his lap as he sucked greedily at her blood—her stupid, ordinary human blood—and she seethed with anger all over again.

"And you aren't even sober enough to see you finally got me into your bed, you jerk!"

She put her hands on either side of his head, about to push off and away from him, but just as she was about to swing one leg over his torso, a warm hand grabbed her wrist.

She gasped.

Zagan's other hand found its way to her back and stopped just below the base of her wings, where he pressed her down to him. His beckoning wasn't strong—she could have easily squirmed out of his hold. But instead, she allowed him to press her against his chest and tangle one hand in her hair. She heard the beating of his heart when she laid her ear against his sternum.

"I'm sorry, Coryn," he whispered and tightened his grip.

She smiled but ignored the sensation of her heart warming up and exploding behind her ribs. "I know. Go to sleep, Zagan. We'll talk about it in the morning. I'll … I'll be right here."

She nuzzled into his chest and closed her eyes, the soft sound of his breathing and the slow beat of his heart eventually lulling her to sleep.

CHAPTER 16

Zagan awoke the following morning knowing what Coryn must have felt like when she'd plummeted from the Heavens and slammed into the ground. In fact, he imagined he felt the same way she would have if the gods had reascended her and cast her down several more times until they were satisfied she'd ache for centuries.

Damn angel blood!

But as much as his body and head ached, it was his heart that felt the most pain. His memories of the night before were fuzzy, but he recalled that first shot of angel's blood, the euphoria it had brought him combined with the joy of reuniting with his friends. There'd been more shots. Many more. When everyone began retiring for the night, drunk and high and fuzzy all at once, Oriax had insisted on Zagan staying in Hell, but he'd felt the overwhelming desire to return to Coryn. After clumsily transporting himself back to the cave, he'd been ashamed. But then Coryn's face, shocked at first, had flushed with heated passion. There was no way he would ever forget her pleasured face, no matter what state he was in. He would never forget her mewls and moans ...

His eyes shot open and he stared up at the ceiling of the cave. A feeling of dread washed over him as he recalled just what had happened the night before—his teeth, sinking into Coryn's neck as she'd panted and cried out for him. The bitter taste of her forsaken blood, no different than the taste of a human's. The look of recognition and horror Coryn had worn when she realized why he wasn't acting like himself.

"Coryn!" he called, moving to sit up, but he was stopped by a weight on his chest. He looked down and there was his beautiful, slumbering angel.

He had to give it to the gods; Coryn was perfect in every way. She had a peaceful smile on her face as her chest rose slowly up and down with every breath she took.

He tried to relax back onto the mattress but cursed when she began to stir.

Like him, it seemed to take Coryn a moment after she opened her eyes to realize where she was. He said nothing, watching with fascination and delight as her eyes darted beneath her thick lashes, looked down at his bare chest, over at the wall, and at his tail swinging back and forth over the side of the bed.

When she lifted her head, their eyes met, and the forgiveness he saw there was nearly enough to make him melt. Not that she would ever know that.

"Morning," he said, his voice scratchy. His head throbbed with each syllable.

She smiled weakly. "I notice you left off the *good* in that greeting."

"Hmm. Probably because it feels like my brain is going to implode."

Her smile broadened. "Well, that's good. You deserve a thousand mornings like this then, after your antics last night."

She'd never been more right about anything.

"If repeating this morning includes waking up to you in my arms, then I'll gladly suffer through a thousand more."

He spotted the bruised puncture wounds in her neck and felt a wave of guilt all over again.

She sat up, severing all contact between them, and he felt the instinctive urge to pull her back down to him. He resisted, though. He deserved this punishment.

"There are other ways to get me into your arms, you know." Coryn wouldn't look at him. She avoided his gaze exactly as she had when she'd first fallen to him.

"Angel—"

"Don't call me that!" she snapped, shouting so suddenly he jumped.

The sound echoed in his head, jostling his hungover brain. She took a few quick, deep breaths and stared at him like a wild animal stuck in a cage—a cage *he'd* created for her.

132

"Not only am I no longer an angel, but any evidence that I ever was will die." She looked over her shoulder at the swooping arch of her left wing and frowned. Her bottom lip quivered as she blinked away her tears.

Her profound sadness made him want to stab himself through the heart with his own claw. "You're right."

He couldn't believe how stupid and ignorant he was being. Her face, so recently filled with forgiveness for him, had turned so quickly to sadness. And while he struggled to find the right thing to say, her sadness transitioned to rage.

"Coryn, I'm sorry for the pain I've caused you. I will have Lamia push back the infection in your wings a thousand times over. She doesn't know for certain it won't work. And in the meantime, we can find other ways for you to keep them. I am so, so sorry."

"Good," she spat.

He noted the quick rise and fall of her chest and the flush in her cheeks as she glared at him. He wanted so desperately to kiss those cheeks and redden them even more, but that would sacrifice the delicate relationship they had begun to forge.

Instead, he sat up, groaning as the whole world spun. He pinched the bridge of his nose and took a breath before he noticed Coryn studying him out of the corner of his eye.

"Just how much angel blood did you drink?" she asked.

He met the question with a cringe. "A lot," he admitted, hating how she turned away from him.

Silence stretched between them for a time until Coryn strode to his dresser and picked up a glass and pitcher. Where had they come from? Her wings twitched as she poured water into the glass, then made her way back to him.

"What does it do to you, exactly?" she asked, then offered the glass to him.

He let out a small laugh. "Destroys my head."

Coryn rolled her eyes; he owed it to her to go on.

"It is a high I cannot even begin to explain. Angel blood is poison to a demon's brain, but not in the same ways a demon's poison is to an angel or human."

It hurt to tell her these things, but she deserved to know and needed to understand.

He sighed. "And since I'm being so honest, the other knights are concerned my infatuation with you is jeopardizing my chance to take the throne."

Coryn's eyes widened. "Is it?"

"Hardly. If anything, I want it more." He would tell her more about that plan later; he didn't want to overwhelm her now. "I needed to prove to them that you will not be my undoing." He leaned close, his voice growing husky. "You will not be my undoing, will you, Coryn?"

She shook her head, clearly mesmerized by his gaze, and he smirked.

"That's a good girl." He pulled her toward him, enveloping her in his arms as he stroked her wings.

"I am sorry," he said again, his throat vibrating against her head with each word. "Everything I do, it's to make us more powerful. Make *you* more powerful. Do you wish angel blood still ran through your veins?"

She didn't hesitate before responding. "Yes, I do."

He pulled back, distancing himself enough to look into her eyes.

"I miss my wings, my golden ones. Being forsaken feels too different, too in-between."

He couldn't hide his hurt, and she softened immediately.

"That said, I would never wish any of this away. You're a demon—and a pompous ass—but you're my pompous ass. And I like being yours."

More beautiful words had never been spoken. Was Coryn finally telling him she cared for him? He tightened his arms around her and, all at once, was consumed by his own emotions. The fuzziness of his head was replaced with a high sweeter than even angel blood could give him.

He had to tell her. The words were bubbling to the surface, and she needed to know.

"Coryn, my sweet female—I love being yours, too." He straightened up and studied her intensely, feeling as if he were bracing for a punch.

"Coryn … I … I *love* you. I need you. And whatever I need to do to prove that, I will."

Coryn's mind came to a screeching halt. *Did Zagan just say he was* in love *with me?*

When had she risen off the bed? He stared at her, looking more scared than she'd ever seen him. She wished she could put his mind at ease, but her head and her heart were fighting to make sense of her feelings.

She had never run from anything in her life, but his words instilled in her an overwhelming sense to flee. She took a couple of tentative backward steps toward the mouth of the cave. Though her heart was eager to tell him how she felt, her head knew better. He would never make her, a creation of the gods, his queen, even if she eventually lost her wings. Did she really want to be his concubine?

When she lengthened the distance between them, Zagan held out his hands. "Coryn, wait."

Another command. She froze immediately, and Zagan's pained eyes widened further. Her emotions flooded her, and her whimper halted the apology he was surely about to utter.

"Do you mean it? That you'll do anything to prove you love me?" she asked.

"Despite the reputation of my kind, I never lie."

She couldn't have scripted a more perfect response than that; he was walking right into her trap. "Really?"

There was a flash of suspicion in his expression—and perhaps mild amusement—but he never wavered. With the way he was looking her up and down, she figured he must have thought she'd request something sexual to prove himself. *Typical male.*

"Yes, Coryn. I did promise that to you, did I not?"

Why yes, Zagan. Yes, you did. She smiled up at him, noticing his slow intake of air through his nose as he braced himself for her request.

"Then release me from this cursed bond." As she watched the words register, she took in her own lungful of air and continued to inhale until it burned. Breaking their bond would guarantee her freedom. Though she would remain forsaken, she would no longer be under his control, and they would be able to see if the curse really was the driving force of their feelings for one another.

As Zagan's expression turned from surprise to contemplation to regret, Coryn knew the answer to her request before he even opened his mouth.

"Coryn …"

She wanted the world to hear her scream. Her chest felt as if it were collapsing in on itself. "You said you would do *anything* to prove you loved me. You promised it again, just now!" She grew more hysterical as she spoke. "I'm telling you, prove it by releasing me."

"I also told you that I do not lie." Zagan kept his voice infuriatingly calm, and he brought his hands up in front of him, exposing his palms as if approaching a scared kitten.

"Believe me when I tell you this, ange—Coryn. There have been many times when I have regretted forcing my bond on you. I look at your wings"—there was extra pain in his expression when he said that—"and I see the longing you have for them to be golden again. Seven Hells, just to have them remain *attached to your back*! I would storm the Heavens and pluck feathers from the wings of every seraphim, erelim, cherubim, and god if it meant earning yours back again.

"I have looked for ways to remove the bond—I know you must have as well—but it's not possible. I know you hurt when you see other angels, but I also see how conflicted you are when they preach their ideals. Our bond may be a curse but know that for every moment I regret forcing it on you, there are a hundred more moments where I could drop to my knees and thank the gods for sending you to me."

His words were sweet and honest and true, but she couldn't keep her emotions from overwhelming her.

"I hate that you did this to me," she said, trying to keep her voice from wavering. "I hate that demons now heal me when I'm sick, and that you have complete autonomy over everything I do. And I hate that I can't move from this damned spot until you say otherwise!"

He looked surprised, as if he'd forgotten he'd told her wait. He rose to his feet but kept his distance, as if she were a wild animal about to be released from a cage.

"You may move, Coryn. I'm so sorry for that part of the bond, but I wouldn't take it back if it meant losing you."

Though she was now free to run, she stayed in place as he approached.

"You know now that I love you. I want to protect you always. I wish you would tell me you feel the same, or at least what your true feelings are, but I will not force you. I'm still trying to figure out how to speak in a way that won't affect you, because I never want to force you to do anything ever again. To force you means to lose you. I see you care for me less and less every time you have to follow one of my commands. This bond is my curse as much as it is yours."

She burst into tears, overwhelmed by the weight of the curse and his words and hating that the eternal sun wasn't there to dampen her emotions. He was trying; she knew that. She'd always known that, which was why she chose to forgive him.

When he took a few more tentative steps toward her, his expression matching the pain she felt, she opened her arms up. He breathed a sigh of relief as he closed the distance between them and enveloped her in a tight hug. Coryn wrapped her arms around him, but they only reached halfway up his back.

He held her as she cried, lightly stroking her hair with his claws and letting her unload all the tears she'd been holding back onto his warm skin.

"You're so strong," he rasped, one hand losing itself from her waist to cup her cheek as he coaxed her to look up at him. "There's a lot of bravery in that small body of yours."

"Hmph." Coryn wiped tears from both her cheeks. "Looks can be deceiving, you know. I also pack quite a punch."

His hold around her tightened. "Don't I know it."

"So watch out, or I'll kick your ass."

"I know that, too."

His tail came along her side, slowly trailing up her ankle, calf, then beneath her tunic to her thigh.

"So ... how many times will I have to tell you I love you before I get any kind of response?"

"How about I tell you how I feel once demons stop coming by to bother you or challenge me."

137

He looked around without relinquishing his hold on her waist. "Well, I don't see any now."

When he met her gaze again, she gave him a long and assessing look. Zagan, demon knight and the next King of Hell, squirmed beneath her gaze.

"You're too quiet," he said and tugged on her hips, pressing himself against her. "If all I had to do to silence you was tell you how I feel about you, I would have done so as soon as you fell to me from the sky."

He slid his hands from her hips, up her sides, and into her hair. Bunching it in his fists, he yanked on the locks, making her gasp. His eyes grew dark and his voice dropped into a low, gravelly tone.

"I long to hear you speak, Coryn."

Her breath quickened as she looked up at him. Whether she wanted to admit it to him or not, she loved the possessive hold he had on her. Maybe she hated the idea of this bond, but she was sure he could see it in her eyes—and smell it on her body—that this was all too forbidden and erotic for her to ignore. But as he pressed his arousal against her stomach, she stifled her moan.

"You are to become the demon king, Zagan."

"I know."

"To love someone means you should commit to them."

"I know that, too."

He couldn't possibly. "I will not be your concubine while you make another demon your queen."

He looked surprised, confused. "Who said I would take another to be my queen? You will—" He hesitated. "I *would like* for you to rule Hell beside me, if you wish. Hell's army, its knights, the throne … I am Hell's prince, but I did not want any of it until I met you. I want to give it to you. All of it. You wanted to be an archangel? I will make you my queen. Think about it, Coryn. Legions upon legions of demons will race to follow your commands. The curse can't be undone, but the crown … that can be yours. I can give that to you."

He looked at the ground. "I don't want any of it if I don't have you with me. Please be my queen, Coryn. Please be mine, forever."

I could be queen. Zagan's *queen.*

Despite the careful wording of his proposal, she knew this was not a request—nor did she want it to be. She could be with Zagan forever, have him all to herself, and rule Hell with him. She would be more powerful than she ever imagined. Ouranos would have never promised her anything like this. He'd probably never intended to nominate her for archangel, either.

Funny how it took a demon for me to see the light.

As if he'd read her thoughts, Zagan narrowed his eyes and suspicion laced his voice. "I want to be your god now, Coryn. I want to be the one you crave, and if I had my way, you would never think of that former lover of yours again."

She wanted to tell him Ouranos no longer mattered, yet she couldn't find her voice. He wanted her to be his queen. To rule Hell by his side. But in his eyes she could see a spark of rage as he misread her silence.

His trembling fists tightened in her hair. "Listen to me, Coryn."

He growled in frustration, realizing he'd uttered another command.

"I would like for you to listen to me. I will become king. You can be my queen. Together we can eradicate every god ... starting with *him*. Under my rule, the Heavens will not stand a chance. We could end this war, once and for all, and all the realms would be corrupted with our passion."

Coryn's heart raced at the idea and a chill of delight rocked through her.

"Please, if you want to be mine, tell me."

"Yes, I want to be yours, Zagan. And I want to be your queen."

"Thank you," he whispered as his head fell back and his shoulders relaxed. When he regarded her again, he had the widest, most euphoric smile she couldn't help but return.

"That almost makes me want to praise the gods before we obliterate them," he said, then kissed her tenderly on the forehead. "Now, will you give in to what your body craves?"

She had to give him credit; he was being careful not to issue commands. Although, she kind of wished he would so there would be no need to decide what she wanted—all her pitiful body did was ache for him, and he knew it.

Damn this demon and the incredible power he had to taint her soul!

But as she stared up into his red eyes, she felt as if he were the only one her body and soul had ever craved.

What is this demon doing to me?

No one, Ouranos included, had ever made her feel this way. Though they had been brought together by obligation and a cursed bond, they had truly grown to care for one another. Her resolve to fight her feelings grew weaker; there was no sense fighting them.

"Yes," she whispered, "I will give my body what it wants."

Then, rising onto her tiptoes, she connected her lips with his.

CHAPTER 17

Sunlight spilled into the cave when Zagan woke the following morning. Coryn, small and delicate and warm, lay curled up in his arms, her head on his chest and her soft auburn locks tickling his skin. She still was an angel, *his* angel—if he could wake up to this every morning, he'd wake up among the Heavens.

He stared up at the ceiling and gently traced the ridges of Coryn's spine. Her wings still felt soft, and their color was a healthy gray—if gray could ever be described as such. They were a far cry at least from when they'd been black and dying.

Sex was good; they should probably continue with that. Four or five orgasms a day would keep her wings strong, wouldn't it? He chuckled softly, then stopped abruptly when Coryn's even breathing paused.

After a brief moment, her melodic inhales and exhales resumed, and he was happy to find he hadn't woken her. In fact, Zagan had never felt so elated. Like he could take on the Heavens, Hell, and everywhere between, all at once.

Coryn had willingly given herself to him, and that was worth any kingdom. And though he hadn't demanded she be intimate with him, his sexy commands had been fun. There were certainly some perks to this bond outside of having a powerful, competent warrior angel as his queen.

Closing his eyes, he craned his neck and inhaled her scent, feeling like all of Manusya was feeding off of his elation and spreading his corrupted demon taint, much like the seed that now filled his beautiful angel.

She finally began to show signs of stirring. With his tail, he picked up an apple from the bowl on the bedside table and sank his teeth into it. The crisp sound was louder in the serene cave than he'd anticipated, and Coryn opened her eyes. He took another bite and, with his arms still protectively around her bare form, held the fruit a few inches from her lips.

"Good morning. Care for some breakfast?"

He watched with delight as her sleepy eyes blinked a few times, then focused on the apple. She stared at it as if she was assessing where she was—not in her bed, but his, and not alone, but in his arms. Beautifully naked, rested, and ready for the taking again. His erection surged against her side at the thought.

It twitched again when he watched her sink her teeth into the apple. She chewed thoughtfully and swallowed, extending her neck as she did so, then looked up at him. Her smile was enough to brighten the sun.

"Good morning." She glanced at the small bite she'd left in the apple. "And thank you."

He brought the fruit to his lips and covered her bite with his own. "Did you sleep well?"

"Mmm," she purred and took another bite of the apple. She nuzzled against his chest and purposely brushed her stomach against his erection.

Zagan shuddered and, moving his tail and the apple away from her lips, caught her smirk.

"I thought *I* was the demon here," he said, matching her expression as he placed the fruit back into the bowl.

With his arms wrapped tightly around her, he slipped his tail beneath her chin and coaxed her to look up at him. He fused their mouths together, sweet apple scent wafting between them as he kissed her deeply.

If only he could bottle this feeling of power. Having his angel wrapped in his arms was sweeter than the purest drink of her blood. Of course, her other fluids would be even more delicious ...

Coryn giggled on a sigh, and Zagan realized that while he'd been lost in thought he'd nipped her bottom lip. He licked over the spot, not minding the coppery taste on his tongue, and pressed his forehead to hers, smiling as he stared into those otherworldly eyes.

"You like it when I bite, don't you?" he rasped, and her shiver was his answer. His cock twitched again, and this time he arched his back off the bed and groaned loudly, nearly spilling his seed without her even touching him.

What in the seven Hells was going on!

Coryn, the little vixen, purred in response and began kissing down his neck. Every kiss and every lick was magnified on his skin, almost to the point of pain.

"Stop!" And she had no choice but to obey.

He panted as he looked into her eyes, a mixture of confusion and disappointment and hurt reflected back at him. He met them with equal emotion. She ceased touching him and moved to lay beside him.

He propped himself up on his elbows. "Something is wrong."

Otherwise, he would have sunk to the hilt within her and filled her with his seed by now. And they both knew it.

"What is it?" she asked, her voice small as her eyes jumped back and forth to his.

"I ... every touch, every sound, the light ... everything is intensified right now."

It was sensory overload times a thousand. Even the sheets hurt. He kicked off the blankets, exposing his aroused, naked body, and sucked in a breath as they cleared his foot and settled in a heap at the end of the bed.

As much as he was in pain, Coryn's look of concern was the worst part of this.

He arched his back again and cried out, feeling as if a red-hot brand had just been pressed into his spine.

"Zagan!" Coryn shouted.

Dark figures began to cloud his vision. He blinked, watching them turn white on the backs of his eyelids before he opened them and saw a new scene—the dark horde was before him. Blink, scene change. Blink, scene change.

Instantly, he knew what was happening. "Someone else is trying to claim the throne."

As if confirming his suspicion, his vision returned and his skin felt less sensitive. He pushed to his feet, collected his clothes, and quickly pulled on his pants.

Coryn wasn't far behind. She raced to the dresser and pulled out a fresh tunic. "I thought demons weren't like angels. That they can't feel what others are doing around them."

143

"Not usually," Zagan said, "but a king knows when his kingdom is under attack. The throne might not yet be mine, but it's mine to defend."

And Coryn would fight right alongside him this time. Since her fall from the Heavens, she'd fought in tunics and robes, but for this battle, he would gift her with something special.

***

"It was the best the human blacksmiths could do," Zagan grumbled as he handed the armor to her.

But each piece was perfect. He must have spent a lot of time with the blacksmith, describing her angelic armor in detail, to get a set this precise.

"Zagan, I love it," she whispered as tears welled in her eyes. He'd even given her a sword, too, a close match to the one Pahaliah had confiscated.

He bowed in response, but she could see he wished it was true angelic armor. His expression made her own pain dissipate.

"There isn't any chance you'll remain here and wait for me, is there?" he asked.

But they both knew she wouldn't. Zagan's rise to the throne was just as important to Coryn—she needed to fight for the right to rule by his side as queen.

"You wanted me to be your angel of darkness," she said, "so let me be your angel of darkness."

They flew for what felt like hours, but it allowed Coryn to prepare for battle. She watched Zagan before her, giving one flap of his wings for every three or four of hers. He looked back every few minutes, making sure she was still behind him. Eventually, she met his gaze with one of displeasure—she was strong enough now to keep up with him—and so he stopped checking on her.

After flying across the ocean, they came to a large island. Zagan pointed his clawed hand, and Coryn spotted Lamia, then her old foe Oriax. They were with another demon, who was about Zagan's height, and all three were fighting against five more demons who were too fast, strong, and calculated to be part of the lesser demon army.

It looked as if Zagan wanted to tell her something, but it was clear he didn't want to waste any more time. He let out a roar, which Coryn felt in her bones, then he swooped down to join the battle. Coryn drew her sword from its sheath and dove after him.

She landed beside Lamia—Zagan was already assisting Oriax—and lifted her sword to meet that of Lamia's opponent.

Lamia took the reprieve, giving Coryn a small nod to acknowledge her arrival before turning her attention back to her attacker—a skeletal figure with charcoal-black bones and glowing orange eyes. He lacked horns and a tail, and instead, donned a heavy hooded cloak.

Coryn withdrew her sword from his and brought it back in again. She nearly faltered when metal met metal and a vision of a man flashed over the skeleton's form.

Lamia knocked the demon's sword away from Coryn's. "His name is Dantalion. Don't be fooled by what he projects onto his bones."

Dantalion returned his attention to Lamia, this time projecting a vision of a warrior woman as he swung his sword at her. Coryn had no idea a demon could take the shape of a human. How many demons could be posing as humans on Manusya unbeknownst to the gods?

But shifting wasn't Dantalion's only trick. Just as Lamia deflected the demon's sword and went to parry it with an attack of her own, Dantalion vanished.

"Son of a bitch!" Lamia cursed, swinging around.

Coryn looked everywhere, but there was no sign of the demon.

"To Zagan!" Lamia called, running over to Coryn and grabbing her by the arm. "Quickly!"

Coryn tore her arm from Lamia's grasp but ran alongside her. She didn't need to be told twice to join her king. They fought through the horde of lessers together, desperate to get to Zagan and protect him—Lamia because he was her king, Coryn because he was her everything.

Dantalion had teleported into the midst of the main battle, though it seemed Zagan and the other knights had that situation under control. Coryn spied Zagan with a male demon pinned against his chest, his strong arm crushing the demon's throat, while Oriax and the tall knight each faced two more opposing demons.

Lamia and Coryn glanced at each other, an unspoken agreement to take the extra enemies off the knights' hands. Lamia moved behind Dantalion.

"There you are, asshole," she said with satisfaction, snakes forming in her hair to slither forward and around Dantalion's arms in a vice-like grip. A few sank their teeth into the demon just as he went translucent, keeping him from flashing away and causing him to howl in pain. Lamia laughed a sinister, contented laugh.

Coryn approached a male demon, roughly her size and almost human-looking with no horns or wings. He jerked forward and growled when the sharp steel tip of her sword met the skin of his bare back.

"Careful, little one," Zagan's tall knight warned her. "Raum can shift into a raven and take to the skies faster than you can blink."

"She has him, Jinn," Oriax said.

Ah, so this was let's-all-get-drunk-on-angel-blood-at-his-club Jinn. Coryn was surprised by Oriax's faith in her, though, and she gave him a nod, her sword still aimed at Raum.

The demon in Oriax's hold was a tall, stunningly beautiful female, and all Coryn would think was how glad she was that she wasn't the demon currently pressed up against Zagan. The female seemed complacent, unlike the other opposing demons that were eyeing each other as if waiting for someone on their team to be the first to make a move.

"I am going to ask you one more time, Phenex," Zagan warned, eyes locked on the demon standing before Jinn—she wasn't as beautiful as the demon in Oriax's hold and looked the most nervous of them all.

"Who dare challenges the throne of the king and its rightful successor? Who are you brave enough to represent, if not me? I will not hesitate to kill your twin if you are not with us. You know I do not lie."

He tightened his grip on Phenex's brother, crushing his windpipe and causing him to gasp in an attempt to inhale whatever oxygen he could. A long polearm lay by their feet; a weapon Coryn could only assume belonged to Phenex's brother.

Frowning, Jinn stepped forward. "No one benefits from this," he pointed out. "She can just resurrect him."

Zagan smirked. "She can, but Furcas wouldn't be the same. They never are the second time around, are they, Phen?"

146

Phenex took a slow, deep breath, but let out a whimper when Zagan tightened his hold on her brother. Her eyes locked on her sibling's, and his on hers.

But Zagan gave Phenex no further time to reply. In a move so fast Coryn almost missed it, Zagan flicked his wrists. There was a crack, a gasp from Phenex, and Furcas's lifeless body dropped to the ground, his neck broken.

Phenex screamed, her bird-like screech reminding Coryn of a cherubim angel in distress, and as she ran for her brother's corpse, Dantalion spun on Lamia, and Raum shifted into a large black bird and flew into the sky just as Jinn had warned.

Coryn expected bedlam as the raven screamed in the sky, but the fighting did not resume. Oriax and his beautiful hostage exchanged hushed words before he released her.

"Seere has agreed to accept defeat. Zagan?"

Zagan nodded. "I accept."

With Raum hovering in the sky above, Dantalion, and Seere retreated behind Phenex, who cried out and set murderous eyes on Zagan. Her reddish skin grew more vibrant and began to glow. Coryn felt the heat on her own skin when Phenex suddenly ignited, engulfing Furcas in white-hot flames. The smell of burning flesh assaulted Coryn's nose and she gagged, but as quickly as the stench came, it was gone. When Furcas had turned to ash, the heat and flame immediately ceased.

With her eyes still wet with tears amid the flames, Phenex glared bitterly up at Zagan. "Let me resurrect him in peace."

Zagan shrugged, his eyes still locked on Phenex as he ran his hand down Coryn's arm and entwined her fingers with his. "Just remember who your real king is. You do not get off so easily the next time you challenge my throne."

He led the others away, and though Coryn did not turn back, she heard demonic whispers and the sounds of the wind and bone grinding on bone. She felt Furcas's soul passing through her on the breeze, and she shivered.

Her king was not merciful.

CHAPTER 18

"Why didn't we kill them all now if you won't be so lenient next time?" Lamia asked once the trees were thick enough to block any sign of Phenex and her fallen brother.

"They're good knights, Lam," Oriax replied.

"Not good enough if they're too stupid to side with an opponent of Zagan."

"Just who were they, anyway?" Coryn asked. "I thought the four of you were the only knights."

"The only knights who count," Jinn said with a wink. "Shit went down between us all a while ago and we split. Seere, the pretty one, leads them much like your beau leads us. Unlike your beau, however, nothing ever seems to bother her."

Zagan growled and Jinn chuckled.

"Raum is the little raven shifter asshole, and Dantalion is the skeletal one. He can project any kind of body onto those bones, so be careful if someone strange approaches you. I think you got a pretty good idea of Phenex and Furcas, the phoenix twins ..." Jinn trailed off as he and the others looked uneasily at Zagan.

"We had to send a message," Zagan said, his arm wound tightly around Coryn, protecting her in case another attack fell upon them. "They needed to know I will not hesitate to end any of them. When this is over, they will serve me or their souls will be sent to the Lake."

"Got it, boss," Jinn said. "Come on, let's go to the club to regroup and see what others may know."

But that gave Zagan pause. He looked from Jinn to Coryn to the closest portal back to Hell that lay in the trees beyond.

148

"You all head back and see what you can find out. Coryn and I will go home."

His knights understood there was no room for argument or discussion. Coryn opened her mouth to challenge him, but he cut her off.

"You will descend to Hell when I say you are ready."

He could see her disappointment, but she didn't refute his demand. He glanced at his knights and, quick to obey his silent order, they each bowed to him and scattered.

Coryn spun from Zagan's tight hold. "Why do you think I'm not ready?" she asked, her tone thick with the defiance that made him love her all the more.

"To descend to Hell now is to challenge the current king and this new opponent. Leave the investigating to the others. We have a few things to do here to prepare."

He spread his wings in sign of their departure.

Coryn did the same, her fists balled at her sides. "So it's not about my preparedness at all. It's about your own lack thereof."

He could only smile before he took off into the air, then heard her growl and follow after him.

Lack of preparation was partially the reason they were staying on Manusya, yes. But there was another reason they'd flown to the scene of the battle instead of using a hell portal. A reason why, had the battle been in Hell, he would have commanded Coryn to stay home—one look at the realm she'd been previously programmed to destroy, and he was certain he would lose her. They'd come so far together as a united pair on Manusya, but it was a world Coryn had been familiar with as an erelim. Nothing would prepare a former angel for a descent into the underworld.

Demons, lessers and superiors alike, would surround her, vying for a taste of her blood—not that he would let them have her. But when he presented his queen to the underworld, it would be on his terms, not because some idiotic demon below had a death wish and was forcing his hand.

They flew for another hour before Zagan dared look back at his queen. "We have one stop to make before we head home," he said and banked north.

***

Zagan wondered what Coryn would think as they descended upon the former village of Dellview. The wooden houses still lined dirt roads. Signs advertising custom tailoring or fine fabrics swayed in the wind. The makeshift table that had been erected in Zagan's name still sat in the square. The human bodies were all gone; Zagan presumed angels had come to cleanse the area of his taint.

Maybe Coryn was thinking about how she'd been too late to save the people that had once lived here. Perhaps she was imagining their blackened souls rising from their chests as their bodies disintegrated and turned to dust; how each one of those tainted souls had been one more point for Hell in its war against the Heavens.

Maybe she was contemplating all these things, but Zagan chose to focus on the moment he'd bound Coryn to him forever. Her lips had pressed against his as his poison, thick with the binding curse, slipped down her throat.

Neither of them voiced what they were reflecting on as they walked through the abandoned Dellview streets. Perhaps others would move back here someday, perhaps not. For now, the abandoned homes served as tombstones that marked the deaths of the people who'd lived here. Well, all but for one special young man—the one who had been the center of it all.

"Alexander's grave?" Coryn stripped down to the robe beneath her armor. Though she spoke softly, her voice seemed amplified in the abandoned town. "Is this the reason we're here?"

"Yes," Zagan said, pulling Coryn to him once again.

They stayed silent for a while and gazed at the stone Zagan had set over Alexander's final resting place. Funny how his soul was the only one Zagan hadn't wanted belonging to Hell.

With his claw, Zagan traced *Alexander Hillyard* into the stone, then a circular symbol that had a Z surrounded by lines and circles in the middle. He knew Coryn would have an idea of what it stood for.

"Is that your mark?" she asked.

Zagan nodded. "To be marked by a demon of rank means you're under that demon's protection, and to challenge a mark-bearer is to challenge the demon himself. Our marks are used not only for claiming a mate, but also territories, landmarks, anything we wish to protect. The other knights have placed their marks all over, but I have made my mark only once. Here, on this grave."

He coaxed her before him, then slid his hands up to her shoulders and pressed his thumb into her right shoulder blade. "I want to place my second and final mark right here."

The way she trembled when he rumbled in her ear made him want to take her right then and there. He groaned against her skin. "Do you want me to mark you, sweet queen? Claim you as mine once and for all?"

"Yes," she whispered, her quick, heavy breathing exciting him further.

"Yes," he echoed. The word was bliss to his ears.

With one hand still digging into her shoulder, he spun her around and pushed her toward the table in the square as he cut through the back of her robe with his claws and tore it from her shoulders, exposing her smooth skin. The perfect canvas for his symbol.

"Coryn." He kissed her neck, her bare shoulders, and hiked up the bottom of her robe. "I will mark you, and you will be forever mine."

As hard as a rock, he panted, aching to claim her while he carved his symbol into her skin. With the way she was grinding her ass against his lap as he bent her over the table, he knew she wanted the same. Holding her down with one hand, he slid his pants down with the other and positioned his cock at her entrance.

"If you want this, tell me you're mine," he said against her ear. "Say who you belong to."

He nearly released at the desperate way she moaned his name.

"You, Zagan. I'm yours." She sank back, eager for him to fill her, and he would not deny his queen. He slammed home, burying himself to the hilt inside her, and they groaned together in harmony.

"Fuck, Coryn, so tight." He pressed into her as deep he could go while her muscles spasmed around him. He breathed short and shallow, trying to hold back his orgasm, to gain control long enough to mark her.

"Open your wings," he commanded, and she obeyed, granting him access to the milky skin that would forever bear his insignia.

"Master."

Zagan stilled. *No!* He'd been so focused on claiming his angel that he hadn't felt the presence of his greatest curse.

He opened his mouth, about to tell Coryn to look away, but her head shot up and the damage was done—she and the messenger were face to face.

The bastard knew exactly what he was doing. For the first time in years his hood was down. He wanted Coryn to see his face, to see how mangled Zagan had made it. But whether she recognized him or not, Zagan knew she would recognize his voice.

Arms braced on the table below her, she exhaled a breath that was no longer heady with pleasure. The name on her lips was a curse to Zagan's ears, and it was as if he was no longer there, buried inside her.

"Ouranos?"

Swearing, Zagan quickly withdrew from Coryn and pulled her against him, holding her robe together as he moved a short distance from the table.

Ouranos, messenger to the demon king, had a smile so smug that Zagan would have punched it from his face had he not been holding Coryn's clothes to her form.

"I'm sorry. Did I interrupt something?" Ouranos asked, tilting his head to the side. "It's nothing I haven't seen before. Finish if it pleases you."

Zagan roared. He'd never been more tempted to kill the former god, but to kill the king's messenger would mean forfeiting the throne. Had he not wanted to make Coryn queen so badly, it would have been worth it.

When Zagan didn't launch across the square at him, it was evident Ouranos knew he had immunity—for now. The white-winged asshole nodded his head at Coryn, who stood frozen in Zagan's grasp.

"Hello, Coriel," he greeted, and Coryn shuddered at her gods-given name. "I see you've met the God Slaver."

Zagan had never been so ashamed of the accomplishment. Yes, he was powerful, and yes, he was the only demon to have ever downed a god. Enslaving Ouranos had solidified Zagan's claim to the throne, and it was the reason every other demon regarded him so highly. But Zagan didn't have to look at Coryn's face to know the anguish he would see there. She didn't have to say anything for him to know just how betrayed she felt.

"Do not talk to her!" Zagan barked.

He quickly tied the excess fabric of her robe together and attempted to guide her off to the side. In classic Coryn form, however, she squirmed and pushed away from him.

"Coryn, I—"

"God Slaver?" she cried, looking from him to Ouranos and back. "This is who you've been shielding me from? Because you knew?"

She threw a hard punch against Zagan's chest, and all he could do was allow the blow.

"You never lie, but that doesn't mean you speak the truth, either." Her voice was broken, shaky.

Ouranos shook his head in mock surprise, and it was everything Zagan could do to keep from strangling him.

"Oh, I'm sorry. Was she unaware she is not the only creation of the Heavens to be bound to Hell by you?"

"Just tell me what it is the king wants, damn you." Zagan pulled Coryn closer to him, but she was either too shocked and shaky or was also interested to hear what Ouranos had to say because she did not fight him.

Ouranos cleared his throat. Why wasn't he showing more emotion at seeing Coryn? Had Zagan been in Ouranos's shoes—not that he would ever wish that—they would have been in a battle to the death for her by now.

"The king is most upset," Ouranos said, "by your blatant disregard for his last command."

"The command you delivered to me?" Zagan let out a dry, humorless laugh. "You told me to return to Hell, and I did. If that wasn't what I was supposed to do, that's on you. Why don't you tell the king you're the one who blatantly disregarded whatever it was he actually told you to pass on to me."

"Regardless," Ouranos said, "you are now summoned to the castle by order of the king. You may refute your insolence there if you wish, though I would advise against it." He glanced at Coryn, and Zagan growled low in his throat.

"Would you like me to watch your pet for you while you're away?"

Zagan roared. "Fuck off, Ouranos, before I take the title of God Slaver to God Slayer."

The former god's lips quirked up in a smirk. "As you wish, Master." He bowed, then spread his white wings and took off into the sky.

"What did you do to him?" Coryn whispered as she watched him disappear.

Zagan fought to keep his emotions in check. "We met on Manusya. We fought. I won."

"His face." She shuddered. "And the color of his wings has faded …"

"He caught hellfire to the face, and I suppose his wings are dying just as yours are. All is fair in war, Coryn. I did what needed to be done to protect Hell."

"But you knew all this time who he was to me. You used our bond to hide him from me."

Zagan dropped to his knees before her and took both her hands in his. "Coryn, I am so sorry. Yes, I knew what Ouranos meant to you, and I couldn't stand the thought of you choosing him over me."

He gripped her fingers, but she did not reciprocate. His heart wrenched as he peered into her endlessly blue eyes.

"What can I do to repent? What will it take for me to prove my devotion to you?"

Even on his knees his horns came to the top of her head, so he sank back on his calves to make himself smaller.

"Anything. Please, Coryn. My queen."

But she narrowed her eyes and said, "You should go, Zagan. Your king beckons you."

CHAPTER 19

Coryn felt so angry and betrayed she could barely see. When she'd heard Ouranos's voice, she'd thought she was hearing things, as if her heart had been saying goodbye to him one final time before she devoted herself completely to Zagan. But when she'd looked up and had seen the gods' face, had felt Zagan's reaction behind her ... it was as if her vision had gone askew, as if she'd been tilted sideways and dunked underwater, forced to listen to their conversation through a thick and murky sea.

God Slaver.

The demons called her knight God Slaver—because he'd indentured *her* god. Had Ouranos been in the Heavens just weeks ago, would he have allowed Pahaliah to confiscate her sword like Michael and Azazel had? Would he have allowed her to be sent and bound to Zagan?

She wished he would have reacted to seeing her. Despite her anger, she blushed wildly when she thought about how the scene would have looked to Ouranos—Zagan pinning her to the table, about to claim her in the most permanent way he could, his hardness pounding into her eager flesh.

Yet Ouranos hadn't been angry or jealous. He hadn't tried to pry Zagan off her or make sure she was safe. Instead, he'd mocked them both. She wasn't sure which of them made her angrier.

God Slaver. The words echoed in her mind, drowning out all other thoughts.

"Coryn ..."

Why was Zagan still trying to talk to her?

"I said go to Hell!" she cried, unable to hold back the barrage of tears that had been threatening to fall.

As Zagan stood, Coryn fell to her knees, but he let her be.

He sighed heavily. "I wish I didn't have to, but I do. I will return to you as fast as I can. I will fix this ... I swear it."

"Go!" she shouted.

He spread his hands in surrender, then turned on his heels. But he wasn't three steps away before three glowing red portals appeared around them and lessers began spewing from the ground.

Zagan turned back to her, his eyes filled with apology. "Get your armor. We are being challenged."

"By the king?" she asked, moving quickly and willingly to follow Zagan's order.

"No, by whomever wants to be king next." He reached into his pocket, scattered three beads on the ground, and they exploded into portals.

"Knights, to me!" he shouted.

Jinn, Oriax, and Lamia each emerged from a portal, weapons drawn and ready for battle. As much as Coryn wanted to tell Zagan to fend for himself, she was more than happy taking all her anger out on a bunch of lesser demons.

It was almost like old times, with her armor on and sword in hand, shouting as she beheaded, dismembered, and stabbed through weak demons. As dozens crawled from the portals and surrounded Coryn, Zagan, and his knights, she allowed herself to become lost in the battle. The only difference now was that her former enemy was now her only ally—and a poor one at that. Yes, she and Zagan were protecting one another from the barrage of attacks, but he'd betrayed her trust. He'd been about to claim her, knowing full well her former lover was still alive.

Shing! A demon's head rolled.

Clang! Her blade hit the hard surface of a horn, then sliced through it.

In each demon, she saw a piece of Zagan. Barbed tail. Red eyes. Bare, muscular chest. Fangs. She may have even killed some of the demons on Zagan's side, but she didn't care. She hated them all. As she fought, she not only shouted with the efforts of battle, but screamed at the top of her lungs as if every single demon was to blame for her pain.

The only thing that silenced her was a booming clap of thunder in the sunny sky above. Every demon jumped and stopped to look up. But Coryn knew what was coming.

Angels.

It was only the second time she'd seen Heavenly beings descend from this vantage point. From the ground, the spectacle of the winged warriors descending to the earth was truly a sight to behold. When she was erelim, she'd always been the first to fall from the sky. The first to hit the ground. The first—and last—to take a demon's life before reascending to the Heavens. This time, the first angel to arrive was a familiar golden-winged green-eyed female archangel.

Coryn roared as she charged through the sea of demons, eyes set on Pahaliah, who sliced effortlessly through two lesser demons with one swing of her sword.

Pahaliah turned toward her scream, eyes widening as Coryn closed the distance between them, her sword at the ready, while angels continued to fall in all around. Paha defended Coryn's attack, her panting breath on Coryn's face as angelic steel met Coryn's weaker human blade.

"Coriel," she said, other angels turning to look at them and advancing before Paha shouted, "Stand down! I have her."

Coryn's laugh was dry and held so much spite that Zagan would be proud. "You most certainly did have me, didn't you?"

Pahaliah's confused expression wasn't the reaction Coryn expected.

"Admit it! You did this to me. You were afraid I would replace you as arch, so you took my weapon and deployed me to fight against Zagan on my own."

He'd been an even better target than a thousand lessers—it was his bond that had damned her to this miserable fate after all.

"There's nothing I can do to be archangel now, so just admit it." She shoved into Pahaliah, knocking her back a few paces, their swords pressed tightly against one another.

Coryn's chest burned as images of impaling Pahaliah with her sword consumed her. But even if it killed her, she was ready to defy Zagan's command not to take the life of an angel.

"You think *I* deployed you?"

Paha swung her sword around, slamming the hilt into the neck of an approaching lesser before an erelim plunged his sword through its heart.

Coryn moved to strike, but Paha caught her blade with her own.

"Coriel!"

Coryn leaned into her sword, making Pahaliah's blade shake with the force. "It's Coryn. I can't use my angelic name, remember?"

Pahaliah winced. "Coryn, then. I swear to the Supreme God that I was not the one who sent you to Manusya that night. You've always been a thorn in my side, but I would have never sacrificed you to the demons. None of us did!"

Coryn regarded her suspiciously. Unlike Zagan, angels weren't strangers to lying ... but Pahaliah seemed genuine in her words.

Coryn let up on their swords but couldn't tell now if the burning in her chest was from the curse or her rage. "Bullshit, Paha! Someone deployed me, and I know you know who it was."

"I thought you had descended to prove something to us and failed. I thought it was your own fault." Paha's eyes searched Coryn's as if she were trying to peer into her soul. She took a few backward steps and lowered her sword. Coryn did the same.

"Are you telling me that's not what happened?" Pahaliah asked.

"Paha!" someone cried.

In the next second a large demon slammed into Pahaliah's back and a single horn exploded through the front of her armor, mid-sternum. She didn't even have a chance to look surprised before the demon reared back and flung her upward, sending her like a rag doll into the air. Coryn sliced her blade across the demon's exposed throat, and it gurgled out a roar, then fell to its side on the ground in a pool of sticky black blood.

Paha's body landed a few feet away, and beyond it stood High Archangel Michael, a shocked expression on his face. His gaze lifted to Coryn, full of accusation.

Coryn shook her head. *No!*

Michael pointed his blade at her and shouted, "Eliminate the forsaken!"

The angels surrounding them finished off their demon targets and then turned toward her.

Zagan fell in beside Coryn. "Over my dead body," he growled.

Michael shook his head and shrugged. "That's the idea."

As high archangel and demon knight charged one another, Coryn fell to her knees to protect Pahaliah's body. All the hatred and spite she'd had for Paha melted away as she studied her expression, which looked troubled by

Coryn's accusation even in death. Her final question to Coryn had been so rich with disbelief that Coryn knew without a doubt that Pahaliah was not the one to have damned her to her fate.

Then who was responsible?

While Michael and Zagan continued to fight, the other knights stayed close to Coryn, protecting her from the angelic onslaught as she lay over Paha's body. A dead lesser demon fell on top of Coryn, covering her in blood and forcing some of the air from her lungs. She hurled the demon off her back, launching it a safe distance away from Pahaliah's body, then gave her former superior one last, hard look.

"I'm so sorry, Archangel Pahaliah."

Coryn felt as though she should murmur a prayer, but the Heavens didn't deserve her prayers. All she could hope was that Pahaliah would be reborn far away from its corruption.

Panting, Coryn stood and grabbed her sword. Dead demons and angels surrounded the portals lessers were retreating to, marking the end of the battle, but it wasn't clear who was victorious. Michael was leading dozens of angels back to the Heavens, and while Coryn was surrounded by bruised demon knights, none of them were dead—and that was certainly something to be thankful for when up against a high archangel and his army.

Zagan was on her immediately, ripping her armor from her body and inspecting her for wounds. "Are you hurt? I will slice him into bite-sized pieces and feed him to the lessers if—"

Coryn placed a steadying hand on his chest and shook her head. Despite how confused she was about Ouranos, Paha, and what the Heavens were up to, she knew Zagan loved her—and Pahaliah had just proven that Zagan was all she had.

"I'm fine." She stood on her tiptoes and kissed him on his bloodied lips, then turned her attention to the other knights. "How are all of you?"

After assuring her they were fine, they exchanged glances with one another. Finally, it was Jinn who spoke.

"Zagan, we gotta go. It's time to claim that throne."

Coryn let out a short, cold laugh. "Well, that's convenient. The God Slaver was summoned to Hell by the king you're about to overthrow anyway."

"Ah," Oriax said, shuffling as he looked back at the other knights. "So she knows."

"Yeah, I do."

Zagan growled, taking her by the arm. "I wish you would save your insolence for when we are alone," he murmured as he walked her across the field.

Coryn shook her head but let him lead her. "I'm sure you would. So I'm allowed to descend now?"

"I know you're upset about the archangel, but I need you to redirect that anger from me onto our next opponent. We have no choice but to descend, and I need you to prepare yourself. You will remain by my side unless you are in danger. We need to keep the amount of fighting we do to a minimum until we reach the king, and any demon would surely attack an angel on sight."

"Let them try."

"We will save our strength, Coryn."

She shuddered as the command took hold, but Zagan nodded.

"If using our bond is the only way to protect you, then so be it. Unless we enter battle, you will lay low and stay close to me until we are in that throne room. Do you understand?"

She pursed her lips and offered only a slow nod in response. He tightened his grip on her arm.

"This is for your protection, Coryn. Please trust me. The king is feeling threatened now. There's no doubt about that. We won't be able to enter his halls without a fight. Every servant and every beast in that place will want to attack us, so he won't be our only challenge."

"I'm confused," Coryn said. "Aren't you the king's knights? Why would he attack you?"

"I am a knight, but I am also his successor. We have protected him and fought for the realm in his name until this point, but he knew that when the time came, we four would stand against him."

He smiled as he regarded each one of them, Coryn included.

"Five now," he added. "And we fight well as a team. We have each other's backs. Tonight, you will have a new king." He gripped her hand. "And a beautiful queen. Then we will make sure the Heavens know what a mistake it was to let her go." They arrived at a small cliffside and Zagan placed his palm against the gritty wall. Much like the glowing red portals that had appeared on the ground earlier, one began to glow on the rocks.

Zagan took one last, longing look at Coryn before leading her by the hand into Hell.

CHAPTER 20

Falling through the portal to Hell was *nothing* like descending to Manusya from the Heavens. Coryn felt as if she were stretched, then compressed, and finally squeezed as she was plunged into the depths of the ocean. Her lungs weren't getting enough air and began to burn.

A deafening *whoosh* filled her ears as if she'd been thrown into a wind tunnel, and her veins, lungs, and skin returned to normal. She heard a sharp popping noise, which was followed by the instant stench of sulfur, and she was bombarded by fire and soot. The sensory overload caused her to stagger and scrunch her nose, and she covered it with her hand.

"Are you all right?" Zagan was in front of her, hands planted firmly on her shoulders. He leaned down so their eyes met, and he examined her, gripping her tighter as she tried to focus on him.

"Y-yes," she said in as sure a voice as she could muster, "I just ... wasn't expecting that."

Oriax let out a short laugh. "I guess none of us considered what traveling by portal would feel like to an outsider. Our apologies."

Coryn smiled weakly and nodded. "I'm sure plummeting from the clouds would be a new experience for you, too."

She winced at her words as soon as she'd said them. The last thing any of them needed was to acknowledge that she, a former angel, had been brought into the realm of ultimate sin.

"Here is the plan," Zagan said, and they all circled around him. They stood beside the closing portal on the cobblestone wall of a castle, in a dark courtyard with muted-colored flora, immersed in a permanent haze.

Who knew Hell had gardens?

"We'll slip in through the eastern corridor," Zagan said, pointing his clawed finger to a closed wooden door beyond Jinn. "It's midday, so the servants will not have returned to their quarters yet."

He turned to Coryn and rested a hand casually against the small of her back. "We need to get you a servant's robes to cover your armor. You'll have to press your wings close to your back until we get to the throne room."

"One with a hood," Oriax said, nodding. "Her clothes aren't her only giveaway. No demon is that beautiful."

Zagan glared at Oriax, and his nostrils flared. "Yes, O, one with a hood. Once we get to the throne room, you and Jinn will dispatch the guards. Lamia, you will cover Coryn while she removes her robes for the fight."

He turned his attention to Coryn. "You will be beside me when the fight begins. The king is out of practice, so the battle will be quick and smooth. I want us both to deal the killing blow."

Coryn didn't need to look around to know that Zagan's knights were surprised, and perhaps outraged, by the idea.

Zagan turned to them. "If she is to be my queen, she needs to have a hand in taking down the king. It is the only way she will gain respect here."

Coryn scowled. Oh, she would make sure every one of these beasts knew who was in charge.

"Remember what I told you, Coryn. Stay close and make yourself scarce until we are at the throne."

"Yes, yes, the bond won't let me forget that. You don't have to remind me." Her tone was harsh, but Zagan nodded in approval.

"Let's go."

They entered the servants' quarters, and just as Zagan predicted, the hallways and chambers were empty. They slipped into a bare and narrow room, where the beds were stacked three high and the wardrobe contained identical robes. Lamia tossed a set to Coryn.

She threw it on, straining her muscles to flatten her wings against her body. She probably looked like she had a hunchback, but with all the shapes and sizes demons came in, she was confident she would go unnoticed. Zagan covered her face with the oversized hood before they slunk back into the hall.

The castle was much like the ones on Manusya—gray stone walls and marble floors with red carpet runners everywhere. It was kept meticulously clean, including the air—Coryn's lungs didn't burn as they had outside. She could see herself ruling here if this was to be her sanctuary.

She was about to comment on how quiet it was and ask if they had the right realm and castle when a shadow materialized in the distance. Coryn's first instinct was to hide, but Zagan gripped her arm and stopped her from making any sudden movements.

"I know I said to stay scarce, but remember, you're the least recognizable of all of us," he whispered in her ear.

She shivered at the feel of his breath on her skin and he gripped her tighter in response. "Walk with confidence and you won't call attention to yourself."

The shadow passed down another corridor and the knights resumed their advance.

"If just one lesser picks up on your scent, Zagan, it's all over," Jinn said, and Zagan nodded.

"You saw how they were above ground," he said to Coryn when she gave him a curious look. "In this realm, their instincts are even stronger."

"Then why not have your army fight with you?"

"Because they are not *my* army. They are the king's army. They will follow my orders and come to me above the surface if the king allows it and, after the upheaval, will support my claim for the throne. But not now, not here in the presence of their current leader."

"Knights and higher-ranking demons aren't prone to that instinct," Oriax added. "The mindlessness of a lesser demon is really the most horrifying thing about them."

Coryn turned her attention to the hallway before them. "How much further to the king?"

"A few more floors down," Zagan said. "It's likely we will fight before we get there."

But the descent into the depths of the castle was far easier than any of them expected. They caught sight a few more times of horns and tails as lessers scurried from this hall to that, but the demons seemed too preoccupied to notice anything around them.

Coryn caught Lamia giving Zagan a suspicious and uneasy look. He nodded, continuing with his claws locked around Coryn's arm.

"You don't need to cut off the circulation," she advised in a whisper. "I can take care of myself."

"I know," Zagan replied. "But you don't have to. I will always make sure you are safe."

It was a sweet response, but it wasn't the one Coryn was after. It was as if she were a human child being dragged along the street by an overprotective parent. She might as well have had a leash—but she knew better than to mention that to Zagan. Something told her he would find far too much delight in obliging.

A loud scream came from behind them, filling Coryn's ears, and suddenly, she understood why Zagan was so concerned.

One moment Lamia was behind them, and the next she was not. Her ear-piercing scream carried down the hall long after she disappeared.

Coryn and the remaining knights sank into battle stances, standing back-to-back as they searched for the attacker and their missing comrade. They found neither, but Lamia's scream still lingered.

Oriax's pointed ears twitched, and he looked up and growled. His dark lips curled back, and baring his sharp fangs, he let out a long, raspy hiss. Black smog exploded from his mouth and traveled upward, rising to the high, rounded ceiling. They heard a male cough, then Lamia's in harmony.

Furcas appeared, stuck to the rough stone of the ceiling with one hand and foot while the others held Lamia against him, her back to his chest so her front was facing the ground. They both coughed wildly, Furcas so violently that Coryn was sure he would drop Lamia. But he had a vice grip on her—it looked like he was crushing her.

"Coryn, remove the cloak," Zagan said in a low voice, and she was quick to obey.

Jinn spread his wings and launched at the pair with a loud roar, aiming his horns at Furcas, who laughed and hid behind Lamia. Jinn slowed, drawing his claws.

Furcas laughed. "I already died once. I am no longer afraid of it."

Lamia let out a choking noise as Furcas hung from the ceiling by one foot—Coryn wasn't sure how he did it; it looked as if he was suctioned there—and wrapped his arms around Lamia, tightening the squeeze. The patches of scales on her skin, usually emerald green, were quickly turning blue.

"Continue your attack and I'll kill her!"

Jinn retreated to the ground immediately, looking helpless. Placated, Furcas lightened his hold on Lamia, and the color quickly returned to her face.

"Aw, what's the matter, Jinn?" Furcas whined, cocking his head to the side as he hung like a bat. "Afraid I might retaliate for what your false king did to me?"

Lamia's face was now darkening as blood rushed to her head.

"Put her down, you twisted zombie," Zagan growled, keeping his protective hold on Coryn. "It's me you want to retaliate against, not her."

Furcas shrugged. "I'll get to you. The king has ordered all of you dead and we will not disappoint." His hair looked a little more white, his orange skin a touch more gray than it had been before Zagan killed him. His eyes, which had been dark with silent fear on Manusya, now looked wild.

Oriax stood beside Zagan and Coryn, his head whipping back and forth as he kept watch on the hallways. Jinn stood directly below Furcas, ready to catch Lamia if she fell.

Lamia had put up a good struggle despite her chest being crushed and the blood rushing to her brain, but she now went limp in Furcas's arms. He began to laugh wickedly, then knocked his chest against her back so they began swinging back and forth as he giggled with glee.

"Catch the dolly!" he cried, opening his arms and sending Lamia plummeting toward Jinn in a wide arch.

As Jinn caught Lamia, Oriax shouted that the opposing knights were approaching. Raum charged Oriax and Dantalion blew past them, targeting Jinn and running a spear through one of his wings. Jinn shouted but didn't lose his hold on Lamia. Zagan let go of Coryn to help them, and Coryn spun to meet Seere and Phenex.

"What, your king is too weak to fight Zagan himself?" Coryn said as she drew the sword sheathed between her wings.

While Seere simply shrugged, Phenex replied, "He doesn't need to waste his time on all of you."

Revenge was heavy in her eyes. She must have liked what she saw when she approached—with Jinn already injured and Lamia unconscious, the fight was now three to five. Well, three and a half. Zagan had pulled the spear from Jinn's wing, and though Jinn groaned in pain, he lowered Lamia to the ground and stood to help even the odds.

"What are you doing?" Jinn asked Phenex through clenched teeth. "The king is done. We fought together as a team once. Help us overthrow the old bastard so we can have the right demon rule."

The other demons exchanged knowing smirks.

"What is it?" Zagan asked, backing up to rejoin Coryn. "Tell me what he has done!"

No one volunteered to answer, but Furcas cackled maniacally and dropped from the ceiling, aiming for Zagan, who sprang out of the way, shooting his barbed tail toward the crazed demon. When Furcas rolled out of range, Zagan set his claws on Phenex, who screeched, welcoming the invitation to fight. Furcas, still cackling with glee, scampered into the shadows and went invisible.

"Watch for him," Zagan warned Coryn as he and Phenex circled one another.

Coryn had her back against Zagan's, and Seere was orbiting Coryn as Phenex was doing with Zagan. As they circled, Coryn could see that Jinn and Oriax surrounded Lamia and were fighting against Dantalion and Raum.

Seere looked the least interested in the fight. She was a knight for a reason, though, and Coryn knew to keep her guard up. Her beauty was difficult not to admire, even in these circumstances. She was the tallest female demon Coryn had ever seen, just an inch or so shorter than Zagan. Not only was she keeping an eye on Coryn, but her dark brown, almost-black eyes kept scanning the room to check on the other fights.

It was during one of those moments that Coryn decided to go in for the attack. If Seere was saving her energy in case things got hairy with the others, Coryn wouldn't allow it. Her sword met one of Seere's two small chakrams—she held one in each hand, and both donned curved blades on either side of their handles. The weapons had decorative cutouts on the flat surfaces of the blades, but the edges also had grooves and nicks to catch attacking weapons. Coryn's sword wedged in one of the cutouts along the chakram, making it impossible to do anything but withdraw the sword.

Seere attacked with the other chakram before Coryn could collect herself, but the demon drew back as well. Coryn growled. Was Seere underestimating her abilities, just as Lamia had on Manusya?

I'm really sick of everyone thinking I'm only Zagan's plaything!

Coryn went in for another attack, but Seere caught every thrust of Coryn's blade with her chakrams. The demon was fast, strong, and her reflexes were impressive. There was no way Coryn would be able to slice her way through the blur of metal to get to Seere. She considered throwing down her blade and fighting with her hands like Zagan, but she lacked claws.

Seere's eyes followed her like a bored cat watching its prey, her uninterested expression further infuriating Coryn.

Coryn stabbed her blade forward a few more times, studying the way Seere manipulated her weaponry to catch the sword in the holes. Sometimes she deflected with the outside of the rings as well, but she never went in for an attack of her own. Did Seere know that harming her would mean death by Zagan?

I'm sick of everyone fearing him over me, too.

With a shout, Coryn went in for a final thrust. Her blade landed on the outside of Seere's left chakram, and the demon deflected just as Coryn had anticipated. She used the momentum of her sword to swing it around and intentionally got it caught in a swirling gape in Seere's weapon. It took more force than she'd expected, but Coryn managed to slide her sword along the metal of the hole, then twisted and jammed the blade through the hole at its thinnest, like a key going into a lock.

Seere gasped when Coryn's blade pierced her stomach. If Coryn was taller, she could have stabbed the demon through the heart. Would Zagan be angry or proud at what she'd done?

A river of black blood began to spill down Coryn's blade, though it was only an inch through Seere's skin. Coryn considered pressing harder.

"Good, Coryn," Zagan said, and her hazy gaze cleared as she stared at Seere's stomach.

"Please, leave this to me now." Zagan guided her off to the side, but Seere made no move to flee.

The only demons remaining in the corridor were Seere, Zagan, Jinn, Oriax, and Lamia. The other opposing demons must have fled. *But when?*

Zagan stood before Seere with his wings spread, a viscous, dominant demon in all his glory.

"Tell me what we're about to walk into," he growled, his tail twitching as if he felt the urge to strike.

"It's not who you are expecting." Her voice held no distress, despite the position she was in.

Zagan growled, poised to dig his poison-barbed tail into her, but Coryn stepped forward and placed a hand on his shoulder. The muscles beneath her touch softened immediately.

"Zagan," she said in a soothing voice, "leave her. We won. She accepts it." The last thing they needed was Phenex raising another dead knight only for them to become as insane as Furcas. "You will gain good warriors in these demons once you are king."

Oriax and Jinn exchanged a look, then nodded to each other. Still crouched on the ground, Lamia pushed to her feet.

Zagan stared at Seere for a long moment, his tail erect and still dripping with poison. "When I am king, you and the others will serve me." He pointed at Coryn. "You will now bow to your savior, your queen."

Seere looked dumbstruck, staring wide-eyed at Coryn as she clutched her stomach. She bowed, but whether she was doing it because she had no other choice or because she truly meant her appreciation, Coryn wasn't sure. All Coryn could do was nod back in response.

"Now fuck off, Seere," Zagan said. "I have a throne to claim."

Coryn had to give it to Seere—she knew when to obey orders. Without so much as an angry glance, she spun on her heels and retreated down the hall

"Let's go," Zagan announced. "It sounds as though the other demon has already claimed the throne, and they will have hell to pay."

They ran at full speed through the castle, no longer bothering to sneak around. A few of the more stupid lessers and servants tried to stop their advance, but Coryn and Zagan fended off their attacks with sword and claw. They slowed to a jog and came to an impossibly tall door. Coryn knew where it would lead—the throne room. It was lined with hellfire and covered in ragged stone.

Zagan let out a humorless laugh. "This pompous asshole thinks they don't need guards against me?" He turned back and eyed Coryn with a haughty smirk. "Let's show them who we are, my queen."

CHAPTER 21

The old demon king was still there—a large, black mass before the throne, limbs hanging limply from his body. His corpse, all hulking muscle and horns, lay on the steps leading to the dais and was surrounded by sticky black blood with an unmistakably Heavenly blade driven through him.

Above him, Ouranos sat on the throne, his legs crossed and an elbow on the armrest, his hand bracing his chin. He looked down at Zagan and wore the smuggest look Coryn had ever seen.

"Oh my go—" But she cut herself off. She wouldn't give Ouranos the ammunition.

Needing to look away from him, she turned her gaze to the former king and the sword stuck through him. How could Ouranos have pulled this off? Whatever he'd done, Zagan beat him once. Together, even after the long battle with the opposing knights, they could beat him again.

"You know what this means, Zagan," Ouranos said. "Demon law is clear. The slayer of the king becomes king himself. I allowed myself to be captured by you in hopes of getting here, but I didn't anticipate you and the king being so strong. Even though you spent so much time on Manusya, I couldn't make a move for the throne—you felt every disturbance in Hell no matter where you were and always came running. I needed to bide my time, and all you needed was to be sent a little … distraction."

He smirked as his eyes traveled to Coryn. "You did well."

Her eyebrows knitted together. What? Ouranos had let himself be captured by Zagan? And had made sure she met the same fate? Her heart dropped into her stomach.

Zagan turned to look at her and the shock in his face matched her own. "Did you know of this plan?"

The mixture of suspicion and hurt in his tone made her tear up—she still wasn't used to feeling her emotions in full force—but she made sure her eyes never left Zagan's through the blur.

"No, I promise," she replied with a small shake of her head. Her tears kept falling as she turned to Ouranos. "You're saying ... I was sent to Zagan on purpose?"

Ouranos stood but remained on the platform, above them and the dead former king. "Rest assured, Zagan, Coriel—I mean, *Coryn*—had no idea. She was a gift created just for you by the Heavens. Is that not reason enough to worship us?"

So that was why she'd always been so drawn to Zagan. He looked over his shoulder at her, nearly on the verge of tears.

He blames himself for falling into this trap, she thought. *For falling for me.*

"She's perfect," he whispered, so quietly that Coryn wasn't sure if anyone else had heard him.

But, of course, he would think her perfect—the gods had done well creating her specifically for him. Everything about her, from her looks to her personality down to her inability to resist him, had been customized for him. She was a fallen angel he could have, mark, and be distracted by while Ouranos moved in on the king. She'd never felt so used.

She turned her gaze to Ouranos. "So Paha really had nothing to do with this?"

He nodded. "Smart girl. She was always too by the book for anyone's liking. Would you believe it was your beloved High Archangel Michael who sent you to Zagan that fateful night?"

Reeling, she looked away.

From the rafters dropped five gray-winged beings—more forsaken—and Coryn realized they were an addition to Ouranos's army.

"I am still in control of angels, and now I control demons. I am still a god, and now ... I am Demon God King Ouranos. Yes, that has a nice ring to it, don't you think?"

Zagan winced. "That is a terrible title, and it is my duty to relieve you of it." Next, he spoke quietly so only Coryn could hear. "Forget about the killing blow and let me handle this. If you find yourself in too much danger, or something happens to me, run. That is an order."

He released a realm-shattering roar, and Jinn, Lamia, and Oriax charged at the former angels.

Coryn moved to join the knights. She wanted Ouranos and his forsaken to fall into a bloody heap on the floor. Her heart jumped and her body jerked back as she envisioned slaughtering one of the forsaken.

You will not kill a being of your kind, Zagan had said, and damn it all, she had to obey.

"Come on," she pleaded under her breath, but the command had a firm hold on her.

He'd never forbidden her to kill gods, however. If she couldn't fight the forsaken, she would fight the poor excuse for a god instead.

Zagan had already reached Ouranos by the time Coryn changed her plan, and she watched in twisted satisfaction as he took a swipe at the god. Ouranos reached back to retrieve his sword, panic setting in on his face when he realized he'd left the blade in the former king's corpse.

Those from the Heavens really need to keep better tabs on their weaponry, she thought wryly as Zagan's claws connected with the god's chest and ripped four large gashes across it.

"Aargh!" Ouranos cried as he fell back.

With her sword heavy in her hands, Coryn rushed at him, but a forsaken slammed into her and sent her falling to the ground. All she could do was deflect the barrage of blade attacks, parrying them this way and that as she cried for help. She landed a few kicks, but her body jerked back each time she tried to fight Zagan's orders.

Finally, Lamia pulled the forsaken off her and pierced him through the back with her blade. His red blood exploded over Coryn, but she was safe. Lamia dropped the forsaken's corpse to the ground and extended her hand to Coryn.

Coryn took it gratefully. "Thank you."

She looked past Lamia to Zagan and Ouranos. The god had somehow reclaimed his sword, and he and Zagan were blow for blow.

Coryn tried to join the fight, but Lamia caught her arm.

"The forsaken are dead," she said. "Let Zagan finish off the king."

Zagan felt the hot metal of Ouranos's blade far too many times as they battled. He was fatigued from fighting the opposing knights and shaken after
learning the truth of Coryn's existence, but those were no excuses. Cuts and
gashes covered his chest, abdomen, and arms, but Ouranos looked no better.

It's time to end this once and for all.

Zagan licked his lips and bared his fangs, growling as he walked backwards
down the steps of the dais. Ouranos was above him, sword hilt tight in his
hand, his eyes as wild as Furcas's had been. Zagan finally reached the bottom
step and continued walking backwards, knowing from the silence in the room
that Ouranos's forsaken were dead. But what about *his* forsaken?

He spotted her in his periphery being held back by Lamia and sighed in
relief. Even though she was a weapon of the gods, she still belonged to him—
and no matter what, he would never let anything happen to her.

"You dare to challenge a demon god king?" Ouranos taunted.

Zagan let out a humorless laugh, then retracted his claws and picked up
the blade of a dead forsaken.

"It's time I earn my title," he said, then charged forward and swung the
sword at Ouranos's chest.

The god parried his attack, then made his own charge. They battled for
several minutes before Zagan stopped, laughing as he looked down at the
sword in his hands.

"You know what? This won't do. This won't do at all." He tossed the
sword aside with a loud clang that echoed off the stone walls and extended
his claws. "Yes, this is better, my claws. These are what will tear you apart.
Do you remember, messenger? Do you remember how it felt to have them
rip through you?"

He ran at the god again, whipping out with his tail. Ouranos seemed
stunned by his words—no doubt he was reliving that horrific day from so
long ago—and by the time he went to block, it was too late. Zagan wrapped
his tail tightly around Ouranos's throat and tossed him up the stairs, causing
him to land in a heap over the corpse of the dead king. Before he could

recover, Zagan was by his side, and he wrenched him to his feet and shoved him up the stairs to the throne.

"Take your seat, King!" he roared as he pushed him down and brought his tail around again, but Ouranos caught it between his hands this time. Zagan laughed, thoroughly enjoying himself.

"Do you see, Coriel?" Ouranos cried, arms shaking from the effort of keeping Zagan's tail away from his face. "He's a barbarian! An animal! This is what you are damned to be with!"

Zagan would make sure that was her choice. "Coryn! Would you join me up here?"

He nearly purred in satisfaction when he felt Coryn's presence beside him. He pushed his tail further into Ouranos's grasp, and the god gasped.

"Please, Zagan! Mercy!"

Zagan's lips twisted into a wicked smirk as he stared down at the now trembling king. "I will make you an offer, messenger. Accept it, and I *may* allow you to live."

Ouranos exhaled a shuddering breath. "Yes, anything."

Zagan relaxed his tail, blindly sought Coryn's hand, and grabbed it. "You are a god. Reascend her."

A gasp escaped Coryn. She shot him a look of surprise and squeezed his hand. "Zagan ..."

"Give Coryn back her status as erelim," Zagan repeated.

Ouranos looked as shocked as Coryn, but he knew better than to question Zagan. "Y-yes, okay," he said.

"Knights!" Zagan summoned, and they ran up as he knew they would. He removed his tail from Ouranos's neck and took a step back. "Make sure he doesn't try anything stupid."

Ouranos sighed with relief, then stood slowly, his palms up, and Zagan moved Coryn before him. Ouranos held his hand at Coryn's chest level and began waving it around in patterns, murmuring something in a language Zagan didn't understand. Coryn's grip on Zagan's hand got tighter and tighter, then fell away as her wings transitioned from gray to brilliant gold.

It was the most beautiful yet painful thing Zagan had ever seen—no, not just seen, but *felt*. He only just managed to keep his composure as he felt their bond fall away.

When Ouranos completed his chanting and his hand fell back to his side, Coryn's wings were not the only thing to have changed—she had more color in her cheeks, more life to her. She stood straighter, carried herself with greater confidence. She was stunning.

"Zagan," she whispered.

"Kill me," he said, then cursed himself for the trepidation in his tone.

This was the moment of truth—she would either follow his order because the bond still stood, or she would choose her own path.

"Kill me ... Coriel." The change in name caused his heart to ache.

He stared at her as she stood there, frozen. He watched the realization of the command register on her face, but her body did not react, aside from the widening of her eyes.

"My name is Coryn," she said, "and I could never."

Before he could even smile in response, a brilliant and blinding light surrounded them—and he heard his erelim scream.

CHAPTER 22

I am here, O gods. My bones are dismayed. My soul is dismayed. Hear the words of my groaning and grant me my strength.

As a forsaken, Coryn hadn't understood Ouranos's prayers, but now, as erelim, she recognized his whispers.

On her hands and knees, she furiously blinked away the flashes that had momentarily blinded her. Once the power faded, she regained her vision, and when she looked up, a scream tore from her lungs. Though she was a member of the Heavens once again, what she saw was nothing short of a nightmare— Zagan, Jinn, Lamia, and Oriax were levitating in the air above her, struggling against invisible bonds, their backs to one another.

The short freedom Ouranos had been given to exercise his godly powers and reascend her was all he'd needed to end the battle for the throne, and he had won. His shoulders shook as he laughed.

"I will make you an offer, Coriel," he said, echoing Zagan's words. "Accept it, and I may allow you to live."

She didn't know what that meant for the others, or whether Ouranos thought she still cared for him ... maybe she could use that to her advantage.

"My name is Coryn, Ouranos. And yes, please tell me what it is you offer." She couldn't demand he tell her; his patience was likely too thin for her to take the chance. She thought of Seere and channeled the demon's indifference.

He smirked. "I know your thirst for power, little canary."

Coryn winced, his former pet name for her no longer caressing her heart. Instead, it stabbed through it.

"Give up the run for archangel," Ouranos said. "Remain here with me, rule as my queen, and together we will command angel and demon alike. The war between the Heavens and Hell may end yet."

Did he really think that she would bow to his every whim just because she was an erelim again? But if she didn't obey, Zagan and the others would surely die. She needed to play on Ouranos's assumptions.

"And what of them?" she asked, avoiding Ouranos's proposals and motioning toward the bound group of knights instead.

"What would you like done with them, canary?" He pointed at Zagan. "That demon defeated you, bonded you, made you his pet. If it makes you happy, I could kill him and his fighters right now. Unless you'd like to end them yourself?"

With the wave of his hand, she saw that the invisible rope around them was tightened. It took everything she had not to shout, "Stop!" Groans and gasps came from the demons as they were squeezed tighter, but Coryn kept an unreadable expression as she looked up at them.

"Say the word and I will give you their corpses," Ouranos said gleefully.

"No, no. I would like to get my revenge, but I'd like time to decide how."

Ouranos laughed again, as if he'd fully expected she'd say that. "Of course, my vengeful queen. Good. I will put them in the dungeons and we will play with them later."

Coryn couldn't look at the group as they were seized by lessers who erupted into the throne room at Ouranos's command. Nor could she stomach the idea of sliding her hand into Ouranos's when he extended it to her.

With a slow intake of air, she walked toward him, lungs burning with the breath she held as she slipped her hand into his.

"Throw them into the pit," Ouranos instructed the lessers as he led Coryn to the throne and pulled her into his lap.

"All of this is ours, little canary," he said, running a hand up and down her spine between her wings.

She used to tremble with pleasure whenever he did that. Now she tried not to cringe.

"Yes, my lord," she said, catching sight of Zagan's spiked tail before the doors closed. "Ours."

Though the demons were painfully constricted in an invisible wire and traveling as one mass, and despite having just lost the throne of Hell to a god from the Heavens, all Zagan could think about was how quickly Coryn had turned her back—her golden-winged erelim back—on him.

She'd called him her lord, he thought, and the ache in his chest was worse than any torture Ouranos could inflict on him.

He'd made a mistake, trying to give her back the one thing they'd thought she could never have again. But they'd been winning the battle, he'd seen the opportunity, and he'd taken it. He'd wanted to give everything back to Coryn.

Including me as her enemy?

He'd never considered she would turn on him, and he couldn't believe he'd been so stupid. He'd also never imagined Ouranos would have had enough power to capture them after battling and ascending Coryn; Zagan had grossly underestimated the power of this demon god king.

He cursed under his breath, and at the noise, the lesser guard in front of him stabbed a spiked weapon into his abdomen, right where Ouranos had already struck. The entire group of knights was propelled forward as Zagan jumped at the rat-like beast, roaring hoarsely and baring his fangs. The little bastard only continued to grin at him. Once Zagan took back the throne, this thing would be the first to die.

"How can you accept a god from the Heavens as your king?" he demanded. Though Ouranos had spent three decades serving Hell, it didn't make him one of them. "He said that the war between the realms would end. A god and his"—he grit his teeth—"angel queen? Hardly seems like he will fight in favor of demons."

"Oh, but he will!" the guard before Lamia said.

As they walked toward the dungeons, the cluster of demons rotated like a planet. Jinn was now leading the front of the line.

"No just creature from the Heavens could ever stand living in Hell," the guard continued, looking proud of himself for knowing something he didn't think Zagan realized. "Our liege has been down here for years and corruption has set in. If he were just, he would have died long ago. Do you have the powers of a god? Hm?"

Zagan ran his tongue over his teeth. Ouranos had forsaken warriors, not full-blooded angels, either because he no longer had access to the Heavens, or because angels couldn't tolerate this realm.

A flash of concern crossed his mind when he thought of Coryn, now an angel in Hell. It angered him to think of her erelim form wasting away down here, Ouranos unwilling or uncaring enough to help her. Would she call to Zagan then?

She was made for you, and you alone. If you can't have her, no one can.

His jealousy was overwhelming; the corrupt thoughts he'd always projected onto human souls were now seeping into his own. He'd never felt more like a creation of Hell than when he'd been fighting against Ouranos, but now he felt an even stronger evil bubbling up from the depths of his soul. Never before had he hated angels and gods with such ferocity.

He was quiet throughout the rest of the journey to the dungeons. The knights continued to revolve in their invisible bonds as they made their way down, passing floor after floor of cells, torture chambers, and corruption rooms. It was at the bottom of the castle, the deepest level of anywhere in Hell, where the passion pit lay.

Three stories up from the bottom, Zagan broke into a sweat. By the time they'd reached the edge of the circular cliff that dropped into the pit itself, his body began to cook.

"You heard your ... king," Jinn rasped, already sounding desperate for water, "he wants us alive."

"Oh, you will be," said the rat-like lesser in charge of guarding Zagan, "albeit just barely."

All five guards gathered together and pushed against Jinn, sending the group teetering on the edge of the stone cliff before they fell over.

It felt as if they plummeted for ages, then they hit the bright red sand of the pit with a loud thud and several groans. As soon as the invisible wire binding them disappeared, they all scattered, distancing themselves from one another so that no more heat was passed between them. It was truly hotter than Hell down here.

"They won't live to see the morrow," Zagan murmured.

He spread his wings, but they captured heat and immediately began to bubble. Kicking off the ground, he gave a few hard flaps, but there was no rising thermal air to lift him. Everything was stagnant, torturous, and there was no way he could fly. He landed clumsily on his knees, then he shouted and pummeled at the sand as if each grain were to blame for him ending up there.

"Stop. Stop!" Oriax pleaded, running over to Zagan before reaching out to pry him off the ground.

The skin-to-skin contact was unbearable and Zagan shrugged him off. He stayed on the ground with his hands before him on the sand and bowed in apology to the others.

"I have failed you."

He was so angry with himself. For falling for the gods' ruse, their secret angelic weapon ... for putting her happiness before his entire realm. He was especially mad that he should hate her but couldn't. He slapped his thigh and roared in frustration.

Annoyingly in tune with one another, his friends knew what was bothering him most.

"Yes, you're an imbecile," Jinn offered, meeting Zagan's stare, "but I also know that once we're out of here, you will never make that mistake again."

Jinn extended his hand to help Zagan up, and it was clear in his expression that he wouldn't let Zagan get away with shrugging him off. Zagan gripped Jinn's burning hand and winced as he rose to his feet.

"You know she only accepted Ouranos's offer in order to protect you, right?"

Zagan paused, humbled by Jinn's faith in Coryn.

Oriax shook his head. "Don't be a fool, Jinn! If she were still forsaken, I would agree with you. But she is erelim now, an erelim with a propensity for revenge and a thirst for power. She has no reason to want to save Zagan, not when he bound her and she now serves a god from the Heavens. I fought against her on Manusya. I have seen her hatred."

He looked at Zagan, his eyes dark, his face hard. "I'm sorry, man. Without that bond, she has no reason to care for you. If anything, she'll want you to pay for what's happened."

"Even after finding out she was created specifically for Zagan?" Lamia argued, her face growing red. "If I were her, I'd be pretty fucking pissed to know I was only a pawn in their game. If she wants revenge on anyone, it will be on Ouranos."

She waved her arm toward Zagan, her voice softening. "The way she looked at him, that was real. She cares for him. And even if she's angel now, she's still here, in Hell, ready to rule ... with our rightful king."

They all turned to Zagan, seeking his opinion.

"I want to believe she still cares for me now that the bond has fallen away. But she is erelim again, and I don't know what kind of command gods like Ouranos can have on her. We will need to tread lightly. I will not make the same mistake with Coryn that I made with that bastard god."

He took a deep breath, hoping that, should the time come, he would be true to his next words. "If at any point I feel she is no longer with me, I will strike her down as I would any other angel."

He'd almost rather stay suffering in the pit than find out the truth of Coryn's allegiance, but it was time to rise.

"Now, let's find a way out of here."

CHAPTER 23

"Come to me, Coriel." Ouranos turned to sit in his throne for the thousandth time since he'd defeated Zagan, clearly pleased with himself.

And he should be, she supposed. As cheap an attack as it was, Ouranos had been about to lose the battle for the throne—and his life. He'd seen the opening, and he'd taken it. She would have done the same thing.

Yet, she had been the cause of Zagan's moment of weakness. He'd done her a favor, knowing just how much she missed her wings and her free will. Had he been that confident she would remain with him after getting back her golden down? It was enough to bring her to tears, thinking about how much he must truly care for her to take such a gamble.

What must he think of her now, though? She was no longer bound to him, a god of the Heavens sat upon his throne, and he'd watched her pledge herself to the cheap victor.

"Coriel," Ouranos called again, snapping her from her thoughts.

"Coryn," she corrected, then added quickly, "my lord."

He raised an eyebrow and braced his temple against an index finger. "Oh? You still wish to keep the name the demon bestowed upon you, do you?"

Perhaps it was a poor decision to fight for it, but the name meant too much to her.

"It is ... my punishment," she lied, though felt she was doing an excellent job in looking pained by her false confession. "It will always remind me of my insolence against the Heavens. I know now it was what I was meant to do"—how hurt she felt that Ouranos and Michael had used her all this time—"but never again will I disobey an order."

Ouranos's smirk was dark and wicked. "Excellent, angel. You have done well, and the Heavens will thank us for what we've done for the war. Now, thousands of souls will be led to salvation by our hands."

He spread his arms, beckoning her to him, and she flashed back to years ago, when he had done the same thing in the Heavens. How strange it was to now be going reluctantly to him in a throne room in Hell.

"I missed you, Cor," he said as he pulled her into his lap.

He fisted her hair as he drew her close, inhaling the scent of her against her neck, and she resisted the urge to pull away.

"I have been down here for so long, waiting for you, for this very moment. And now all of this is ours."

He trailed his hand between her golden wings and let it linger there as he surveyed the throne room, smiling as if imagining his vast kingdom that lay beyond its walls. But Coryn wondered, now that he had this power, was he really going to fight for what was good?

All demons sought to do was taint souls and strengthen their numbers. It was a matter of survival. They had systems and stuck to them. They were genuine in their emotions, even if those emotions were sinful. But the Heavens were far more corrupt than Hell. Angels and gods were manipulative, even among their own ranks—Ouranos and Michael were proof of that. While they were claiming good, it was at every necessary expense—including creating life for it to be a pawn to do their bidding. She would never forgive them for that.

And now, she would exercise the same manipulation that had been bestowed upon her.

"The color in your wings is returning," she said.

How she had always admired his wings, but now she was sad to see the bright oranges and reds seeping back into his feathers.

Ouranos smiled. "We are both free. We are exactly as we should be now. Everything has fallen into place."

She bit her bottom lip. "I didn't know where you'd gone." Bracing her hands against the throne on either side of his head, she hovered over him but did not press her body against his as he glided his hands over her. "One moment you were in bed, the next you were gone, and no one heard from you again. They said you'd gone to Manusya to find me. Imagine my guilt and pain when I returned."

"We had received word that Zagan was on Manusya. Michael was going to sacrifice himself for capture, but I went in his place. He is not as strong as you and me, Cor. As a human once ascended, I didn't think he could survive down here and maintain the light. Plus, with him gone, you would have been nominated for archangel and never would have fought against Zagan. I wanted to tell you the plan but couldn't. You understand, don't you? Though I don't like that you're down here now, truth be told. Not as an erelim. You are strong, much stronger than Michael—we made sure of it at your creation—but Hell is not a healthy place for an angel."

Oh, even though she was not a god, she was plenty strong and could handle Hell, thank you very much … but she bit down on the urge to argue. The last thing she needed was to anger him when he seemed so willing to give insight into everything that had led up to this point.

"I think Michael killed Paha," she confessed, trying to sound sad as she purred into his ear.

He nuzzled her neck and wrapped his arms tighter around her, no longer allowing distance between their bodies. She settled into his lap, helpless to do anything else.

"I thought she was the one who had sent me to Zagan alone, all because she wanted to stay archangel. I hated her for so long after that, and when it finally dawned on me that day on the battlefield that she wasn't to blame, a demon ran her through and Michael just stood there, watching the whole thing."

"Your work wasn't yet complete, angel," Ouranos said, speaking as if he was explaining something to a small child. "You're a clever little one. We couldn't chance you piecing everything together until the time was right. Pahaliah was sacrificed for the greater good, and she will be remembered as a model archangel for all future creations."

Coryn couldn't believe what she was hearing. She wanted to scream and was taken aback by her own resolve to suppress the urge. Ouranos was right, she certainly was strong—but also much smarter than he gave her credit for.

"So what do we do now?" she asked, her voice barely above a whisper. If she'd spoken any louder her voice would have wavered, exposing the emotion she couldn't allow Ouranos to hear.

"You will return to the Heavens. I am sure you are eager to return, are you not? You will deliver the message to Michael that we have conquered Hell and will begin purging its tainted souls immediately."

Coryn nodded, gaining enough resolve to put distance between them and look into his eyes with confidence. "Were you and Michael the only ones who knew of this plan?"

"Yes. And as far as any others will ever know, this all happened by chance."

She was hoping he would elaborate, but he didn't offer an explanation and she'd pried enough. He was pleased when she simply nodded in response.

"That's a good girl. Now ascend and tell the others what we have done."

She was all too happy to climb off his lap and stand on her own two feet, and once she did, he made no move to kiss her or wish her a good trip. Zagan would have, but she was grateful Ouranos did not.

"Yes, my lord," she said, "and I will return with Michael's response."

CHAPTER 24

To leave Hell meant leaving Zagan behind, but Coryn would strengthen and come back for him. Plus, she couldn't deny her excitement about ascending to the Heavens, especially when she thought she would never see the place again.

It was a much more cumbersome trip from Hell than it would have been from Manusya, as she first needed to travel by one of those painful portals to the human realm before she could take off into the sky. But when she was finally making her way through the clouds, exhilaration flooded her. There was something about golden wings that made flying better. They seemed to catch the thermals better, took less effort with every flap, and damn if they didn't look good in the eternal sun of the Heavens!

It was also particularly satisfying to see the shocked faces of all the angels that watched her explode through the clouds and land on the plush ground. She smiled, albeit a bit too smugly, and they whispered among themselves as she made her way to archangel headquarters. Her first order of business—a chat with Michael.

The eternal sun calmed her nerves and warmed her face; it was unlike anything she'd experienced in the other realms. Everything was illuminated by soft red and orange glows, like embers. Perhaps she'd been living in Hell all along.

Coryn saw a bustle of activity among the angels—they were posting campaign signs for an upcoming emergency archangel election. A pang seared through her and nearly stopped her in her tracks. They were looking to replace Pahaliah, and her former leader would not be greeting her at Michael's door.

Then who would be?

"Coriel?"

Coryn spun around.

"Archangel Azazel," she said, giving a slight nod of her head. It wasn't as deep a bow as she was sure he was expecting, but he was the last angel she wanted to greet upon her return.

He circled around her with one eyebrow raised. "Last I saw you, your wings were ashen and your falling ceremony had just been completed."

He swiped a hand over her wings and glanced at his palm, as if checking to make sure they were truly gold and not just dusted with color.

Coryn matched his raised eyebrow.

"Who allowed you in?" he asked.

Ouranos's words to keep quiet until addressing all of the Heavens echoed in her mind.

"I apologize, sir, but that is a matter for High Archangel Michael and me to discuss first."

As an archangel for the cherubim, Azazel had no authority over the erelim race and was powerless to argue.

"I see. Well, he is not in his office currently, but you are welcome to wait for his return there." He motioned toward the marble building before them. "I understand you witnessed Pahaliah's demise during the battle against your captor."

Coryn cringed at the emotionless way he spoke about Paha's death. Could he, too, know something about the plan to infiltrate Hell? He and Michael were good friends, but good enough for Michael to confide in Azazel that he'd taken a gamble and knowingly sent a god into Hell? That he'd helped create an angel designed for a demon?

Her silence hung between them for a moment before Azazel continued. "What a tragic and needless incident. Run through by a demon while she was trying to defend you."

Coryn couldn't stop her mouth from dropping open, but she again suppressed the urge to argue. Had Michael spread this rumor? Was he going to continue making her an enemy of the Heavens? To what end?

"It was a terrible thing to have witnessed," she said quietly.

"I'm sure. And now Michael is without a proper partner until the election." He smiled wickedly, letting out a short, obvious bark of a laugh. "But don't bother throwing your name into the ring, Coriel. It's useless now."

Heat rose to her cheeks, but she kept her eyes on the building before them as they walked, getting closer but not quickly enough.

"Yes, High Archangel. Thank you for your thoughtful advisement. Though I go by Coryn now. A punishment for the trouble I have caused."

A tribute to the only male who had ever truly cared for her.

Azazel seemed most pleased, impressed even, by her words. "I see. Well, *Coryn*, I look forward to seeing what other reparations will be brought upon you."

They ascended the stairs to the front hall of the building—why couldn't he just leave her alone?—and made their way to the erelim wing.

"Since Paha's untimely death, and with other erelim currently running for archangel, Michael has employed a new angel as his assistant. One just created, still green. Michael said he saw something of you in him. I hope it wasn't your stubbornness."

Azazel pushed through the golden doors to Michael's offices, and a lean black-haired young angel with bright eyes looked up from the desk where he worked.

For the second time in only a few minutes, Coryn's jaw dropped.

Alexander!

"Coryn, meet Alexandrael. Alex." He took Coryn by the shoulders, shepherding her further into the reception area.

Her legs felt like lead as she approached the angel. He had the small white wings of a malakhim.

"Hello … Alex," she said, the name making her tongue feel numb. "It's a pleasure to meet you."

She hadn't known the boy when he was alive—she'd only seen him as a limp creature in Zagan's arms—so there was no way he would remember her. But would he remember Zagan?

The young man studied her from behind that looming desk, his eyes large and green.

Azazel shuffled Coryn forward a bit more. "This angel will be waiting for Michael until his return," he said, steering her into a seat along the wall before Alex. "You will make sure he sees her, yes?"

Alex nodded, and Azazel smiled a warm smile that made Coryn's skin prickle.

"That's a good boy." Azazel turned to make his leave. "I look forward to hearing more about how you've returned to us, Coryn," he said, then pushed through the golden doors again and was gone.

Silence filled the room once the doors closed, but Coryn found it rather peaceful. She remained in the seat Azazel had placed her in, and it was all she could do not to stare at the fledgling malakhim before her. Were the Heavens a better life? After everything that had happened, Coryn wasn't so sure.

"How long ago were you created, Alex?" she asked gently, her voice just above a whisper.

"I have been in this form for six days, lady erelim." His voice lacked emotion.

Because all angels were created fully formed, it was rare to have such a young-looking creature in the Heavens—the rest of the angels looked at least ten years older. Why had they chosen to reincarnate him so exactly?

"I see," she said, watching as he scribbled something on a long scroll. "I was on Manusya for a while, with a demon knight … Zagan."

She let the name hang in the air, wondering if he would react. Alex didn't so much as look up from the paper.

She hesitated, inhaling a deep breath before finally asking, "Do you know that name?"

Alex stopped writing, then looked up and locked eyes with Coryn. "Yes, lady erelim."

There had been more emotion in his voice this time. Did that mean he remembered, or only that he'd been taught what every angel comes to learn about the formidable demon? It was difficult to tell, especially with such a timid angel. Coryn doubted he'd been like this when he was human; otherwise, Zagan wouldn't have held him in such high regard.

It took Coryn a while to follow up on her question, so Alex had gone back to writing by the time she asked, "Do you like being an angel, Alex?"

He shrugged as any young adult would when they weren't sure of the best way to answer a question.

Coryn chewed the inside of her lip, and Alex kept his eyes on his scroll. Had she and Zagan made a mistake, sending Alex here? She was surprised the boy had been brought back as an angel; after all that had happened, she wasn't sure how much weight her blessing would have carried. That made Coryn suspicious; even when she'd been newly forsaken and in the care of a demon to whom she'd been bonded, she'd felt more comfortable.

Coryn sat quietly, listening to the sound of the pen scrawling across Alex's scroll. Something shiny to his left caught her eye, and she nearly let out a squeal.

My sword!

So, the bastard Michael had it in his own chambers. Coryn stood, crossed the room in a few strides, and walked behind Alex. He said nothing as she picked up the weapon, but she could have sworn his lip quirked into a small smile as she set it into her invisible sheath. The sword's weight rested against her back, and she sighed with relief. They were reunited.

Coryn returned to her seat, and a few moments later Michael entered the room.

"Coriel," he said, though it was obvious Azazel had told him she was waiting here. He'd either left out the part about her name change, or Michael had chosen to ignore it.

"Coryn," she corrected. She would correct anyone who dared call her by her Heavens-given name. Her new name was a tribute to Zagan; it would keep her grounded and prevent her from fully absorbing back into the hive mind of the Heavens.

"My apologies," he said, offering a friendly smile—a smile that used to make her swell with pride every time she received it—but now she saw the plotting beneath it.

"Old habits die hard, you understand. You know how fond of you I am." When Coryn said nothing, he cleared his throat. "Tell me, how were you ascended?"

"You know exactly how I was ascended," she replied, not bothering to hide the hurt in her voice. "Ouranos told me everything. The purpose of my creation, your plot to take over Hell. He's down there, now, and has become king. Zagan ... he wanted me reascended, and so Ouranos restored me to erelim before taking the throne."

She wanted to punch the satisfaction right off his face.

"And where is Zagan now?" he asked.

"In the dungeons of Hell," she said, not wanting to divulge everything by mentioning he and his knights were in the pit, whatever that was. She noticed that Alex had stopped writing, though his eyes and pen were still on the scroll.

"Ouranos sent me to tell you everything is in place and to make the announcement. Is it true that the two of you were the only ones who knew of all this?"

"Alex, if you would?" Michael said, and Alex slid slowly off his chair, bowed low to the two of them and exited the office.

Michael's expression hardened. "You have been part of a great plan, erelim. The greatest you could have hoped ever to be a part of ... and you played the biggest role of all."

He was playing to her love for praise and importance, and again, she saw right through it. She looked down, afraid her eyes would reveal her thoughts.

"If we'd let the other gods know, none of this would have transpired. They would have found the idea ludicrous, impossible. Think about it. To willingly send an archangel or god into Hell for servitude? It was a great gamble, but after decades of investment, it has finally paid off. We have harmed Hell more since you were sent to that demon prince than we have in centuries fighting against him and his army on Manusya. You have no idea just how perfectly you played your role. Today, after our announcement to all the angels and gods of the Heavens, you will be the one to take Pahaliah's place as archangel. Make no doubt about it."

He patted her on the shoulder, that warm smile and the fire in his eyes more menacing than any flame in Hell.

"We will tell them you found Ouranos upon your descent, worked with him to betray Zagan and set him free, and he won the battle to become demon king. He is king, and you are his champion. Well done, Coryn. Well done."

Coryn studied Michael's fire-eyes. "And what's in this for you, Michael?" she asked as innocently as she could.

Michael let out a laugh that caused lines to form at the corners of his eyes. "I need nothing, sweet angel. Knowing that we have aided the realms in the war against darkness is more than enough."

She didn't believe him for a second but nodded. "That is most selfless of you, High Archangel," she said, putting some distance between them. "I will remember such humility when I share my victory in the square."

Upon exiting the archangels' headquarters, she was greeted by a sea of curious and murmuring gold-, silver-, and white-winged onlookers. It seemed all the beings in the Heavens knew that Coriel, now Coryn, had returned to them and bore exciting news. What were they thinking? Did they believe she was still a demon's pet, or Ouranos's hero? Only time would tell.

Led by Michael, and with Alexander trailing closely at the rear, the sea of angels parted as the trio made their way down the steps and into the square. The last time Coryn stood in this place had been when she'd said goodbye to Diniel and was reprimanded by Pahaliah.

Paha. The vision of her being impaled by the demon and the look of fear in her eyes played in Coryn's mind for the millionth time. And where was Diniel now? Perhaps, like Alexander, he had been reborn as an angel and was here among the crowd, though he would look different and have no memory of who she was or what had happened.

She wondered if the rest of the angels continued to tell their terrible tale about her—that she'd slept her way to erelim, had put Diniel and dozens of others in danger, and had got herself bonded to a demon. Based on Azazel's attitude toward her, she was sure they all blamed her for Pahaliah's death as well. And she was supposed to bear this blame and falsity on her own when Michael and Ouranos were the ones who had caused all this in the name of winning the war. Sacrifice came with reward, but Coryn no longer knew if the reward was worth it.

She flew to the top of the fountain in the middle of the square.

"Brethren!" she greeted.

The angels' faces were unreadable, but through her restored tie to them she could sense their trepidation, suspicion, and excitement. She took a deep breath, trying to rid herself of their feelings; she had been gone so long the connection threatened to overwhelm her.

She fisted her hands and made an *X* with her arms. "Grace, mercy, and peace be with you all."

Although she'd offered the traditional opening for a public speech such as this, instead of responding as one loud congregation, the angels murmured their responses and not all at the same time. She closed her eyes, willing herself to maintain her composure despite the lack of faith the others had in her. Quite frankly, they were right to doubt her. She doubted herself.

"As you may know, I was once known as Erelim Coriel, a top-ranking warrior in our war against Hell and the corruption of souls. You may also know that I was recently captured by and bonded to Demon Knight Zagan, forced to become forsaken and cast from the Heavens. As you can see, my wings, recently gray and dying, are now golden and thriving once again. I come to you today, reascended to join your ranks, and, at the behest of High Archangel Michael, to deliver you good news. While I was bound to Hell, I found our god of the sky, Ouranos."

Gasps sounded from the crowd, but this time they were excited. Some angels cheered, others began to weep. She had fallen for the god's ruse before too, but had she truly been as blind as these angels? The thought disgusted her.

"I learned that Zagan was known to the underworld as God Slaver, and that God Ouranos had been forced to serve the demon king. It was by chance that we found each other and were able to help one another rise from our enslavement and rebel against the demons."

The lie weighed heavy on her heart, despite that she was now winning the angels' love and respect. Every word made her tongue feel numb, and she swallowed hard to wet her drying throat. Her fellow angels would normally pick up on these emotions, but there was so much elation and hope among them that her feelings were being washed out with the tide.

She took in a deep breath, such strong feelings from the angels making her dizzy. Here she was, back in the Heavens, an erelim only moments away from securing a position as archangel. All she had to do was continue the lie. Ouranos would rule Hell, she would rule his army, and everything she'd dreamed of would come true.

Coriel would have continued that way—but not Coryn. She was in love with her demon, the true leader of Hell. The one for whom she'd been created. And it was time the realms knew it.

"I can assure you, I was created specifically for this purpose. It was my pre-determined destiny, and Ouranos's wish, to present me as a gift from the Heavens to Zagan."

The murmuring suddenly stopped and feelings of confusion were now swirling. Eyes wide, Michael began to push through the crowd toward her, but Alexander's hand shot out and gripped his robe, stopping the archangel from continuing his approach.

"Ouranos and High Archangel Michael planned for Ouranos to be captured as well, endangering the Heavens and Manusya alike by risking the influence of evil on a god."

Realization was dawning among the angels, and Coryn could feel them gaining hold on the truth in her words. She held her head a little higher when Michael began his approach again and more angels aided Alexander in holding him back.

"Brethren, I fear that after three decades of serving Hell, Ouranos's soul has been corrupted and he poses a true a threat to all. He does not have the best intentions of the Heavens in mind, nor is he truly the work of Hell. He is something in between, which could mean the end of us all. Many of you have joked about my former relationship with the god to my face—I can only imagine how much crueler those words turned behind closed doors—but you know the respect I had for him. This is not me being a scorned angel. This is me, a wiser angel, who has seen more of these three realms than any of you, and I am concerned for our future."

"Coriel!" Michael ground out, wrenching himself free of the hold the angels had on him.

"Coryn," she corrected.

He shoved his way through the crowd, gaining no friends as he caused angels to stumble into one another. When he spread his huge wings and took to the air, Coryn braced herself on the top of the fountain.

"Hell will always belong to the demons," she continued. "Ruling their realm on behalf of the Heavens will never work! We must put a stop to Ouranos's reign. The only way for you to win this war is to bring joy and purity to Manusya, though the Heavens may not have as much joy and purity as you once believed."

Michael barreled into her, forcing her to open her wings and catch herself mid-air lest she crush the crowd below her.

Her story was out, and the angels were left to make their own choices on who to believe—a rebellious angel who had been bonded to a demon and was then reascended, or their tried-and-true high archangel, leader of their elite warrior class. The odds were certainly not in Coryn's favor. Still, there was enough doubt exuding from the angels around them that she felt hopeful.

"The time to strike is now!" Coryn shouted as she dodged another advance from Michael. "The demons are disorganized while Ouranos settles into the throne. We can purge their fighters, dethrone the god, and bring him back here. I will deliver him to you on Manusya by sunrise tomorrow. If you believe me, fight with me against him! If not, then I will see you in Hell after the demons send you all to your rightful place."

The crowd parted as she dived through the clouds on which they stood to make her descent to the human realm.

CHAPTER 25

"We're going to die down here, aren't we?"

"Just. Fucking. Climb. Oriax!"

Demons all over Hell would no doubt disown them if they could see that their elite warriors were stacked one atop the other, pushing the smallest member of their group as high as they could up the side of the passion pit wall. At the base was Jinn, then Zagan, followed by Lamia, the one who was being truly motivational.

"When we get out of here you're going on a diet, my friend," she said through a strained groan.

She rose up on her serpent tail as much as she could as they desperately tried to lift O high enough to grab onto a stone jutting out from the side of the wall. As it was with most things, their ticket to freedom seemed just out of reach.

"Stretch, you damned demon!" she growled, and with one final, desperate hop, Oriax missed the stone and they all tumbled back onto the sand.

While Lamia roared in frustration, Oriax gasped and coughed on his back.

"This is hopeless," Jinn said, a pessimist from the start of this plan. "O's right. We're gonna die down here if we don't get water soon, and that little exercise didn't exactly help us conserve energy."

"If it means killing Ouranos, I would go without water down here for weeks," Zagan said, still eyeing the stone. "Usurping him is reason enough to keep me alive."

"That's if you survive the beasts they throw down here with us," Oriax added, voice hoarse from coughing and gasping in the dry heat. "Speaking of which, I don't know why they haven't let anything loose down here yet. How long's it been, a couple hours?"

"Who knows," Jinn said, head down. "I wouldn't wish for anything like that, though. That's just what we need, some raging bull demon entering the ring."

So they sat in silence, trying to conserve as much energy as they could in case they were attacked. But the more time that passed, the more Zagan fantasized new ways to kill Ouranos. He feared having to challenge Coryn if it came down to it, which he knew made him a fool, but he wasn't sure he'd be able to harm her.

"Hey!" a voice called above them, and a rope fell from the top of the cliff and slapped Oriax in the face as he looked up. Jinn snorted in a feeble attempt to contain his laughter.

"Shut up," O said, his voice nearly gone. He gripped the rope and tugged on it. "It's sturdy. Let's get out of here!"

But Lamia placed a hand on his shoulder. "Wait."

Zagan and the others looked up at the top of the pit. The heat caused the air to ripple, making it difficult to see the shadowy figure above.

"Who are you?" Lamia called.

Using the rope, the figure descended into the pit and landed gracefully beside Oriax.

"Seere?" Lamia asked, and both she and Oriax backed away from the other knight. "This is a trap."

Zagan and his knights extended their claws, and Seere held up her hands, showing them that she was weaponless.

"Easy, easy," she said, and there was something in her eyes that compelled Zagan to listen.

"Stand down," he said, and once he lowered his hands, his knights did as well. "What are you doing here, Seere?"

"Getting you out of this hellhole. I know when we've lost a fight and when our new king is a cheap bastard. Furcas, crazy ass that he is now, followed you inside the throne room in case our new leader required protection. Even he admitted we may have made a mistake by backing Ouranos."

She nodded. "We lost to you fair and square, and you've proven more than once that you are the better choice to be king, God Slayer." The demon bowed her head and kept her eyes trained on the ground. "Will you accept us into your army once again?"

The other knights were more intelligent than he gave them credit for. Smirking, he exchanged satisfied glances with his knights, then nodded.

"I did tell you that you would serve me, did I not?" He held out his arm to Seere and they gripped one another at the elbow. It was easy to read her; Zagan knew this was no lie. Like him, he knew she prided herself in sparing those around her from that one sin.

"Where are the rest of your rotten bastards?" he asked, and Seere's smile grew.

"Ready to save your fried asses."

With a whistle, Raum, Phenex, Furcas, and Dantalion threw themselves into the passion pit alongside them. Though Zagan would never admit it, he was grateful for the assistance; after roasting in the pit for who knew how long, he wasn't sure he could make the climb on his own.

While everyone climbed, and his knights argued with the new recruits over who was the most rotten ass, Zagan pressed Seere for information.

"What's happening in the castle now?"

"It's chaos. Ouranos has every demon he can giving the place a complete overhaul. Instead of addressing his new subjects, his first order of business has been to make the castle just the way he wants it."

Zagan shook his head, though he was more concerned about Coryn's state than Ouranos's. He must have had some expression of longing or contemplation because Seere picked up on his thoughts immediately.

"There's been no sign of the angel since Ouranos sent her back to the Heavens. He seemed concerned about keeping her down here now that she was no longer forsaken."

He could only nod as he fought to keep his breathing steady. At least Ouranos and Coryn weren't together—though if they were, the rage he'd feel would be motivation enough to climb faster.

Seere did what she could to encourage him, climbing with ease while his slick, sweaty skin hindered his progress. Eventually, they got far enough from the blazing heat below for him to open his wings and get some air beneath them. Giving his arms and legs a rest, he flew the rest of the way. When he got to the top he lay on the cold stone, wings outstretched, and caught his breath as he looked up at the ceiling. They needed to scale many more stairs to complete their journey, but just beyond that ceiling was the throne room. This time, he would make sure Ouranos got what was coming to him.

***

"Ah, my angel. Returning so soon?"

Coryn had entered the throne room, no longer needing to sneak around in servants' clothes, and now approached Ouranos.

He had made quick work of his power over the demons. Though she had only been in the castle once, and hadn't spent her time taking in the decor of the place, she recognized it had changed. No longer were the tapestries on the walls red, but blue and orange. The throne, which had been cold, bare stone before, was now covered with plush orange upholstery. The room was less a dedication to Hell, and more a tribute to the god of the sky. The color in the plumage of his wings had fully returned and matched the bright orange color with which he'd decorated the castle, but it was clear the scars on his face from Zagan's hellfire would never heal.

"I would have liked you to stay in the Heavens for at least a day," Ouranos continued as Coryn made her approach. "Hell is no place for an ange—"

"They're coming for you," Coryn said, doing her best to exude panic and fear with her wide eyes and her quick stride. "The angels. Some approve, some do not. If you try to ascend, you will be stopped. We are to meet on Manusya at sunrise."

Ouranos's amused gaze turned cold. "What did you say to them?"

"Exactly what High Archangel Michael told me to say," she said with fake bewilderment. "That after I was captured by Zagan, you and I found each other by chance. That I have been freed from Zagan's curse, and you have risen to power as king. But some are suspicious."

"Suspicious? Why?"

"You've spent more than thirty years down here, directly serving the king and his knights. Everyone knows how influential demons can be on one's soul. They fear that yours may not be salvageable."

"What!" Ouranos rose from his throne and spun, arms gesturing widely around the room. "I have finally procured Hell in the Heavens' name, and they dare challenge my motivations?"

"I know. It makes no sense to me, either." Had she really admired this god? He was gullible, too blinded by his own power to question her lies. "I believe you're still the god I knew in the Heavens all those years ago." *Corrupted long before Zagan got to you.* "You're good, and strong, and did what you had to do for the war."

She hoped her words didn't spur his lust for her; she was acting enough as it was. If he touched her, she wouldn't be able to help flinching.

His eyes were smoldering as he looked at her, and her heart fell into her stomach, but he made no move to close the distance between them. "So you'll stand with me tomorrow?"

She nodded. "I will stand for the betterment of Hell."

Her words were met with an angry roar, and she thought Ouranos had seen right through her. But as the cry echoed around the chamber, Ouranos jumped as high as she did.

They both spun toward the throne room doors.

Zagan and the knights had returned.

***

Zagan had prepared himself for meeting Ouranos, but he hadn't known how he'd react to seeing Coryn again.

She's a trick. She was made specifically to take me down. But that knowledge did nothing but make his emotions stronger.

The knights exploded into the room behind him, now nine strong to eliminate their false demon god king. He didn't want to think about what may happen to Coryn.

The confusion and horror that registered on Ouranos's face was something that Zagan knew would bring him joy for decades to come.

"What is the meaning of this!" the god demanded of Dantalion. "Why have you brought these infidels here?"

It was Seere who answered. "Because Zagan is the one true king."

Zagan couldn't help but smile as Coryn took a few steps away from Ouranos, exposing a glimmer of hope that she may still want to be his.

Ouranos's shocked expression disappeared as he looked at the group. "Is that really what you believe?" he asked, then shrugged. "Why don't we settle this once and for all, then? Tomorrow."

Lamia barked out a humorless laugh. "Tomorrow?"

"The Heavens have challenged us. We, of Hell. We will fight them, and each other. Winner takes the throne."

Zagan stared at Coryn as Ouranos spoke. It was difficult to tell what she was thinking. Was that hope in her eyes? Was she eager for him to fall into the trap Ouranos was setting, or did she know something and want Zagan to become Hell's king once and for all?

Coryn stared down at him from atop the dais. Ouranos had so graciously fashioned a throne for her to match his, and though she didn't occupy the seat, seeing her so close to a chair fit for a queen made him want to cry out.

"Accept the challenge," she said.

His confusion at her words kept the roar from escaping. He hoped the look in his eyes didn't betray the stern tone he forced into his voice as he addressed Coryn.

"Why would we wait until he has rested overnight and gained even more strength, then face an army on Manusya a hundred times stronger than what he's amassed here? Surely you and your kind will be joining him."

Coryn remained stoic as she glared down her nose at him. "Are you suggesting that you fear taking on the greater army of angels?"

"Hardly." Though his answer was quick, embers of unease ignited inside him. He really was losing her. Maybe he'd lost her already. She now stood beside her former lover—perhaps current lover?—as a queen atop Hell's throne. And who was Zagan to her? Her arch nemesis, her former captor, and a demon. Though she'd been made for him, she didn't need him anymore. Unease turned into rage.

"Aren't you concerned we'll wipe the Heavens out?"

Finally, she showed a glimmer of emotion. The slight quirk of her lip turned into a humored smile, and she flashed her glittering teeth. "Not in the slightest."

Though their bond was gone, there was something in her tone, in the widening of her eyes, that made him understand the true meaning of her words—*Trust in what I'm telling you to do.* He was certain it was imperceptible to everyone but him, and he hoped beyond hope that it wasn't his blind love for Coryn that made him believe it. Was he walking into another trap? But he couldn't resist; they would have to find out.

"Fine," he said, "you want us to wait so you can have a few more precious hours of life? We will wait." His gaze snapped to Ouranos. "But mark my words, you are prolonging the inevitable, so I will make your death even more painful. The Heavens have more to fear than ever before."

"You will be escorted to the regular holding cells," Ouranos said, chin tilted up as he glared down at Zagan and his knights and put his arm around Coryn.

He regarded Dantalion next. "*All* of you. Considering the pit won't hold you any better and you'll need your strength before I slice it out of you tomorrow."

With a wave of his hand, he ordered a group of guards to surround them and relieve them of their weapons. Zagan gave Seere a small nod and the other knights followed without protest.

Please don't let me have condemned these knights to death, Coryn. Please.

CHAPTER 26

Coryn watched as Zagan and the knights were escorted away. When the guards shut her and Ouranos in together, she stared at the throne room doors, unable to find the strength to exhale.

Please don't let me have condemned them all to death. She wasn't sure who she was praying to, but it certainly wasn't the god behind her.

"He accepted that easily," Ouranos said.

When she heard him step toward his throne and sit down, Coryn collected herself and gathered whatever resilience she could to silently exhale through pursed lips. "He underestimates you."

"You played to his pride. That was well done."

If Ouranos suspected that she'd been sending Zagan a subliminal message beneath her words, he didn't show it. She turned to find him resting his head casually on one hand, one leg swinging and the other tucked beneath him as he sat on the throne. She forced a smile. His face, so recently filled with satisfaction and smugness, changed like he'd pulled a mask away.

Is he letting his guard down now because we're alone? Is he running out of strength to hold up the farce?

Much to her surprise, vulnerability poured from him. He opened his arms wide, beckoning for her to come. Even more surprising, she found herself walking toward him.

"You see now why you were created the way you were, don't you?" Ouranos's voice held genuine concern as he cupped her cheek and studied her eyes.

Coryn stared right back. "Honestly? I want to see, but it's difficult to understand."

He frowned. "You were made to serve a much higher purpose than your counterparts. You are my most important creation. And though you were made to trap the demon"—his eyes traced along her jawline and over her collarbones—"you're beautiful, and smart, and witty. The perfect combination of everything *I* enjoy."

His hands trailed from her waist to her hips, and he pulled her closer. His eyes rolled back, as if he were savoring the familiar shape of her form. She shuddered to think just how many times he'd held her.

"I missed you, angel. You don't know how terrible it's been down here. Not only the recovery from my initial battle with Zagan and healing from the hellfire, but it's been lonely, too. With little to ground me, I've fought hard not to lose my way. The thought of someday ruling Hell with you has been all that's kept me sane."

He buried his face into the crook of her neck. "And now we are here. Now it is ours."

He really believes in everything he's done.

From the way he held her, as if he were desperate to draw comfort, she believed he'd once been scared. He may still be; his hands trembled as he mindlessly stroked her back. She remembered her own fear when she'd faced Zagan as a forsaken for the first time. It hadn't taken him long to take her under his wing—literally and figuratively—but she doubted anyone had ever nurtured or comforted Ouranos during the decades he'd been a servant in Hell.

"Where did you stay?" Coryn whispered. "Where did you sleep?"

Ouranos's hold around her tightened. "I served the king, no matter what time of day or night he needed me, so I stayed there." He hiked a thumb blindly over his shoulder.

Coryn peered around the throne to the back of the room, where an empty pair of shackles lay dangling from the stone wall, and a matching pair, lower down, lay on the ground. She couldn't say anything but wrapped her arms around the god's neck and squeezed, lending him the comfort he sought.

"When I wasn't delivering messages, I was against that wall, waiting for the next order to come from the king."

Ouranos had been shackled behind the throne for more than thirty years? When Coryn had been bound to Zagan, she'd at least been able to move around. She'd flown around Manusya and had been free during the day.

"It's okay," Ouranos said, and Coryn realized she'd yet to respond to his revelations.

He lifted his head, as if he'd finally found the strength to look at her again. "It wasn't all bad. I learned the laws of Hell, how the demon king ruled. And I am ready to take on that role with you."

Coryn resisted the compulsion to pull away when the spell he'd had on her shattered. She would not revert to who she had once been—a power-hungry angel naively pining after a god. While she felt genuinely sorry for what Ouranos had endured down here, she had to remember everything he'd done to her as a result of his crusade. She considered the danger he'd put the three realms into, and what he would do to Zagan if given the chance.

I may have been created to destroy Zagan, but he is the only one I would ever choose to save.

"You need your rest, Ouranos," she said, gently pulling away.

The spell between them fell away from him, too, but she didn't care. Clearly, neither did he, as he simply nodded to her, rose from his seat, and made his way down the stairs. He did not ask her to join him in his chambers as she'd been afraid he might. Without so much as a glance her way, he rapped on the throne room doors with his knuckles.

"Good night, Coryn."

"Good night," she said, then was left alone in the throne room once more.

***

Zagan had been down to the holding cells many times in his life. Not as a captive, of course, but as a younger knight escorting prisoners.

How eager I was then to fight for my king.

And now he was the reason Ouranos had been able to grab the throne.

Zagan had captured an angel and let her into his life, into his heart, but she'd been a trap made expertly just for him. What the gods likely hadn't expected, however, was for him to want to ascend the throne if only to give her the power she'd been denied. Angels were the playthings of gods, and, over their time together, he'd seen Coryn slowly discover and come to terms with that.

Now, she probably resented everything, especially Zagan. She had what she wanted, and she didn't need him anymore. That stung more than the thought of losing his throne for good.

They passed cell after cell filled with defeated looking lessers. The former king, as his rule had been drawing to a close, had grown more and more paranoid of those around him. His constant jailing of demons had been the talk of Hell for months, and the cells were more crowded than usual.

Jinn shouted to him over the sound of the prisoners' protests. "The messenger is so focused on sitting in that chair for as long as he can that he hasn't even started ruling yet. Half of these demons are yelling for him to set them free because they've done nothing wrong. I believe them."

Because of the overcrowding, the nine knights were forced to share three cells—Lamia, Seere, and Phenex in one; Oriax, Raum, and Dantalion in another; and Zagan, Jinn, and Furcas in the last. Jinn stiffened when he realized the crazy demon was going to be with them and went to argue with the guards, but Zagan placed his hand on Jinn's shoulder.

"We're all one team now. We will act like it."

Furcas jumped as the cell door was closed behind them, and he sought his sister's gaze through the bars. Phenex had already been watching him and nodded from across the aisle.

"It's okay," she cooed as the guards rattled Oriax's cell door, ensuring it was locked before walking away.

Furcas hit the bars of their cell with his hands, staring at one of his palms after the clang echoed over the shouting. He grunted, looking helplessly back over to Phenex.

"You can't use your magic in these cells. You know that," she said.

Lamia pushed Phenex to the side of her cell and slammed her own body against the bar.

"Zagan, why are we here?" she demanded. Her eyes were brighter than usual, fueled by her rage. "We should have taken him down in the throne room."

Zagan made sure the guards were out of earshot. Not that it mattered—the lessers around them were making such a racket he was surprised he could hear himself.

"Coryn told me to take the challenge."

"Yes, so they can *slaughter us* after Ouranos regains his full power and all the angels in the Heavens join him."

Zagan shook his head. "No, she's plotting something, and it's going to help us. I know it." *I hope I know it.*

The irony of putting his faith in an angel was not lost on him. The more he thought about it, the more he questioned his decision.

Believe in Coryn.

But Lamia remained unsettled. "You better be right, or you just damned Hell to the Heavens."

"I know." He didn't know what else to say, but his knights were looking to him for assurance. He took a deep breath, gathering his thoughts.

"I know we've had our differences, but you are the strongest warriors I have ever had the pleasure of fighting beside. I wouldn't have endangered your lives if I believed we have no chance against that asshole god. Coryn has unlocked something inside of me, and I'm listening to it. I believe she is guiding us all to victory at the expense of those who created her. If you do not trust her, then please trust me, your rightful king. Now sleep. We need our strength."

***

Zagan awoke to the sounds of dozens of caged, hollering demons slamming against the bars of their cells. From his bed, Jinn leaned sideways and peered down the hall.

"Dinner time," he said. "Or lunch, or breakfast? Who the fuck knows!"

Furcas was already scrambling up the wall opposite Jinn, his mouth watering as he sniffed eagerly at the air. While he was distracted, Jinn caught Zagan's eyes.

"Promising continued knighthood under your rule to this crazy, was that wise?"

Zagan shrugged. "He's fine. He's the one who saved us, remember? Had he not been spying in the throne room, the other knights would never have rescued us. Plus, we slept without him ripping our windpipes out with his teeth, no?"

Before Jinn could respond, a loud shout rang through the hall.

"Quiet!" one of the demon guards sneered. "Quiet, I say. Quiet! Bow before your queen!"

Silence immediately fell over the hall.

Before Zagan realized what he was doing, he'd shoved Jinn out of the way and pressed his face into the far corner of the cell to get a better look down the corridor. Guards were making their way along it. They stopped at each cell, opened the small slit in the door, slid in a few metal trays—Zagan was guessing one per prisoner—then locked it behind them again.

Coryn trailed behind them in all her golden-winged glory, her eyes scanning each cell. Zagan's breath caught, and though it seemed to take days before the guards reached their area, he only just managed to compose himself before Coryn spotted him.

He'd watched her pass dozens of cells, each time hope then disappointment evident in her expression. To anyone else she probably looked stone-faced the entire time, but not to Zagan. He knew his angel. And when her sky-blue eyes settled on him, the relief and emotion he saw in them chased away any doubt he may have previously had about her.

He stood straight, his eyes never leaving hers as Jinn stepped forward to accept their trays.

"My queen," Zagan said with a bow of his head. *Mine, in every way.*

Coryn nodded as a small smile played across her lips. She extracted several small vials from her robes and placed them on the trays before they were distributed to the three cells that held the knights. When she placed the vial on the final one, she took the tray from the guard.

"I will give this one," she said. "Continue to the other cells."

The demon, caught off guard, hesitated for a moment. "Y-yes, Your Majesty," he said, then bowed and quickly shuffled along the corridor.

Zagan stepped forward to accept his tray from Coryn. She extracted a folded sheet of paper from her robe and placed it beneath the vial before handing over the tray.

"Five hours to battle," she said quietly, her voice barely above a whisper.

He reached out and accepted the tray, brushing his fingers over hers for the briefest moment before she drew back. That was all the contact he needed; he could fight for her for decades with just that touch.

"We will be ready," he whispered, unable to take his eyes off her.

She nodded at him and at Jinn, then looked back at Zagan in alarm when she realized Furcas was with them. He gave her a small smile, and it seemed to relax her.

"Enough of this silence!" she called along the hall. "As you were."

A cacophony of plates clanging on metal trays immediately rang down the aisle as the demons all dug into their meals at once.

With one last nod to Zagan, Coryn turned to follow the guards further down the hall.

When she was finally out of sight, Zagan noticed Jinn holding up his vial.

"It's ... angel blood," he said, bewildered. "She gave us angel blood?"

Zagan glanced down at his tray and the vial that lay there, the silver liquid shining brightly beneath the thick clouded glass of the vial. He sat, unfolded the paper and laughed.

A taste of what's to come. Raise Hell.

***

Zagan insisted the group eat their slop before they treat themselves to the angel blood, and then he ordered them to get some rest. They had only a few hours to recharge before the fight of their lives, and Zagan wasn't going to screw this one up. This fight wasn't only about getting Hell back from the gods or claiming the throne. He was fighting for Coryn, to ensure her permanent freedom, and to give her the life she deserved.

They were awoken unceremoniously by a new group of guards, who were violently shoving keys into locks and clanging doors. Demons in the other cells groaned and snarled as the knights were extracted.

"Shut up, all of you!" Zagan yelled when he exited the cell behind Jinn and Furcas. He'd been in the zone before the chaos and didn't want to break his concentration. "Next one to shout or holler will be the last to be released when I am king."

The dungeon quieted, much like when Coryn had been announced. Jinn and Oriax shook their heads and rolled their eyes at each other, and then they were on the move.

Zagan assumed they would be brought to the throne room, maybe for a pre-battle discussion with Ouranos, but they'd taken a wrong turn down the corridor for that.

"Queen Coryn has instructed us to take you to the courtyard portal," the guard explained.

"And that was approved by the messenger?" Oriax asked.

The guard glanced over his shoulder at O. "No. We only need to listen to one royal, yes?"

Zagan smiled. Ouranos had clearly made a few more enemies in the hours since they'd been locked away.

When they arrived at the portal, the knights' shackles were removed and the weapons they'd been forced to surrender were returned. Furcas was especially pleased and, just as Zagan had hoped, was chomping at the bit to raise a little hell.

"The location has already been calibrated," said the main guard, motioning to the red portal beside him. "You will be arriving in Dreadmouth. The meeting will be in the plains due south."

Zagan had to laugh. His angel was a clever one; she'd chosen the same field where Zagan had first laid eyes on her and the last location the demons had won in. Morale would be high.

"Here we go," he said. "Let's go claim my damn throne and my queen once and for all. Shall we?"

CHAPTER 27

As Coryn had predicted, Ouranos was none too happy about the liberties she'd taken to send Zagan and his friends through a portal. Had he known about her little tour of the dungeons, he probably would have tried to kill her. Yet, here she was, beside him as they stepped from the trees and into the bright sunlight of the open field.

"You were never going to let Zagan and his knights join this fight," she said. "They were going to step into a trap before they ever saw a portal."

"All is fair in war, dear queen," Ouranos sneered, calling her *queen* like one might call someone *whore*.

Despite everything, Coryn was genuinely surprised at the sudden change in him.

"We all know why you're here and whose side you'll be on," he said, "so you might as well wait here for him."

That stopped Coryn in her tracks.

Ouranos, his small group of forsaken and the demons still true to his cause, continued walking. When they came to the broken pentagram from their last battle, demons and forsaken alike began reconstructing it for the demon army.

So Ouranos had known what she'd been up to after all and had let her play her little game. Did he really think he had enough allies in the Heavens and Hell to win? He was a confident god, but she had seen him waver on a few occasions. Panic set in—had she unwittingly orchestrated the annihilation of the demon knights? What was Ouranos planning?

When the final piece of the pentagram had been completed and it glowed a brilliant red, lesser demons began spewing from the circle like undead from the earth. So much had changed since the last time Coryn had beheld such a sight, and in this very field. She had once been a proud demon-hating angel, had fallen—in more ways than one—and reascended, and was now about to fight against her own brethren to save a demon. Zagan was the only being who had ever had any faith in her, who treated her like an individual and not just a weapon or a member of an army. The only being to have ever truly cared for her, who loved her. She had never been more confident with a decision in her life and hoped she hadn't underestimated Ouranos.

"My queen," rumbled a deep voice from behind her.

Zagan! Her heart leaped and the words came out before she'd even finished spinning around.

"I love you!"

When Zagan's expression morphed quickly from confusion to shock and then utter delight, Coryn laughed out loud.

"In case something happens," she said, "I needed you to know that. I love you, Zagan. And thank you. For everything."

Zagan snaked his tail around her waist and pulled her into his arms.

"Oh, my sweet angel," he said, slipping his hand beneath her chin before he leaned down and kissed her lips gently. "The pleasure is all mine. But you will thank me later, in bed, when I am king and have finished branding my queen." He kissed her again, his lips lingering on hers.

She couldn't stop the tears that stung her eyes nor her laughter. Commands from her demon weren't so bad after all, she decided.

Zagan hesitated for a moment, then placed his hands on her shoulders and spun her around, bringing her face to face with his knights—all eight of them. Their goofy grins made her blush. Amid her spontaneous declaration of love, she hadn't realized they'd been standing there.

"Oriax, Phenex, keep her safe," he said, gently shoving her forward.

The two knights nodded and stepped up to meet her.

Coryn's heart, which had so recently been soaring, plummeted into her stomach. "Wait, what?" she said, trying to face Zagan, but he held her firmly.

"You will not kill angels, and you will soon rule those lessers," he said close to her ear. "Who will you fight?"

"Ouranos," she said without hesitation, suppressing the shudder that his warm breath on her skin elicited. "And his forsaken. At least let me at them."

"Forsaken are still angels, sweet one," he cooed. "Trust me, I know."

When he kissed her ear, she couldn't hold back the shiver that finally managed to break through. But he pushed her, more forcefully, toward his knights.

"Come on, Coryn," Oriax said with an encouraging smile. "It'll be an easy win anyway. We'll be on the sidelines, just in case."

She stuttered, searching for words as the other knights walked past her toward the pentagram.

"I get it," Oriax assured her, "I want to fight too. But sometimes you have to listen to the people you care about, and who care about you. I've learned that they often know what you need more than you do, no matter how right you think you are."

Coryn's thoughts went immediately to Pahaliah. Though they'd constantly clashed, the archangel had loved her—she wouldn't have always sounded so damned disappointed otherwise. Paha had tried to make sure she didn't do anything stupid, but she hadn't listened. What if she had, though? The opportunity to fight Zagan and getting bound to him may never have happened. Coryn didn't want to consider what would have become of her had she obeyed Paha, had she never been sent alone and weaponless to Manusya that fateful day. But after being forced to follow Zagan's every command and regaining her free will, she knew which orders she wanted to obey.

"*Sometimes* you need to listen," she said, smiling as her stubbornness got the better of her, "but not always."

She ran forward, gripped Zagan by the shoulder and spun him around. "I need to fight with you. As your angel of darkness, and as the Queen of Hell. The Heavens deserve payback for what they did to me, and I intend to help deliver it."

Zagan's red eyes held a mix of pride and trepidation. His chest expanded, and Coryn expected him to fight her once again, but he paused.

"Very well," he said on a sigh. "I can't deny you. But please, be careful. I can't lose you again."

"You won't," she said, leaning in and giving him a searing kiss. "Ever."

As the group walked toward the battlefield, the sun continued to rise, but no sun was bright enough to deliver the flash of light that exploded from the clouds before a loud clap of thunder rocked them.

"Here they come," Phenex said, and light gave way to darkness as a swarm of angels began falling from the sky.

The sky grew dark as countless pairs of wings burst from the clouds.

"Those ... aren't just erelim," Coryn said as emotion exploded inside her chest.

She scanned the sky, trying to sort through her angelic connection. The gods must have dispatched every angel in their arsenal, no matter the type or tier. Even though she'd been disconnected from the angels for some time, she was sure this number was too much even for an archangel to control through their connection.

"Coryn?" Jinn prompted.

"Angels ... we have a connection to one another," she explained, trying to focus on the demons beside her instead of the chaotic interference now flooding her mind. "We feel what other angels around us feel. We know when one of our brethren dies. Archangels can send us orders telepathically, making it easier for us to move in formations or launch simultaneous attacks without giving ourselves away."

She realized she was divulging secrets no demon knew, but if she was going to be Hell's queen, she needed to be open and honest.

"Right now, though," she said, "there are too many of them. It's like the lines are scrambled, and no one can make sense of anything."

"Well, good then," Dantalion said as hundreds of angels landed on the opposite side of the field. "Maybe this will be an even shorter fight than we thought."

All Coryn could do was nod as she felt the overwhelming sense of dread emanating from the angels. They were afraid—but was it because they knew they were going to lose, or because they had planned something catastrophic?

***

"Seems like a good time to invade the Heavens," Lamia said as they stood to one side of a sizable demon army. "They seem to have brought everyone they have."

It would have been a good idea if the demon realm wasn't already at stake.

"Today I will give Coryn all of Hell," Zagan said. "After that, taking the Heavens will be easy."

They were used to seeing a smaller number of angels to demon fighters, but this time the armies seemed to be about equal.

"At least they're taking us seriously," Dantalion offered.

"Don't be so sure," Zagan said. "The messenger still rules Hell, so not everyone behind us will be supporting us. We may be fighting some of our own plus that army today."

He shook his head as he watched the barrage of angels continuing to land, disgusted that he'd let some of the demons behind him be swayed by a god.

"You should have taught that army to revere you when you were their general," Lamia chided. "Just saying."

"Yeah, yeah." Zagan eyed Ouranos where he stood at the far end of the opposing demon army.

"Seven Hells, how long are these angels gonna take to fall?" Jinn growled. "This would take a lot less time if we just attack now—starting with that guy." He motioned with his head to Ouranos.

Zagan had been thinking the same thing, but he put up his arm to stop Jinn. "We fight fair and clean. It makes our victory all the more painful for them when a quarter of their numbers are left to retreat."

"You want to wait for their army to grow larger?" Coryn said incredulously. "They will vastly outnumber us by the time they all land. I don't have a good feeling about the ones who are already here, let alone what may be coming. Best we get started now."

"We fight by the rules, and that means waiting," Zagan said.

"You want to play by the rules? What even *are* the rules anymore?" she demanded. "A god created me to take your throne, and the Heavens are sending every angel they have down here. They aren't playing fair, and neither should we. We're about to define the future of all three realms—now's not the time to flex your pride."

A chorus of *oooohs* sounded around them, and Zagan flicked his tongue over his teeth as he glanced sideways at her. "Who let you come again?"

Coryn rolled her eyes. "Trust me. Let's start fighting now. We may even win the battle before nightfall. The cherubim and seraphim aren't as well-versed in battle. We can pick them off first, but I also recommend going after the erelim that are already on the ground and get ahead of their wave."

Zagan nodded. "Very well. Knights, you heard the queen. We charge and aim for the gold-wingers first. Coryn, my request to you still stands. If you are to go after any beings in this fight, please make them Ouranos's lessers. They'll be as good as dead after this fight, anyway. I will go after the god, but I want you away from that fight and surrounded by your knights, who will kill any angels that come at you and filter the demons to you."

She opened her mouth to protest, then shook her head. "If staying away will keep you focused, then fine."

He'd been ready to defend his decision, but with her words, he let out the breath he was holding. "Thank you."

"Fight well," she said, "and stay safe. I love you."

He inhaled, feeling as if her words were his source of power. "And I love you. Knights, Demon Queen, let's show this battlefield they don't fuck with the rightful king of Hell."

His words were met by enthusiastic whoops and shouts from his team, and he turned to find that the flow of angels hitting the ground had slowed. Six stoic white-and-gold-winged angels landed in front of the rest. They must be high archangels, the tier Coryn had always strived to reach. But why? They paled in comparison to her.

Queen is a much more fitting title for my angel. She deserved a gold crown atop her head to match her breathtaking wings.

"I guess we missed our chance to charge," Zagan said, and Coryn rolled her eyes.

"So we did. The blond-haired male in the middle, that's High Archangel Michael."

From behind Michael stepped an angel Zagan knew but hadn't been prepared to see. It was Alexander—he knew it. They locked eyes instantly.

Michael followed Alex's gaze to Zagan, and his smirk was far too off-putting for Zagan's liking.

What did I damn that boy to?

"Look at that smug bastard," Dantalion said.

"Let's make sure he never flashes that smile again, shall we? Dantalion, Raum, and Lamia, you're with me. Focus on Ouranos, but after him, the arch's our main target. The younger white-winged angel beside him? Spare him if you can."

Lamia growled. "You're in the business of saving far too many angels, King."

Zagan elbowed her. "Just shut up and do it. The rest of you, act as Coryn's shield against the angels."

With everyone now in place, silence fell over the crowd.

"Ouranos!" Michael shouted in greeting from across the field, though Zagan noted the dark tone in the archangel's voice, and while he didn't know the proper protocol when an angel addressed a god, he was sure it wasn't by first name.

"High Archangel Michael," Ouranos replied.

Michael made a dramatic gesture as he scanned the crowd as if Ouranos had lost something. "And where is Coriel?"

"Gone," Ouranos spat, and Zagan held Coryn tighter to him. "She has chosen to ally herself with her former keeper. Her soul cannot be saved."

"Is that so," Michael said, placing a hand atop Alexander's head while he shifted his gaze to Zagan, his eyes then flicking to Coryn.

"Ah, there you are, Coriel. So you've allied with your keeper. Interesting. Three factions will fight today, it seems."

Ouranos's bright orange-and-red wings flew open, and he took a few steps toward Michael. "*Three?* What are you saying, High Archangel? You and I were to fight together! Surely you don't mean—"

"Coriel must have told you that she informed everyone in the Heavens of what you had me do," he said, gesturing to the angels behind him with a sweep of his arm. "I have been shown the light, Ouranos. I have seen the error of our ways and have repented for my involvement in your scheme."

Ouranos drew his head back and scoffed. "*My* scheme? Is that what you told them?"

"Look at you, Ouranos, standing with your army of demons and corrupted angels. If you were truly with us, would you not be standing with us now? You can't even unite one demon and angel beneath you." He stole a glance back over at Zagan and Coryn before shaking his head at Ouranos. "What makes you think you can do so on a greater scale? This *could* be a war between only two groups. Join us, and together we will defeat them."

218

With his tail swishing sharply from side to side, Zagan looked over at Ouranos. Even from this distance, it was obvious the god was shaking.

"I did this for *all of you!*" he shouted to the Heavenly army across from him. "I suffered for *you*! So we could conquer Hell and finally purge its evil corruption from this realm!"

The hair on Zagan's arms stood as lightning snapped off Ouranos's body and his demons slipped into fighting stances.

"I hate to break it to both of you," Zagan chimed in, "but when it comes to corruption, we've learned a lot from you. You want evil? Betrayal?" He motioned between Michael and Ouranos. "It doesn't get any more twisted than this. Now, if you'll be so kind, we have angels to kill and souls to claim. Maybe, when I rule you all in Hell, you'll finally learn what it is to be decent."

Michael roared into the sky, and the field exploded into chaos. Like locusts, winged angels and demons alike took to the air and charged at one another. At Zagan's command, grounded demons surged forward and were met by shapeshifter angels that took the forms of lions and bulls.

Zagan immediately lost Ouranos in the crowd, but going airborne, he prepared to fly to where he'd last seen Michael. He was sure that where he found the high archangel, he would find his own target.

"Protect Coryn!" he shouted, and he and his knights tore forward to end the god once and for all.

CHAPTER 28

Chaos reigned. As Zagan fought his way through the crowd, that much became obvious. Contrary to Michael's belief—or perhaps he'd been hiding the knowledge—some angels did stand behind Ouranos, and as Zagan had expected, the dumber demons were fighting for Hell's current king as well. These supporters were easily identified because they were fighting their own kind—angel against angel, and demon against demon. Zagan made sure to dispatch any angel he saw and any demon that dared look at him with scorn, all the while scanning for Michael and Ouranos.

Finally, he spotted them locked in a heated battle, their swords clashing. They were shouting at each other, but among the chaos, it was too difficult to make out what was being said.

Zagan let out an earth-shattering roar so they would know he was coming, and they broke apart. Zagan extended his claws and took a powerful swipe at Ouranos as he hit the ground. The god jumped out of the way, but only barely, and Zagan's knights then surrounded him.

Ouranos spun, his Heavenly sword in his grasp as he glanced from one knight to the next, his nervous gaze lingering on those who had once sworn their service to him.

"Having a god as your king would change everything!" he pleaded.

"Exactly," Dantalion said. "We were fools to think that having you rule would be for the betterment of Hell. Perhaps a god like you would have truly brought darkness to the Lake of Souls, with your taint and what you did to Zagan's angel, but the Heavens would always call you back."

The dejection emanating from Ouranos was palpable. The god lowered his sword and glared at Zagan with disdain. Weak as he was, he was already on the verge of surrender. Without the support of the angels he'd helped create or the demons he'd coerced into accepting his reign, it was the smartest decision Ouranos had ever made—but that didn't mean Zagan would show him any mercy.

Zagan closed the gap between them, but Ouranos held his chin high.

"Every time you look into her eyes, stroke those wings, or slide into her body, she is taking a piece of your soul. Know that I created her for that very purpose."

Zagan smirked. "And you should know that as she rules Hell beside me, she will be the Heavens' undoing. As your temples in the Heavens burn and the ashes of angels fall to this realm, know that *you* created her. The demon queen. My angel of darkness."

Zagan shoved his claws through Ouranos's chest. He felt the heart in his fingertips beat for a few more seconds as the god stared wide-eyed at him—the new demon king.

"See you in Hell, Ouranos."

***

Coryn may have been created to ensnare Zagan, but the gods also bestowed upon her a damn good ability to fight.

With every angel who fell on the battlefield, Coryn's chest burned like Zagan's curse on steroids. As pain shot through her body, she couldn't suppress every wince, but she remained standing with her chin up as she battled with the knights surrounding her. How strange it was, to feel so many deaths for brethren she truly didn't care about anymore. Maybe there were a few angels she'd want to spare in this fight, but if she'd learned anything from her time on Manusya and in Hell, it was that those in the Heavens needed saving most of all.

Coryn rubbed her chest when she felt another angel fall.

Phenex glanced at her. "How many now?"

"Seventy-four," she shouted and dropped her arm to take a swing at one of the opposing lesser demons. "That last one was cherubim."

Oriax shook his head as he wiped angel blood from his daggers onto his shirt. "That's a fucked-up thing to feel, when one of your own dies."

221

"Yeah, well, I've learned that the Heavens are fucked in a lot of ways."

Zagan and the knights he'd taken with him—Dantalion, Raum, and Lamia—were still nowhere to be seen, but Coryn could hear the chaos they caused in the distance even above the screams and sounds of weapons crashing against each other. Though she'd never admit it to Zagan, she was glad his other knights were protecting her. She was so distracted by what could be happening to him that she wasn't fighting at her best.

As she was about to shout for Oriax to send an incoming lesser toward her, she felt as if a log had slammed into her back. She buckled to her knees and the wind was knocked out of her. Phenex and Seere were by her side immediately, bracing her by the shoulders as she fought to force oxygen back into her lungs.

"What hit you?" Seere shouted.

"They're down. All the angels are down!" Oriax said.

Coryn knew what had hit them all, but it was difficult to catch her breath and voice the reason. She was glad when Phenex explained in her stead.

"Zagan killed Ouranos, didn't he?"

Coryn could only nod as her gasps for air finally began taking hold. "Someone ... did," she forced, but they all knew it was their new king.

Phenex and Seere helped Coryn on to her feet and bowed to her, acknowledging the change of reign. Coryn nodded, unsure how else to respond.

"With Ouranos gone," she said, "there's no reason for us to stay back. Let's get to Zagan."

Most of the angels were still stunned by the loss of a god, and the battle quickly turned into an angel bloodbath. Lesser demons began losing control, drunk on the scent and taste of the silver liquid saturating the ground. Some surviving angels took to the skies.

Funny, there was no command to retreat. And yet, more and more survivors flew away.

Maybe you're all finally smartening up. May the spirit of Wodan be with and guide you all.

There were only a few pockets of fighting left as Coryn and the knights made their way to the center of the field, stepping over feasting lessers, angel and demon corpses, and pools of silver and black blood swirling together like oil and water.

Coryn finally caught sight of Zagan in all his demon glory. He fought Michael, and his trio of knights surrounded him, taking on the angels still fighting alongside the high archangel. By the time Coryn and the others reached them, the knights had the angels grounded, and Michael was on his knees, Zagan holding him by his large, open wings.

"Ah, perfect timing, my queen," Zagan said, and Coryn couldn't help but fall in love with him all over again. Strong, powerful, and cocky, no matter the circumstances.

Zagan stood straight, his chest heaving, looking like the proud warrior he was meant to be. Michael knelt before him and stared up at Coryn with a mixture of fear and hatred.

"Now," Zagan said, manipulating Michael's wings and forcing the high archangel to his stomach, "beg the forgiveness of Hell's queen."

Zagan slammed his foot into Michael's back, forcing a loud yelp of pain from him.

"Aargh! Fine! Yes!" He strained his neck to look up at her. "C-Coriel," he began.

Zagan slammed him into the ground once again. "Her name is *Coryn.*"

"Coryn, I'm so ... sorry—"

Zagan growled and grabbed Michael's hair, forcing his spine to bend unnaturally. "Do not apologize to her shins! Look her in the eyes, winger, and *beg.*"

"Mercy, Coryn," Michael choked out. His eyes glazed over with tears as he stared up at her, but whether it was from pain or genuine guilt, Coryn wasn't sure. She guessed the former; this creature was far from savable.

"I am sorry. Tell me how I may repent. Mercy, Coryn, please ..."

Zagan still didn't look pleased with the high archangel's groveling, despite his tears now falling in earnest. "Tell me what you would have me do with him, my queen."

There was so much anger in Coryn for the ruse Michael and Ouranos had pulled. And yet, everything they'd laid out brought her to this moment—she was now smarter, more powerful, and in love. As far as she was concerned, she'd already won. But it was time to prove she was worthy of ruling Hell by Zagan's side.

"Take off his wings," she ordered.

It was truly the worst punishment an angel could suffer, and even the demons around her cringed in delighted surprise.

Zagan was all too happy to oblige. "As you wish, my love."

She should have known Zagan wouldn't use a blade. Instead, he leaned down and gripped the first wing by its base. When he ripped the appendage straight off Michael's back, Coryn's own back burned, not because of the connection she had to the high archangel, but because of the pain she imagined as Michael's blood-curdling scream filled her ears. The sound of tearing muscles, bone, and ligaments was too much for some—when Zagan tossed the wing and it landed before the other grounded angels, one vomited. Another couldn't look away. The others tilted their faces to the sky, murmuring prayers.

As Michael began to bleed out and die, Coryn felt the pull of his soul making its way from his body, but she refused to look away or protest as Zagan reached for the other wing. The sounds were even worse the second time. Michael's screams died when he passed out. She had to give it to the arch—he'd endured more pain in the end than she was sure even Zagan could handle. But as her demon tossed the bloody wing onto the other and straightened, he growled in disgust.

"Asshole couldn't even withstand this," he said, and he spat onto the open wound on Michael's back.

Silver liquid hemorrhaged from the archangel, and Coryn felt his soul leave his body once and for all.

"It's done," she whispered, feeling a mixture of relief, nausea, and fear.

What would happen to the Heavens now? Not that it was her concern any longer. She would protect her king, Hell, and the demons who now called her their queen from whatever threat the Heavens posed next.

"Um, Coryn?" Oriax asked.

"*Queen* Coryn," Zagan growled through gritted teeth, and Coryn snapped out of her reverie and smiled.

"Coryn is fine."

Oriax looked at Zagan triumphantly before asking, "What would you like us to do with them?" He motioned to the shaking angels the knights still held hostage.

In front of all the gold-and-white-winged warriors stood Alex, the only angel standing straight and with a wide grin across his face. He and Zagan exchanged a knowing glance.

Coryn inhaled a slow, deep breath as she considered the angels' fates. The fear in their hearts was almost enough to kill them on its own.

"Let them return to the Heavens," she said, stunning everyone around her. But as she looked up at Zagan, he gave her a warm smile and a nod that encouraged her.

"You've seen enough today," she said. "The eternal sun will calm your fear, but it will never erase your memory of what happened here. Remember who brought you to this field and for what reasons. You will be our messengers to the others who did not descend today. Let them know of our benevolence, but at the mercy of our strength. If the demon king is threatened again, we take the battle to the skies."

The angels nodded, shaking until they were released.

"Th-thank you, Ereli—Queen Erelim Coryn," one managed to get out before they all kicked off the ground and took to the sky like frightened birds.

Alexander lingered for a moment, then bowed deeply to them all before ascending to the Heavens.

"So, he's okay. Good," Zagan said as he watched Alexander disappear into the clouds. "And Queen Erelim Coryn, I like the sound of that. My angel queen." He pulled her against his chest, preventing her from lingering on the carnage around them.

She melted into his hold.

"Now, let's return to the castle and get washed up. We have subjects to address."

CHAPTER 29

When Zagan took Coryn's hand to lead her away, she finally began to process just what had happened and what they were about to do. Without the crutch of other angels' feelings or a command from Zagan forcing her to calm down, she had no choice but to face her own emotions. It was a frightening, yet very welcomed feeling—she would learn to handle them finally.

When they stepped from the portal into the throne room, they were greeted by another overhaul of the decor—no longer was the room yellow and red like the original demon king's, or bright with Heavenly oranges and blues reminiscent of Ouranos; it was more subdued with charcoal grays, blacks, and golds—could the gold possibly be a tribute to her? She shuddered as goosebumps covered her skin with the thought.

The pair of thrones sitting atop the dark stairs and golden dais were stunning. The back of Zagan's throne was not as tall as Ouranos's, as if it did not need to reach as high up to the Heavens. The top was adorned with spikes that looked like Zagan's wings, and the plush cushion seat and footrest were the same deep red as his eyes. Her own throne had also been replaced with a smaller, but just as ornate, version of Zagan's.

Coryn smiled as Zagan led her onto the dais.

"My queen," Zagan said, motioning for her to sit.

"Why, thank you, my king," she replied, holding her breath as she slowly lowered herself onto it. As if hit by lightning, she immediately felt new power course through her veins. She gasped as a circular crown kissed her head.

"It suits you," Zagan said warmly, taking a step back to admire her. "Your wings are beautiful against that chair, and that crown ..." He purred deep in his throat. "I can't believe you're mine."

She couldn't help but blush.

Zagan took a seat on the throne beside her and grabbed her hand as he looked out over the empty room. He smirked, his tail whipping around with satisfaction.

"So they knew I would win and had already begun converting the place," he said with a nod.

Coryn squeezed his hand. "Of course they knew. Even before we left there were plots to overthrow Ouranos and put you on the throne. He was a terrible king, as short as his rule was. He rarely left this room, nor did he formally announce himself as ruler."

Zagan's eyes lit up and a wicked grin appeared on his face. "Is that right? So you were never announced either?"

Coryn shook her head, smiling at Zagan's sudden excitement.

"No? Then we will have to introduce you to your subjects now." He wrapped his arms around her and pressed his lips firmly against hers. He held the kiss until the deafening noise of beating wings outside the walls drowned out every other sound.

Smiling widely, Zagan grabbed her hand and led her toward the doors at the back of the throne room. He pushed them open, and they were met with their eight knights, who fell into formation behind them. They moved out onto the balcony that overlooked the castle gardens. There were tens of thousands of lessers covering the grounds, climbing atop one another or hovering in the air, pushing each other out of the way to get a good look at their new king.

Zagan released a triumphant roar.

The demons began chanting, a thunderous booming echoing throughout the large dominion. "God Slayer! God Slayer! All hail, Demon King Zagan!"

Zagan held up Coryn's hand. "And I present to you Demon Queen Coryn, angel of darkness and the perfect creation!"

Coryn's arm trembled as Zagan held her hand aloft. She gave his a tight squeeze and scanned the crowd, relieved that the demons accepted the declaration better than she thought they would. The announcement was mostly met by cheers. While she couldn't expect the entire realm to accept an angel as their queen right away, she would work to gain their respect. She wouldn't let her subjects *or* Zagan down. She glanced up at him and smiled as her heart soared.

Zagan roared once more, and the crowd cheered and chanted louder than ever—which was lucky as the noise drowned out his next announcement.

"Now, if you'll excuse me, I need to go fuck my queen!"

Coryn's cheeks ignited with heat as the knights, who were in close enough proximity to hear, laughed and parted as Zagan picked her up and entered the castle once more.

"That was a bit over the top," she chided with a smile as she wrapped her arms around his neck.

"Why? Welcome to Hell, my love. We fuck anywhere, anytime, and there is no reason to be bashful about it." He carried her up the stairs and kicked open a set of wooden doors. "Welcome to our chambers."

But before she could admire her surroundings her king's hands were all over her, and she pressed further into his touch in response. Zagan kissed her deeply and quickly got to removing her armor.

"You don't know how much I crave you," he growled between hungry kisses. "How badly I've needed you."

"Oh, I have an idea," she groaned, her body immediately flooding with heat as the first piece of armor hit the ground.

She frantically worked off Zagan's clothes as the rest of her own fell away. He walked them backward, smothering her body with his when they reached the bed, and moaned as they devoured each other's mouths.

"I will make this castle quake with the sound of our pleasure," he growled, stroking whatever part of her he could get his hands on.

Coryn let out a gasp and began grinding against his hardened length, his new proclamation making her quiver. She *wanted* their screams to be heard. She wanted the entire realm to know that she was his, and he was hers. As he pressed his full weight onto her, her golden down kissed her cheeks as they met the firm mattress beneath.

"Coryn, my queen," he rasped between kisses, in a tone that sounded as if he couldn't believe they were here, now, ruling Hell together.

Zagan slid down her body, making her shiver, kissing hungrily at her neck, between her breasts, above her navel before falling to his knees at the foot of the bed. He ran his fingers along the inside of her thigh, grazing his nails against the soft flesh, and kissed her calves.

"I can smell your need," he said, breathing heavily as he spread her thighs apart.

Before she could respond, his tongue was against her clit and licking her soft folds at an agonizingly slow pace. She let out a wavering moan as pleasure rocked her body. She moved against his mouth, pressing harder against his skilled tongue. Even without the bond, he had her mindless. She arched her back, and her hands found their way into his hair.

"Oh gods, Zagan!"

Zagan laughed against her folds. "We've been through this, my darling. *I* am your one and only god, and you are my goddess."

He gave her another lick, this time sliding his tongue inside of her. His hands moved from her thighs to her breasts, and he gave them a worshiping squeeze.

She yelped in pleasure as her muscles tightened around his tongue. But as incredible as it felt, it wasn't enough.

"Please, Zagan," she whimpered, "I need you inside me. I need you to—"

She took a few labored breaths, moaning loudly as she pressed his head closer to her. One hand flew to his at her breast and she squeezed and cried out his name. The orgasm rocked her to her core, leaving her convulsing as he lost his tongue from within her and licked eagerly at her slit.

He finally pulled away. "Delicious," he mused, "I will need to feast on you daily."

He pinned her hands above her head with his tail and stared deeply into her eyes as they both caught their breath.

"There's one more thing," she said between pants, "that I can offer you to taste."

"Oh, angel—Coryn. You are making all of my wildest dreams come true."

She smiled, pulling one of her hands free, and ran her fingers through his hair. "Angel is fine."

Purring, he leaned down, and she craned her head back to give him access to the soft flesh at her neck. He licked from her collarbone to below her jaw. "Tell me what you want me to do."

"I want you to sink your fangs into me and taste my blood."

He trembled. "Tell me yours wasn't the blood you gave to everyone in the cells, or I may have to kill all of my knights."

She laughed. "No. I got a delivery from Jinn's club."

"Good … because only I can drink from the queen." He settled his legs on either side of her and shivered, his cock brushing down the inside of her thigh. "Seven Hells, Coryn, I may come just from tasting you." He ran the tips of his fangs up and down her neck, making her gasp.

"We have all night."

"Would you like me to enter you as I drink from you?"

It was her turn to nearly orgasm. "No, I want you to enter me after you finish your mark—but only *after* you drink from me."

"Seven Hells, you are the goddess of torture." He slowly traced over her skin with his fangs, lingering in the curve between her neck and shoulders and pressing lightly down with his fangs until he groaned his approval. He gave the area one final lick. "That's the spot."

He paused, presumably giving her a moment to protest, but when she didn't, he positioned his fangs against her flesh. She scraped her nails across his back and arched into him as he sank his teeth into her skin and squeezed her breast.

"Zagan, my god, yes!"

The bite burned and pulsed as he withdrew his fangs, and as he sucked hungrily at the wound, he thrust mindlessly against her thigh. He indulged for some time before he drew back and wiped the corner of his mouth with the back of his hand.

"You taste so good, Coryn. In every way. And now, with my goddess of torture's permission, I need to mark you and fill you before I go insane."

"Yes," she breathed.

She was ravenous, desperate to ease her need for him to fill her. She flipped over and opened her wings, giving him full access to her body. He gripped her by the hips and coaxed them upward before he slipped his hard length beneath her.

Leaving over her, Zagan used his claw to gently retrace the marking he'd only half-finished before. "You are no longer forced to obey, but I have one more order for you. Stay by my side. For the rest of eternity, I want you with me. Coryn, will you be mine forever?"

"Yes. I am yours forever, Zagan."

"And I am yours. I love you." His answer was sweeter than any cry of pleasure.

Coryn fell to her elbows as he began carving his symbol into her back. The delicious burn of his claws on her skin left her panting as he drew.

"Just a little more ..." he whispered huskily.

She felt the symbol pulse when he was complete. She'd been branded by him, and she wanted it no other way.

He leaned down and nipped the tip of her ear. "You are my everything. I am your everything. We belong to one another in every way."

He positioned his hard cock at her entrance, and she moaned and leaned back, taking him inside of her. The bliss. The completion. It was almost too much to bear.

She threw her head back as he rubbed her clit, and she continued to thrust back against him. Her breasts dragged along the cool sheets beneath them, and she whimpered, begging him to never, ever stop.

"I'll never stop, angel. I will never stop loving you, fucking you, wanting you. It will never end. I'm *addicted* to you. And I am so close to coming ..."

That was all she needed. She slammed back against him as hard as she could and felt him spill inside of her. It sent her over the edge, and with another loud scream that left her breathless, she collapsed forward.

"Zagan."

He sat up, still buried inside her, and enveloped her in his arms. He brought her down to lay beside him, groaning as he kissed her forehead and pulled out of her. They stayed there for a while, staring into each other's eyes as they caught their breath.

If this was what Coryn had been created for, then she was completely okay with that. This moment of pure tranquility, of them both being content to lay in each other's arms, was worth her entire existence.

Zagan lifted his hand and gently cupped her cheek. "I hope I have pleased you, Coryn."

Letting her hand fall over his, she sighed. "I'm so much more than pleased." She traced gentle circles on his chest before she kissed him again, lingering on his sweet lips. "I hope I have pleased you, too, but how much we pleasure one another pales in comparison to what you've done for me. I hope I can give you a gift as special as all of this someday."

She pressed her hand to his where it rested on her cheek, wriggling her fingers to interlace with his. This was truly the happiest day since her creation. She was falling more and more in love with him with each passing moment. Her eyes stung as tears of pure joy threatened to spill down her face.

He gently wiped away those that succeeded in falling, and he smiled against her lips, happiness clear on his face. There was no mistaking that he loved her with the entirety of his beautiful soul. He would live for her, until his last breath, just as she would for him.

He kissed her again, and she laughed against his lips. Even though she was no longer bound to obey him, she knew she would—*most* of the time. She would always be with him, would always be hopelessly in love with him, and would always want him.

As she held his cheek and gazed into his gorgeous red eyes, she traced little hearts on his chest and flashed him a goofy grin. "I love you, Demon King Zagan. Thank you for saving me."

"You were the one who did the saving, angel. I don't think the gods who created you could have ever anticipated how much I love you." He leaned in to claim her mouth once again, but paused when a knock at the door echoed throughout the chamber.

"This had better be important!" Zagan boomed. Coryn moved to cover herself, but his arms locked her in place.

"Sire," a demon hissed through the door, "are you ready to hold court with your subjects?"

Zagan's hold tightened on Coryn, and he took a slow, deep breath against her neck while stroking her wing. "Ah, yes, I suppose that's part of the job, isn't it? We will be there shortly."

They luxuriated in the warmth of each other's arms for much longer than the demon behind the door anticipated, she was sure. And as Zagan finally led her back down to the throne room, he couldn't stop touching her. When they reached the top of the dais, Zagan wouldn't let her take her own throne; he pulled her onto his lap instead.

Coryn smiled, swiveling so *he* was now her throne. She raised her chin and pulled his arms away from her middle, placing them on the armrests and draping her hands over his. "Show them in," she declared.

"At once, Your Majesty." A bull-like demon on two legs swung the doors open to allow their subjects to filter in.

She grinned as demons of every shape and size entered and bowed before them. Images of them corrupting Manusya and storming the Heavens in her and Zagan's names made her dizzy with excitement.

"Raise Hell, my queen," Zagan said as he ran his fang over his mark on her shoulder and gave it a nip.

She raised her chin. "Oh, I will."

ABOUT THE AUTHOR

Alyson Caraway is a debut author of paranormal romance. When she's not writing, you can find her indulging in retail therapy, playing video games, studying Japanese, or stuffing her face with something deliciously bad for her health. She lives on Long Island with her husband, daughter, and maltipoo.

Get the latest updates on Alyson's books:
    Website: www.alycaraway.com
    Facebook, Twitter, or Instagram: @alycaraway

CPSIA information can be obtained
at www.ICGtesting.com
Printed in the USA
BVHW080744080820
585851BV00001B/287